A KINK IN THE DEAL

AN MMF ENEMIES TO LOVERS ROMANCE

KRISTIN LANCE, APRIL CROSS, ALEC LAKE

TWISTED ROSE
PUBLISHING

TWISTED ROSE PUBLISHING

PREFACE

A Kink in the Deal is a collaborative project between three authors. Each of us wrote the point of view of one character with very little influence from the other authors.

Kristin Lance wrote Jeremy.
April Cross wrote Faith.
Alec Lake wrote Tristan.

Writing this story was a fun project. We had a direction we wanted the story to head (it's an erotic romance, after all). We wrote it round robin, feeding off the chapter written before ours. The story took an unplanned path, but it's only the better for it.

We hope you enjoy the spirit of this collaboration, and appreciate the distinctive voices of the separate characters.

CONTENTS

PROLOGUE

Faith - August

"What if I don't want to go?" I grumbled at my husband, Tristan, while attempting to overstuff my new Louis Vuitton rolling luggage. Tristan didn't say anything while I stood back and eyed the fuchsia suitcase critically. How in the hell would all of this fit? I tried to hold back a sigh, but wasn't successful.

"Remember, we talked about this. The doctor thinks some down-time will help you with your insomnia. You'll burn out if you don't take a step back from work stress."

"Not if my work stress is being replaced by packing stress." *And by missing him*, but I wasn't going to say that, because I was sure he'd drop everything in an instant and blow the Japan deal we'd worked so hard on.

"That was the largest size they accept as a carry-on," defended Tristan, his eyes twinkling with humor, though he kept a straight face. With his sexy British accent, he only needed to speak and I'd melt. Marrying a guy from the UK was the best decision ever. I was pretty sure I had a voice kink.

I didn't want to seem ungrateful, especially since Tristan booked me a spa and yoga retreat week at Lake Tahoe and bought me lovely new luggage. He wanted me to get away and unwind, but how could I do that when just the act of packing for the trip infuriated me?

Another attempt at getting all my clothes jammed in proved pointless. I considered getting my other bag from the closet, but then I'd have to check my luggage. The private plane wasn't available, so I was flying commercial today. Dealing with the hassle of lines and baggage claim was not on my to-do list. Plus, Tristan wasn't going to be around to help carry my suitcases. That thought made my heart flip in my chest. *Tristan wouldn't be there.* How was I supposed to relax without my husband?

I removed a few more items and it would still only zip halfway. I snatched a fistful of random clothes and tossed them on the bed. Fuck it, I would buy new clothes if I needed them. Didn't retail therapy count as a relaxation technique?

The suitcase finally closed, I sat on the edge of the bed, contemplating my situation. Wild strands of my long brown hair stuck to my face from my struggle, and I huffed and blew them out of my eyes. This wasn't about a suitcase, at least not really. The actual problem was I was about to leave on a trip without Tristan for a week. We had minimized the time we spent apart during our ten-year marriage, but sometimes it was difficult to avoid.

Together, Tristan and I headed up the acquisitions department of his family's company. We spent most of our time locating and vetting resorts to add to their ever-growing portfolio of luxury destination travel properties. It was a high-stress job that required a lot of travel, and occasionally we had to travel separately when we were juggling more than one deal. A few days apart here and there was common, but rarely a week. Sure, we could talk on the phone and video chat, but how was I going to live without sex?

Tristan glanced at the time on his phone. "Faith, are you ready to go? We need to head out."

Ugh, what? Where did the time go? I'd planned on jumping his bones for a quickie before we left and I'd wasted all my time being cranky. I quickly switched my facial expression from mutinous to coy as I stood up, slinked over to him, pressed my body against his, and reached down to cop a feel. He wasn't hard, yet, but I could get him there easily.

"How about you lie down and I ride you for five minutes first?"

Tristan barked out a laugh and stepped back out of reach of my roving hands. "No time, love. We really need to go. The airport might be busy, and you know the traffic in Sea-Tac is horrendous this time of day."

When you lived in Seattle, traveling revolved around the time of day. I enjoyed the amenities of a big city, but less traffic would be nice. Tristan hauled my suitcase off the bed. I sighed dramatically and mumbled to myself all the way to the car. Who said I'm not a chill person? I don't need a dang yoga and spa retreat to teach me how to relax. Whenever I want to relax, I just fuck Tristan until we're both happy.

Before I knew it, I was bustled through the first class line and on my way to Northern California, my knee bouncing as I worried about Tristan handling the deal on his own. It wasn't that I didn't trust him to manage it; more that I had this near-constant need to prove myself to his family.

Okay, so maybe I was a little burnt out.

The plane trip was quick, and soon I was in the back seat of a glossy black car, staring out at the brown, desert-like mountains outside of Reno, which didn't bode well. As the road wound higher into the mountains, the brown grass gave way to tall pines, and I gasped softly as we went around a bend and the pristine blue color of the lake came into view. It was bigger than I expected, stretching off into the distance, edged by tall, dramatic peaks. In a flash, tall pines blocked the lake again, and I looked forward to see we were entering a housing development.

Tristan had rented a luxury condo for the week. As lovely as it was, at first, being alone made me antsy. I tried reading, then catching up on one of the shows everyone in the office had been raving about, but nothing seemed to settle me. My mind spun horror stories about Tristan alone in Japan, and my fingers itched to check my work laptop, but I only had my phone and tablet with me. Tristan had signed me out of the email app, so I couldn't even check that.

I spent the afternoon shopping, finding a nice selection of luxury and activewear brands in the cutesy little downtown area. As I went to bed early, I still couldn't see how a solo trip to the mountains would cure my insomnia, and the first night was a restless one — I wasn't accustomed to sleeping alone.

The next morning, I decided to try to relax. My first step was to take my coffee and yogurt out to the balcony and soak in the atmosphere. The cool, dry mountain air was so different from Seattle, and the condo had a lovely view across the lake. For the first time in a long while, I felt like I could just sit and breathe. The mountain view from the balcony was a balm to my restless spirit. That might sound corny, but it was the truth.

At the doctor's recommendation, Tristan had signed me up for a yoga class, pointing out via a quick text that with my insomnia, I was up early, right in time for the morning session — my first yoga class ever — and I sat on the balcony, thinking about whether to blow the class off. Clearing my mind had never been easy for me. And although that made a bit more sense since my recent ADHD diagnosis, I didn't see how yoga would be any different.

In the end, I decided it was worth a shot. I headed inside, set my coffee and breakfast down on the kitchen table, and grabbed my purse. I admired myself in the full-length mirror on the way out the door, turning around and bending over so I could check out my ass in the new skin-tight leggings I'd bought yesterday. I had to know what other people would see if they were behind me in class. Not bad at all. Tristan always said he loved my legs. And while I may not have been super fit, I looked good in the leggings.

The yoga class wasn't what I expected — it was just three other women and me, plus a sexy young male instructor. He led us outside to a grassy lawn area next to the yoga studio after handing out yoga mats to the one person who didn't have their own — cough, me. He started by teaching us a few different positions, and assessed our skill level. According to Tristan, the resort had touted the class as a beginner's course, but it was soon apparent that I was the only real beginner there.

Since I didn't know what I was doing in the yoga class, I felt clumsy in every pose. While bent over in an awkward downward dog position, with the yoga teacher behind me trying to show me how to position my feet properly, I tried to not snicker. The instructor was fit and hot. After three days of no sex, my pussy perked up at the thought of any guy behind me, even one not standing that close to me. Tristan and I should try this position sometime. It had potential. My mind wandered to thoughts of signing up for a sensual couple's yoga class.

"Faith, you need to relax more. Breathe into the position."

The instructor had a calming and helpful tone, but whenever someone told me to relax, it only made me want to punch them in the gut — or the nuts, depending on how much I disliked them. Since this guy was cute, and probably trying to help, I'd stick to his stomach. But instead of doing any of that, I did my best to breathe as he requested.

Sometimes I think guys don't understand the challenges women face at work when they have a prominent position. There was a ton of pressure on me, and I had the added stress of trying to prove myself to my husband's powerful family. I couldn't just mellow out on command. After only a few minutes at this class, I could tell yoga wasn't helping me. My mind kept wandering back to work, or to Tristan. No matter how many times the instructor told me to be present in the moment, I couldn't seem to do it. I was feeling a distinct lack of relaxation.

I was about to bring myself up and out of the position when a real estate sign across the lawn caught my eye and I read the words 'condo for sale' while upside down. The box attached to the real estate sign was full of flyers, and my mind wandered again. I wondered if I could make an excuse to run over and grab a brochure right then. I was curious about property values in the area. I knew California was pricey, but wasn't sure how much a place like this would cost.

At the end of class, I darted over to the sign and slipped a folded brochure down the front of my leggings when no one was watching. I pulled my t-shirt over the top of it so I could hide what I was doing. I don't know why, but I felt weird taking the flyer. I'm sure none of them would have cared, but it felt like I was violating the relaxed atmosphere of the yoga class thinking about a real estate purchase. Besides, I wasn't serious about buying a place.

Later that night, I removed all my clothes and eased into the hot tub with a glass of Merlot. As the warmth from the water loosened my muscles, I sighed and found some peace. I savored the wine for a few sips before gulping it down and setting it aside. I'm a lightweight with alcohol, so I usually tried to be careful, but since I wasn't going anywhere tonight, who cared?

I leaned my head against the back of the hot tub and let the water jets work their magic. It would be pretty fantastic to own one of these condos. I doubt I could ever get bored with the mountain views, and the air had a crisp, clean freshness that Seattle lacked. I should take the sales flyer home with me and tell Tristan I found my inner peace, and for a specific price point, I could fly down and find it again whenever I wanted.

As the alcohol took hold, I noticed the jets hit me in several interesting places that made my pussy tingle. If I could just slide over to my left an inch or two I'd turn this into a naughty hot tub experience. I was tempted, but I also liked the idea of denying myself all week to make the return-home fuck with Tristan amazing. Sex with him was always off the charts, which I believed was a huge contributing factor to our happy marriage. When you were sexually satisfied, it was easier to overlook little things.

I wished the Japan deal hadn't been so important, and that he could have come on this trip with me. We could be having crazy monkey sex in the hot tub right now. THAT would have relaxed me. I grumbled to myself a little longer, but the cool fall evening and wine made it impossible to stay cranky. When I finally climbed out of the hot tub, my pussy protested with a throbbing ache and I wanted to go into the bedroom and finger myself to thoughts of Tristan and those jets.

I didn't realize the time until my phone rang. It was Tristan calling me for our nightly video chat. I smiled and swiped accept, greeting him with a view of my naked upper half.

I teased him in my most sultry voice possible. "Oh, hey big boy."

By the look on his face, he wasn't expecting to be greeted with my tits, but he warmed to it quickly. I kept the view screen at chest level as I chatted with him and carried the phone into the condo towards the bedroom. I couldn't be with him in person, but maybe we could have fun in other ways.

But first, I had a request to make. "I think we should consider this area for our next acquisition."

"The yoga class was that good?" Tristan asked.

"No, the yoga class was a disaster, but there's something about this place."

"You like it that much?"

"I do."

CHAPTER 1

Jeremy - January

"I think you should meet with this woman."

I automatically reached for the business card Tom handed me.

Rather terrible advice from my friend and employee who usually had good ideas. He had been our lift operations manager at Emerald Bay Mountain Resort since before I was born, and he liked to meddle, especially now that I had inherited the ski resort. At that moment, I wanted to fire him. I couldn't, but still.

I flipped the card around in my fingers, frowning. Honestly, I hadn't known people still used business cards, but this one was thick and fancy, with heavyweight cardstock and gold lettering.

"Faith Vaughn, Vaughn Resort Group. More corporate assholes here to fuck things up."

"Jeremy, think about it. She could have a plan that would work for everyone. You don't know until you talk to her." Tom leaned forward and whacked me with his ski gloves, a habit he had picked up when I was a kid, when he used to babysit me a lot. He had been a weird choice for a babysitter, really. A grizzled old mechanic, even then.

I looked out the window, losing myself in the scenery for a moment. It was snowing, and clouds obscured the mountains in the distance. Lake Tahoe was visible, but looked dark and ominous under the heavy cloud cover. I hoped that wasn't a sign. Even in the worst of conditions, the resort was beautiful, and it was my home. I wouldn't sell it to some random lady from Seattle. I sat back on the bench of the gondola and searched his expression, trying to guess where he was going with this. Taking a stab, I said, "I'll figure it out. I'm sorry I fucked up last year. It was unexpected."

I should have known this was a setup when Tom had suggested we take a few runs. Tom hated the gondola. He found the little car too claustrophobic and preferred open chairlifts. But ever since I was a kid, he used the confined space of the gondola to trap me into stern lectures that made the most of the fifteen-minute ride to the top of the mountain. I checked the lift towers. We were a bit over halfway up. That meant five more minutes of hearing about how much I had fucked up my father's legacy. Great.

"I know last year you were reeling. We all were. But you don't need to do this without help. If someone wants to invest in Emerald Bay, I say why not?"

"Because I said no." Right, that wasn't the most adult argument, but I couldn't put it into any kind of eloquent words. It was mine. My responsibility. My fuck-up. My mountain.

"Look, I'm not saying you need to sell, Jeremy. Hear her out. Maybe she has good ideas."

And that was an interesting thought, one that sent my mind spinning in a whole different direction. "Ideas, huh? Do you think I could milk her for ideas?"

"That was not what I was saying." Tom pinched the bridge of his nose, looking more than a little frustrated with me.

This time, when I looked towards the top of the mountain, I saw the gondola building looming out of the clouds. The ride was almost over, and I was done with this lecture, so I shoved my helmet and goggles on.

"Too bad, man. We're at the top." I fled, racing out onto the snow like the wuss that I was, strapping into my snowboard and taking off. I couldn't chase away the thoughts Tom had put in my head, but I knew how to deal with them. An idea was taking shape. This woman knew business and knew how to turn a profit, so I was going to learn everything I could from her. My best plans always came to me when I was out on the mountain, and this was no exception. At the end of my run, I shot my assistant a message to reach out to this Faith person.

The Vaughn Resort Group lady must have been eager, because it didn't take long for my assistant to arrange a meeting. By the time I pushed into the offices at the base of the mountain, she was waiting. There was no time to change out of my snowy outerwear, but hardly anyone in the resort offices ever did. I didn't think twice about it as I wandered down the hall towards the back conference room, depositing my snowboard in my office and filling my water bottle before heading back.

In the hall, I passed Steve, the head of the ski and ride school, and stole a vape pen out of his front shirt pocket. I had an act to put on. He tried to snatch it back, but I took off at a jog, slipping into the conference room and closing the door with a laugh as he crashed into it behind me. I snickered as I locked the deadbolt, forgetting for a moment that I was adulting today.

Behind me, a throat cleared, and it was the most irritated, meaning-laden throat clearing I had ever heard. "There's a meeting happening here."

I grinned, pausing for a minute before turning around, looking down, and noticing that my snowboard pants and boots were dripping on the carpet. She sounded like an uptight bitch, and I was ready to hatch my plan. Then I straightened my face and faced her with my most serious expression. Which wasn't that serious.

I wasn't sure what I had been expecting — a pantsuit wearing middle-aged lady, maybe — but this was not it. She was young, probably close to my age, and she was gorgeous. She was standing by the window writing in a little notebook and the sun glinting in her dark hair. Sure, she was dressed like a moron who didn't understand the weather, but those impractical heels were making her legs look a mile long. And that skirt, fuck me. I blinked and cleared my throat. And even though I supposed it didn't matter if she caught me salivating over her killer legs, I forced my eyes up and met her intense, green-eyed gaze.

"Want a hit?" I held out the vape pen.

She stopped writing and her brows lowered sort of adorably. "What? I said there's a meeting scheduled in this conference room. Are those drugs?"

"It's legal in California. Does weed really count as a drug anymore?" I asked. Then, because I was pretty sure she wouldn't be able to tell the difference, I pretended to take a hit.

"Of course it's a drug." She folded her arms over her chest. "I'm supposed to meet with the owner of Emerald Bay Mountain Resort. Jeremy Kuan."

"Yep, that'd be me." I smiled and held out my hand, letting the damp mitten I'd left dangling from my wrist fly out and thwap her arm. She barely contained a squeal.

"Why are you wearing mittens on your wrists like you're a little kid?"

I laughed and showed her the straps that held them in place. "They're kind of handy. Keeps me from losing them." I peeled them off, then tossed my wet jacket over a chair and sat down. I set the vape pen out in plain sight. "So, what did you want to meet with me about?"

"You're Jeremy Kuan? Is there a Jeremy Kuan Senior?"

"He died last year." I let my genuine emotions show there, because no acting was required to make her feel awkward.

She flushed, her eyes darting around, no longer so intense. "Oh. Yes, I remember that from my research. That was part of what interested us in the resort."

"My dead father made you interested in the resort?" I blinked at her for a long beat, then took a slow sip of water. I probably should have offered her coffee, but... fuck no.

"No, I mean. When I decided a few months ago to research resorts in Tahoe, I read you weren't that interested in taking Emerald Bay over. It seemed like you needed help from someone more business-minded." She finally sat, placed her notebook and pen on the table, and crossed those long legs... and fuck, I needed to stop staring at her. She took a deep breath. "Sorry, can we start again? My name is Faith Vaughn, of Vaughn Resort Group. I have spent the past few months researching potential investments in Tahoe, and we'd love to discuss opportunities for Emerald Bay with you."

I gave her a mocking salute. "Jeremy Kuan of Emerald Bay." Then I leaned back in my chair, staring mournfully out the window with a long sigh. "It's my father's legacy. I can't let it go out of business."

"Right," She leaned forward, those lovely green eyes sparkling. Was she buying my bad melodramatic acting? "That's why I'm here. The right person could bring the resort into the twenty-first century, make it profitable. Build on your father's legacy and his dream."

"Huh. I didn't think it was possible to make it profitable. We're happy when we don't run at a loss."

This was clearly feeding into her strengths, because she looked almost giddy. "Oh no, I've been spending a lot of time learning the ski resort industry, and what the most profitable resorts are doing." She reached down into a fancy-looking bag and pulled out a folder. "I have a five- and ten-year improvement plan and earning forecast mapped out."

"No shit? I didn't even know that was possible." How could I get my hands on that plan? From looking at her, I wasn't convinced she knew the business, but it didn't hurt to learn if she thought we could turn things around. Shifting towards her, I tried to read it, only moderately distracted by the soft, feminine scent that surrounded her.

She frowned. "How are you running this resort without a plan, exactly?"

"We just kind of wing it?"

"You wing it?" She looked like she might stroke out as she flipped open the plan, pointing at the pages for emphasis. "No, you don't wing it. You need to forecast and project earnings to determine your profit centers."

I snatched the paper out of her hand and flipped through it, reading over her numbers and data. Some of it was pretty brilliant. Other stuff was obvious or lacked an understanding of the industry. "Interesting. I have no idea what any of this means." Lie.

She snatched the paper back. "Of course, we'd keep you on board in a managerial role. To help keep things..." She looked around the conference room and shuddered a little, though I wasn't sure why. It was just a conference room. "Authentic."

"Right. Authentic. This all sounds so incredible."

"If we move forward, we'd schedule a formal proposal and an offer. We'd love to make a full presentation. Later in the week?"

I sat back and steepled my fingers, grinning. "Nope."

"I'm sorry, did you say 'nope?'" The bitchy tone in her voice was back, but I liked her feisty.

"Thanks for gathering all of that data, though. Your Q2 projections are a little off, too. Spring break reservations already exceed that number. The idea for the zipline is good, though."

"You're not interested in selling?"

"You catch on fast." I held my hand out for a high five. She left me hanging, her face turning a rather interesting shade of red. Perhaps a little past red, even. Puce?

"Why did you agree to meet with me?"

"I wanted to know what you thought of the financial viability of the company. For my information."

"You can't just..." she huffed and stood, then started stacking things in her bag, pulling on a wool coat that didn't look warm at all. "You don't even know how to run a business."

"Don't I? If you talk to Tina on your way out, she'll give you some complimentary lift tickets so you can explore the resort."

"I don't ski."

I smirked at her. "Precisely. Lovely to meet you, Ms. Vaughn." And I turned and walked out of the conference room, smiling a little, only to find Steve in the hall.

"Vape pen," Steve snapped. "It's medicinal."

"Don't make me go back in there. She's terrifying," I whispered, right as the door clicked open behind me. Shit, I hoped she hadn't heard that. I speed-walked out of the hall without looking back.

CHAPTER 2

Tristan

As good as it was to be back in London, I always winced a little at how small my apartment was. The view was stunning, and being in the center of the city helped with business, but even a millionaire didn't get much bang for the buck in the capital. Truth be told, the apartment wasn't much bigger than the house my father had lived in before his business had taken off and they moved out to Oxfordshire and the country house I was raised in. And yes, it wasn't as if I couldn't afford a bigger place. Considering this was my work apartment for when I was in London, I only used it maybe four or five times a year. Buying anything bigger would be a waste of money.

At the end of another night of negotiations on the new Shiga Kogen development, any place would do to relax. I was sure there were other people in the company that could be sorting out the details of the deal, but the only other person I really trusted was my wife Faith.

She wasn't here.

On entering the apartment, I noticed the Jack Vettriano print had arrived and been installed above the mantle. Faith took a shine to it when we saw it at the Hawksmoor Gallery. I decided to get her it as a little gift, although not the only gift that I had planned for her.

I looked at my watch and saw it was coming up on 04:00 in the morning. Negotiations with Japan had been keeping me up all week, but I had other reasons for being up so late. Every night I phoned Faith and we talked about our day. She may have been thousands of miles away, but that was no reason for us not to talk and decompress together. In the ten years we had been married, we had never gone a day without talking, even when on the opposite sides of the world.

I decided I had time for a drink. I poured myself a whisky and looked out at the blinking light of Canary Wharf, a distinctive sight in the London skyline, like a lighthouse guiding Londoners home. The whisky slipped down my throat, warmed me up, and gave me a little buzz. Just right for talking with my love.

Sitting down in my armchair, I dialed the number and waited for her to answer. As always, she replied within seconds, her face filling the screen. Her usual smile was replaced by a frown. I instantly knew something was wrong.

"Hi love," I smiled and waved my whisky glass at her.

She sighed, and I could tell that whatever it was had really got to her. She could handle most things that life threw at her, so for her to be reacting like this, it had to be something major.

"Hey gorgeous. I thought you were supposed to be in New York today, but it looks like you are in London?" I could hear the strain in her voice.

"New York is tomorrow. What's going on there? Did the meeting go well?"

She leaned back in her chair, then came back with a glass of red in her hand.

"No. It did not go well. It went the opposite of well. I don't even know why they bothered having a meeting with me. They turned us down without even hearing me out." She took a deep drink from her glass, a sure sign she was upset.

I gave her time to calm down before I asked her my next question.

"And you don't think that the owner will budge? Maybe more money would...."

Faith waved away the question. I could see how tired she was.

"No. The owner is a child. You should have seen him. Wearing mittens to the meeting. Mittens. He had no plan, and as far as I can see, he's going to keep on doing what he's doing till the place becomes so unprofitable that he has to shut it down. He might wish it would turn a profit, but wishes don't pay the rent."

I knew the type—owners of family businesses who would rather see it all go to ruin rather than sell to a bigger company that could actually help the place. Misguided people who thought bigger meant evil or heartless.

"Are you going to get some sleep?" I knew that once she got something stuck in her mind, she could stay awake for hours worrying about it.

"No, not yet. I might watch Beauty and the Beast first."

I smiled. That was her go-to movie to help her calm down. When we first met we had watched it at the cinema together here in London, her all cuddled up against me and quietly singing along to the songs. Whenever she seemed stressed, I would sing a tune from it to her, let her cuddle in, and drift off with the song in her head.

"Ok, love," I said, knowing that she would probably be up all night.

We said goodnight, and I clicked off the phone, wanting nothing more than to have her in my arms so I could make her feel better. Although truthfully, that usually meant us going to the bedroom and me exhausting her with intense sex.

I thought for a moment and reached into the bag I had brought with me and took a box from inside. I ran my fingers over the Coco de Mer name embossed on the lid before opening it and looked at the contents. It was a work of art, as much as the print on the wall. This was certainly a different sort of gift, one that she was not expecting. She had a wish list for Coco de Mer but this treat wasn't on it, being quite unlike the lingerie and leather that she had bought from there before.

She would have to wait to see the painting, but maybe she wouldn't have to wait to get this gift.

Eleven hours later, I knocked on the door, waiting for her to stumble out of bed. As soon as the door opened I threw my arms around her and lifted her up.

She was overjoyed to see me, drowning me in kisses and wrapping herself around me. I half lifted, half carried her to the sofa.

"What are you doing here? You should be in New York," she squealed. I love seeing her like this, the side that those she faces in the boardroom never glimpse.

"You looked like you could do with the company, and it's not *that* far from London when you have a private plane. Besides, it's been how long since we last had sex?"

She was already pulling at my clothes when she mumbled, "Far too long."

I pushed at her hands. "Faith, wait. First things first. I have a gift for you."

"I know. That's what I'm trying to get to." She giggled as she pulled at my trousers.

"You are incorrigible. I leave you alone for a few days and you go sex mad. I hope you haven't been harassing the ski instructors. It wouldn't be proper." I laughed as I pulled myself free and fetched my bags from outside.

"Why would I when I have all I could want right here?" she called after me.

By the time I returned with my bags, she had moved to the table in the main room. I put down the luggage, holding up the Coco de Mer bag and waving it in front of her.

"Oh, have you bought me something nice to wear?" she asked.

I laughed. "Yes, in a manner of speaking, I have."

I reached into the bag and pulled out the wooden box, placing it on the table in front of her. For a woman who could buy anything she wanted when she wanted it, she always loved gifts, especially when they were bought with love. She reached out and ran her fingers along the edge.

"Is it something I asked for?" she said, giving me a questioning look.

"No, not the items. But it is something you've asked about before," I replied with a wink.

"Oh!"

I could see the surprise in her eyes, closely followed by trying to work out what it was.

"Just open it," I laughed.

She looked at me, then back at the box, and reached to flick open the latches. Then she slowly lifted the lid.

"Oh. OH!" she gasped.

"I thought we might try something for a change, and you said a couple of times you wanted to try this." I was loving the smile that spread across her face. "So I thought maybe it was time to give you your wish."

CHAPTER 3

Faith

I slowly lifted the items from inside the wooden box. There were only two things to take out: a black silicone dildo and a matching leather harness. I first examined the harness, and thought, 'Oh, fuck, that's awesome!' immediately followed by, 'Oh shit, how am I supposed to use this?'

Tristan and I had talked about me pegging him for a while, and we progressed to me sticking a finger in his bum occasionally, which he seemed to enjoy. But we hadn't yet agreed to the actual pegging, and he didn't exactly jump for joy when I first brought it up. He was always non-committal and would say, "We'll see. Let's work up to it."

Part of me wondered why he brought it with him now when he knew I had a rough meeting with Jeremy. But fuck it, I won't look a gift horse in the mouth. This could be the perfect thing to get my mind off crazy-mitten Jeremy. Tristan was such a sweetheart for flying all this way to support me.

I turned the harness in my hand and played with the buckles until I noticed Tristan was silent. I needed to double check he wanted to do this tonight before I got too excited. When I looked over at him, he was watching me with the eager glint in his eyes that he gets whenever he's turned on.

"Are you ready for this?"

Tristan nodded. "Yes, love, let's do it."

I dropped the harness on the table and rushed over to him, wrapped my arms around him, and tipped my head up for a long, sensuous kiss. He nipped and toyed with my lips while I pressed against him, grinding my pelvis against his now-hard cock through his trousers. My wet pussy twitched the longer the kiss went on, and the need for his cock to fill me grew to where I had to break off the kiss. Too much more of that and I was going to beg to be fucked instead of fucking him.

Tristan picked up his travel bag while I wandered back over to the table to fondle the harness again and marvel at the intricate straps. Tristan paused with his bag in his hand and glanced at me. "Faith, I want to freshen up. I'll be a bit."

I murmured, "Sounds good," while I held the harness up to my pelvis and wondered how it worked. "I'm going to try this sucker on," I sang out to him as he closed the bathroom door.

The more I studied it, the less complicated it seemed. By the time Tristan came back out of the bathroom, I was naked except for my panties and the harness with the attached dildo.

I stroked my fake penis and wiggled my hips obscenely at him. "How does my cock look, baby?"

Tristan laughed. "Bigger than it looked in the store."

I peered down at my new appendage. Yeah, now that he mentioned it, this was a lot thicker than my finger. Remembering my first-time anal experience, I knew I needed to be slow and cautious with him, yet still make it hot. Neither of us wanted an unpleasant experience.

I winked at him. "Don't worry. I'll be gentle."

He snorted at me and stripped off his clothes. Once he was naked, an almost vulnerable look passed over his face. I hoped he wasn't regretting his decision. He stood by the bed and shifted from foot to foot.

"How do you want me..." Tristan faltered, and I wanted to wrap my arms around him and reassure him I'd be tender this first time.

The position was something I had thought a lot about. Yes, I had a fantasy of pounding into his ass and calling him filthy names, but that wasn't something for a first-time experience. I didn't know if he'd want it. Tonight called for a variation of the missionary.

"Oh, on your back, please."

Tristan crawled to the center of the bed and lay on his back. I was about to join him, but paused.

"Uh, did you bring any lube?"

This was going to be a brief experiment if he didn't bring any lube. Tristan indicated it was in his suitcase. I bent over with my ass towards him, unzipped his luggage, and dug around. Dang, this felt so weird, but I was turned on and wet by the entire scenario. I've never been anyone's first for anything, so this was unfamiliar territory for me. My stiff appendage brushed against my legs while I was looking for the lube, and I figured this probably made for an interesting view from the bed. I wiggled my ass at him to entertain us both.

Once I found it, I giggled and triumphantly raised the bottle in the air. "Success!"

Setting the bottle on the nightstand, I crawled into bed and snuggled against his side. I had to shift the silicone penis out of the way, but first I wanted some cuddles and kisses to relax us. When it became obvious what I was after, he rolled onto his side and brushed his lips against mine. I hummed a lusty "Mmm" when he deepened the kiss, and I reached down to stroke his cock.

He was already wet with pre-cum, and I hoped he wouldn't orgasm quickly. I wanted an extended session tonight, slow and sensual. The mental shift of me pegging him was odd, and I tried to get past the awkwardness. I'd never been in the position where I had to be the director of sticking something inside of him other than my finger.

He was definitely holding back and letting me run the show. Usually when I was the dominant one, it turned into me demanding he fuck or lick me. But I was wet and flushed, so I knew I want this and his rock-hard member told me he wanted it as well.

My pussy tingled from the kisses. When he started tugging on my nipple, I knew it was time to move to the main course. Again, I didn't want to get so turned on I begged for his cock. I was in the perfect zone: horny, but not out of control to the point of pleading and offering anything under the sun to get him inside of me.

I pushed Tristan away from me and grabbed the lube before getting on my knees and climbing between his legs. He brought his feet up so his knees were bent, and spread them further apart so I could settle in comfortably. I put a generous amount of lube on the fingers of my left hand and tossed the bottle aside. Using my right hand, I stroked his cock while I slowly coated his ass with the liquid. He inhaled sharply at first, but the more I teased and fondled his shaft and nether region, the more he relaxed. I made sure to get the lube into all the important nooks and crannies. I had been on the receiving end of an ass fucking without enough lube with a previous boyfriend. Spoiler alert, it wasn't glorious.

I leaned forward, braced myself on my hands and knees over him, and brushed my lips against his, biting his bottom one gently. When I nibbled my way down his stomach and stroked his hardness, he moaned loudly. He seemed ready, but I wanted to be sure.

Sitting up on my knees, I slipped about an inch of the dildo into him. I paused, looked him in the eyes, and asked, "This okay?"

Tristan nodded with a tiny smile. "Yes, love."

I smooched my lips at him to blow a kiss.

"Let's do this." I eased the dildo in most of the way. Tristan's sigh of enjoyment told me he delighted in the sensation of fullness. Having experienced anal sex from the other side, I could guess what he was feeling, despite knowing it was different for men, since it stimulated a wonderful spot for them.

As I slowly pumped in and out, I watched Tristan's face closely. I wanted to stop at any sign of distress, but the only emotion I detected was ecstasy. Jesus, watching him was hot. My pussy was a wet mess from seeing his obvious pleasure.

Leaning forward again, I braced myself on my forearms on the bed beside him and slowly fucked him in the missionary position, bringing us face-to-face so we could share brief smooches while I picked up the pace. Tristan caressed my upper body and focused on my breasts, running his hands between our bodies so he could reach my nipples. He tweaked them and played with the stiff peaks, making me moan with him.

My voice was husky when I demanded, "Wrap your legs around me and stroke yourself."

He brought his legs up and hooked them around my waist, and I moved his hand down so he could touch his cock. I continued to fuck him at a steady pace. Once he added in the stroking, I could tell he was going to come soon. He tilted his head back and his eyes rolled a little as rapture overtook him, but he didn't slow his rubbing.

Fuck, this was awesome. He hadn't come yet, but I already knew I wanted to do this again because of Tristan's response. I leaned forward, bit his neck softly and whispered in his ear, "I want you to come for me."

He could only nod while he increased the speed of his hand, panting and groaning, until his breath hitched and he shuddered underneath me. Spurts of his warm cum splashed on my stomach, and it excited me to know I was the cause. Sure, it was his hand, but I made it better. It was fascinating to watch him come from this position. The facial expressions, the responsiveness to my thrusts, they all turned me on. My man was definitely getting pegged again if he's up for it.

I eased the dildo out of him as he relaxed his legs back down to the bed, and I flopped over next to him, worn out. My upper arms ached from holding myself up and my abs were sore from the unfamiliar movement. In the heat of the moment, I didn't notice. Now that it was over, I was sweaty and turned on, but also tired. Tristan seemed dazed and wasn't moving. He had a dreamy, contented look on his face.

I kissed his shoulder and snuggled against him. "You okay?"

"Oh, yeah," he mumbled, and I almost laughed at him. *Heh, I think I fucked him so good his mind blanked.*

"I'm going to get this thing off before I'm too exhausted to move."

I scooted off the side of the bed and headed into the bathroom. When I unbuckled the leather straps between my legs, I noticed my thighs were slick with my juices. Tonight was a mental turning point for me, and knowing that I was his first meant more to me than I realized it would. I didn't normally put credence to it mattering if someone was a first-timer with any sexual act, but it made this experience with Tristan more special and intimate. I loved that we explored this together.

There weren't too many things either of us hadn't done, so this was something I could cherish until we were old and grey. I snickered to myself in the mirror at the thought of me pegging him when we're old and grey as I washed the dildo and set it on the counter. Next time, I should shove a vibrating egg inside me when we do this again.

My pussy fluttered pleasantly at the thought. When I got back into the bedroom, Tristan was sitting up on the edge of the bed, drinking water. At least he looked somewhat recovered. I climbed on the bed, laid on my side, and examined the sleek muscles of his back. I made one attempt to touch his back, gave up because he wasn't quite within arm's reach, and dropped my hand to the bed.

He set the glass on the nightstand and turned towards me, eying me speculatively.

"I want you to lie on your back and spread your legs."

His command punched me in the gut and I instantly became a wet, needy mess again. *Hell yeah.* I was down for whatever he planned, especially if I could just lie there and be lazy.

I spread my legs as Tristan climbed between them. I adjusted myself better on the bed so I could open wider for him. He didn't waste any time. His hot breath tickled my inner thigh as he kissed up the length of it, headed straight for my pussy. I was still tired, but also buzzed from the lack of sexual release, so I was perfectly fine with not having a huge dragged-out session for me. I just wanted to come, sleep, and wake up to a big breakfast.

Tristan used his thumbs to spread my lips apart as he leaned in to lick me from the bottom of my slit all the way to my clit. *Holy fuck.* I shivered and almost jumped out of my skin when his tongue reached my swollen nub. I moaned as he swirled his tongue around the bundle of nerves and tilted my pussy towards his face. *Oh fuck, yes.* That was what I needed.

He wasn't gentle, and I didn't want him to be. He attacked my pussy and clit with his tongue, slipping two fingers inside me to massage my cave wall.

"Oh, god," I groaned as I threaded my hands through his hair and pressed his face harder against me.

I lost track of time as he laved my clit and finger fucked me, while ripples of pleasure radiated from my core. When the orgasm hit, the intensity took my breath away. I bucked wildly against his mouth and cried out, "Oh, god, yes," repeatedly as I rode the seemingly never-ending waves of rapture. I might have peaked again, I'm not sure, but it was a long time before the roller coaster of delight ended, and I relaxed, totally spent.

"Holy fuck," I whispered, not having enough energy to do anything else.

Tristan laughed at me. "I'm guessing that was good."

"Uh... yeah."

Vigorous sex and fresh mountain air really were the best for my insomnia — I barely had enough energy to roll over. Fluffing a pillow, I smashed the side of my face into it and announced, "I'm gonna sleep now."

"Hey, wait!" Tristan tried to stop me as my eyes drifted closed.

"Hmmm?" He better speak fast. Fatigue slipped over me, and I didn't open my eyes.

"Faith, I think we should scout out the resort tomorrow and see if we notice anything we can use for leverage. If we see Jeremy, we could talk to him, or just poke around."

Ugh, Jeremy. I cracked one eye open. I was too tired to put up a fight. It wasn't a horrible idea, even though I'd rather not run into him.

I closed my eye again and drifted towards dreamland, murmuring, "Okay, but... doesn't matter how cute he was... still... jerk."

Sleep overtook me and the last thing I heard from Tristan before I passed out was, "You thought he was cute?"

CHAPTER 4

Jeremy

"Faith Vaughn is back." Steve cornered me on my way to the gondola, clearly eager to share his bit of gossip. He was the head of the ski school and was great at that, but he was a doofus the rest of the time.

"No stealing my vape this time. I have it in a secure pocket." He paused and looked behind him with the paranoia of a long-time stoner who kept forgetting cannabis was legalized, the skis on his shoulder pivoting. "It's medicinal!"

"Don't you have some lessons to schedule? I'm not worried about Ms. Vaughn. These big corporate guys always come back. How do you know she's here, though?"

"I know everything that happens here. Well, that and there's a lady standing over there in a funny outfit yelling at Lucy." He turned and pointed towards the gondola building, nearly knocking over the people behind him. Fortunately, they had quick reflexes.

"Why would Faith Vaughn be yelling at a child?" I asked, looking for them on the snow. I spotted Lucy's familiar small stature and bright turquoise outerwear first, then Faith, who was wearing a dark-colored wool coat that was coated in an absurd amount of snow.

Shit. I knew what had happened.

Steve followed my gaze, tilting his head thoughtfully. "Lucy is getting pretty tall. Maybe Ms. Vaughn doesn't realize she's a kid? You'd better intervene, though."

I shook my head and jogged over, ready to deescalate the situation in any manner possible. A man I didn't recognize stood next to Faith. He was tall and handsome, and I couldn't tell if he was annoyed or slightly amused.

"You know, the mittens make a little more sense in context," the tall man said as I walked up. I met his eyes for a moment and tried not to laugh, wondering what that was about.

"What?" Faith frowned, momentarily derailed from her tirade. She turned and spotted me. "Jeremy. This girl shot snow at me with her snowboard. That should be illegal, shouldn't it?"

Lucy was silently laughing her ass off. She was barely holding on, saved because her goggles and helmet covered most of her face. Faith didn't seem to notice Lucy's shaking shoulders. I kind of wanted to laugh, too, but I tried for stern and fatherly instead. "Young lady, we've talked about this."

"Oh, you're no fun. That was hilarious." Lucy's laughter finally spilled out, and it took her a moment to recover and speak again. "Look at their outfits."

"What's wrong with my outfit?" Faith asked, shaking snow out of her hair. "It's my favorite designer, and this jacket is very warm."

I wasn't sure how to explain the impracticality of a wool coat at a ski resort concisely, so I shrugged. "You know, youth and their fashion sense. Listen, I'm so sorry she sprayed snow at you."

"She doesn't look sorry." Faith had a point, and Lucy's random fits of giggling were not helping her case. Faith huffed and brushed at the snow on her jacket. There was a lot, all stuck in the wool and sure to melt and make her wet and uncomfortable later, no matter how warm the jacket was. Something with a little waterproofing would have gone a long way in this situation. I supposed blaming Faith's impractical outerwear for my daughter's juvenile prank would be unfair.

"If this is what happens at this resort, it's no wonder you're doing poorly," the man said. He spoke in a posh British accent that made him sound even more uptight than Faith. It was a sexy kind of uptight, like maybe you could fuck it out of him. I shook myself, wondering where that bizarre thought had come from.

"She will be punished, but she's only twelve, and her judgement is poor." Of course, I was the one who'd taught Lucy how to spray snow at people with her snowboard, but that wasn't relevant.

"You punish children?" Faith asked.

"Only the ones who belong to me." I rethought that statement. "I mean, not like she's my slave or something."

"Dad, you say the weirdest shit." Lucy shook her head.

"You apologize then. Why am I apologizing on your behalf? Then go to the lodge and finish your homework."

"Fine. I'm sorry." It was the least enthusiastic apology I had ever heard. I glared at her and attempted to send stern, fatherly signals. Not exactly my strong suit as a parent. I was much better at the fun stuff, like teaching her to spray people with snow. Which was how we got ourselves into situations like this.

"You have a child? How is that possible?" Faith asked, frowning.

Lucy cracked up, pushing her goggles up onto her forehead. "Well, when a man and a woman forget to use a condom...."

Clearly, being a jackass was hereditary. I slapped my hand over her mouth, muffling the rest of her answer, which was likely to be worse.

"What the hell are you learning in health class?" I muttered—though she had actually described the basic circumstances of her conception fairly accurately. "Faith, this is my daughter, Lucy. Lucy, say hello to Faith and...." I trailed off, assuming someone would tell me who the handsome guy was.

The man's expression turned a bit more assessing as he looked towards us. "Tristan Vaughn. Faith's husband." He held out his hand, and I shook it, ignoring the little spark of attraction there.

"He's, like, really handsome for an old guy," Lucy observed in a ridiculous stage whisper that everyone in a twenty-yard radius could hear. She wasn't entirely wrong, but she was twelve. She didn't need to be talking about handsome old guys.

I shot her a glare. "Go inside, get Dave to make you some lunch, and finish your Social Studies project."

"But Dad." She started working up her biggest puppy dog eyes. Those didn't work as well as they had when she was younger. I pointed at the lodge and held strong, forcing myself to fight the manipulation.

"But nothing. You're in trouble, young lady. Homework. I'll come find you in a bit. After I figure out how to dry off our guests."

"You don't need to go with her?" Tristan asked, as Lucy unstrapped her snowboard and moped off at a sloth's pace, heading towards the main lodge to pester the kitchen staff for snacks.

"This is her home. She's fine. You look... less fine." I reached out and pulled a clump of snow out of Faith's hair, not realizing until I was finished it had been a super awkward thing to do. "Er, sorry, I was just, um, worried it might melt on your face."

Yeah, that didn't save me from my awkwardness at all. Maybe Lucy was right when she pointed out I said the stupidest shit.

"I didn't see any mention of a daughter or wife in my research." Faith pulled a tablet out of her purse and scrolled through something, frowning. Her husband met my eyes, his brows shooting up. He looked curious or intrigued, maybe.

"No wife. It's just Lucy and me. So, tell me. Why are you guys standing around the base area, anyway?"

"We wanted to continue our research," she said, glancing at Lucy, who was almost walking backwards, her head slightly tilted like she was trying to catch the rest of our conversation. "To experience more of the resort in person."

"I turned you down. Did you forget that important detail?"

Faith planted her hands on her hips. "Surely you didn't think I'd back down after one conversation."

"Right." I really hadn't, but one could always hope. I shifted awkwardly, wondering if I was supposed to threaten to kick them out or just walk away.

I stared at Faith and Tristan for a moment. They seemed to wait for me to do something, or maybe they were so damn attractive they got off on standing around being admired. Unsure, I backed away, only to crash into someone standing behind me.

I spun around to apologize. I found Tom, who had chewed me out after the meeting, was suddenly there, giving me a stern look. How did he move so quickly and stealthily? Where had he even come from? I avoided meeting his eyes and completely changed my tactic. "Well, since you're here, you might as well ride the gondola and experience more of Emerald Bay Mountain Resort. I have to head up and check in with the manager at the restaurant, anyway."

I started walking towards the building, but turned back when I realized they hadn't followed. I found Faith staring at the gondola, looking slightly horrified.

With only a slight quaver, she said, "I do not ride in cars on strings."

"It's a steel cable. It's perfectly safe, most of the time." That last bit slipped out, my urge to fuck with her uncontrollable.

"She refused to ride the cable car at Aiguille du Midi in Chamonix, too," Tristan said.

"Oh, so you've skied Mont Blanc?" I perked up. "It's epic, isn't it?"

Tristan shook his head. "We don't ski. I wanted to go to the restaurant."

Well, fuck. That left me grasping at straws.

"Ah, we have a restaurant, too." Idiot. I'd just said that. "I'm not sure we can compete with Mont Blanc for views, but it's beautiful.

Also, our gondola is smaller and much lower to the ground, so it's far less terrifying." I winked at him and turned, again walking towards the building. I wouldn't force them to follow me. The offer alone would be enough to satisfy Tom and his incessant nagging. After a brief pause and a hushed conversation, I could hear them following me.

I led them through the staff and ski school line into the gondola building so they wouldn't need lift tickets, heading for the first available gondola as it rounded the curved boarding area. I fist-bumped Carl, the liftie, dropped my snowboard in the rack, then climbed into the glass-enclosed car. Faith followed me, looking a little like she might throw up. She took a seat directly in the middle, facing uphill. I shook my head. Reaching for her hand, I tugged her to the other side and sat across from her.

"I'll be going backwards. Looking at the hill." Her eyes darted around the car nervously.

"Worth it. You'll be facing the view. If you can't even handle a ride in a gondola, why do you need to own a ski resort?" I shot her a look, and she squared her shoulders and shifted in the seat, looking determined. Her husband sat down next to her. I relaxed and pulled off my helmet and goggles, scrubbing a hand through my slightly sweaty hair and stretching out my legs a little.

They were wearing winter boots, at least. Tristan's looked leather and expensive. Hers had a fuzzy layer of fur over them that made them look a bit like she had harvested a Sasquatch's feet and made them into footwear. Compared to my sturdy snowboard boots with a strip of duct tape over the toe, they looked fancy.

The gondola doors slid smoothly shut. Faith yelped as the car jolted a little as the clamps engaged with the cable. We shot out of the building and started climbing the mountain. I held her panicked eyes and reached out and laid my hand over hers. "It'll be worth it, I promise. Focus on me, and breathe, for fuck's sake. I was messing with you. It's not dangerous. Safer than driving in a car or riding in an airplane, I promise."

Her husband was watching me carefully, and I knew I should let go of her hand, but she was clinging to me with a death grip as the little glass-enclosed car rose out of the wispy, low-hanging cloud cover that had formed overnight around the base area. She gasped as we broke through and bright sun streamed through the windows. At this elevation, you could see across the lake, where snowy mountains framed the cloud-covered lake.

"The clouds will burn off in the sun in another half hour. Once you're done with lunch, it should be a bluebird day." I extracted my hand from her death grip. Her other hand had been clenched firmly around her husband's thigh, but it loosened as she took in the view. Faith leaned her head on her husband's shoulder and sighed, finally looking relaxed.

"Don't you want this to be around for your daughter? Her legacy?" Tristan asked as he looked around at the view, smiling a little as we rose higher.

I smiled and leaned back, looking out the window, rubbing a hand through my hair. "It'll hardly be her legacy if we no longer own it. Besides, she's building her own legacy in snowboarding." I felt a rush of pride every time I thought about Lucy's last X-Games finish. I couldn't help beaming like a dork. Tristan was studying me, but Faith frowned.

"If she's such a good snowboarder, why did she almost hit me?"

And that part made me flush. "She did it on purpose. In those clothes, you look like two idiot tourists, which makes you a target for the teenagers."

"This jacket is Burberry," Faith said, smoothing her hands over the wool of her coat.

I smirked. "Yes, exactly my point. I'm sure it's lovely in the city, but in the mountains, we like things a little more waterproof."

Tristan seemed focused on something else. "If the resort goes out of business, it won't be here for her at all."

I snorted. "Come on, you two are barely handling a ride in a gondola. How are you equipped to own ski resort properties?"

Faith scoffed. "The same business principles apply to ski resorts that apply to any of our other resorts. We research the markets, we find out what works, and we invest as needed."

I leaned forward, resting my arms on my knees, frustrated. "But how do you know what works if you've never even skied?"

"We have a beach resort in St. Barts, and I've never surfed."

I snorted. "That's not the same, and you know it. You need to understand what people in these kinds of sports are interested in, and that seems impossible if you've never tried it. Have you mountain biked? Hiked? Done any of the things that make us money?" I was getting a little riled up, but she was irritating, assuming she could do a little Googling and fix everything.

Faith was turning a little red. "You can research things and come to an understanding of the numbers and trends without actually experiencing the sports. The sports aren't relevant. It's a numbers game, and a smart analyst can spot trends in any discipline."

I'd had enough of her arrogance.

"Oh, look. We're at the top. Have a pleasant lunch at the restaurant. I'll radio the chef and tell him it's on me. And then I'd rather you stayed off my property."

I ducked through the gondola door the moment it opened, grabbing my snowboard off of the car and stalking towards the snow. There was a shout behind me. I turned to see Tristan jogging after me, stopping me by the door that led outside.

"I'm sorry, I need to go. As you've mentioned, I have a business to fuck up."

"What if you teach us?" Tristan asked, smiling a little.

I shook my head, confused. "What?"

"Show us a little about the sports. Obviously, you love it all. Teach us what it's about. You're not wrong, exactly. She's not wrong, either. She has a mind for trends and data. She's brilliant at understanding those things. But it wouldn't hurt for us to understand the business on a more personal level."

I paused. This sounded interesting. A meeting of the minds. "But I can't sell."

"Why not? My wife has her heart set on this."

"The closest resort to us sold two years ago to a conglomerate. They fired half the staff and reduced the salaries of the rest of them. It was a disaster. The high-salaried jobs are in some big corporate headquarters in Denver, no longer part of the local economy. The locals get minimum wage, and it's not a living wage."

"What if we come up with a better proposal than an outright sale? Something we can both be happy with."

I frowned, thinking about that. It was difficult to admit that his wife's skill with market analysis was intriguing, as was the influx of cash his company could bring. The risks still felt too great. I had known most of my staff since I was a kid. "I don't know."

"Why don't you show us a little more of your mountain? That will give you some time to think it over." He was handsome and charming, and that plus his posh accent probably won him all kinds of deals just on sex appeal alone. He flashed a quick smile at me, raising his eyebrows. I knew I was being manipulated, that this would be part of a scheme to get on my good side, but somehow, I couldn't resist.

"Faith would be pretty hilarious on a snowboard," I drawled, thinking a snowboard lesson could be the perfect way to get rid of her.

Tristan chuckled. "I can't wait to watch."

I sighed. "Meet me here tomorrow. And go to a ski shop and get some real outerwear. Helmet, goggles, some gloves or mittens."

CHAPTER 5

Tristan

The meal at the restaurant was surprisingly delicious. Whatever other problems the resort may have had, the restaurant was not one of them

Faith had been a little worked up from what she saw as another rejection from Jeremy, but after I told her about my plan to get him to teach us, she calmed down and agreed to go for a meal.

She may have been laughing and talking, but I knew that her mind would be analyzing her surroundings, assessing the restaurant, and working out whether it was running to the best of its abilities. From everything I could see, I knew she would find it to be a great investment possibility.

My thoughts were further confirmed when she pulled a tiny spiral notebook and pen out of her pocket. She always carried one around to jot stuff down, so she didn't forget them. She claimed it helped her stay organized, but it kept her from being able to relax fully.

"Faith," I said, drawing her attention from the notebook, "you're doing it again."

She turned back to me, set her pen down, and picked up her coffee.

"Doing what?"

"Evaluating and planning instead of enjoying the moment."

For a second, I thought she was going to argue, but then her face relaxed and she sat back in her seat, slipping the notebook and pen back into her pocket.

"Yes. Sorry."

"It's okay," I said as I reached out and stroked her hand. "I know how you get when you're excited about a project. You need to relax. In fact, I have something I want you to do for me."

She raised her eyebrows and gave me an inquisitive look.

"Can you try to put aside work for a bit?" I asked.

"Yeah, I think I can do that."

She was quiet for a few minutes, then a smile broke across her face.

"So, you enjoyed the pegging then?"

I smiled.

"If you came over here and put your hand on my lap, you would see how much I enjoyed it. I hope it's not going to be a one-off," I replied. It was true—she had made me come so hard I blanked for a few seconds.

"Are you hard right now?" she whispered.

I nodded my head, and she shuffled her chair round a little and reached under the table, her hand in my lap, squeezing and rubbing.

"Mmmm," she sighed.

"Are you thinking about how hard you used me?" I asked as I sipped my wine.

Her hand rubbed against my hardness, and she nodded her head.

"It wasn't that hard. I was being soft and loving," she said.

She giggled when I told her it felt pretty hard from where I was.

"And talking of which, I want you to go to the restroom. Take off your panties and masturbate for two minutes while you think about pegging me. Then I want you to come back and hand them to me."

Her eyes widened.

"Do you know how difficult it will be to get out of..." she started, but then she saw the look on my face.

Her hand withdrew, she jumped out of her seat, and disappeared. I was left alone with my thoughts.

It wasn't unusual for us to play these kinds of sexual games, but I had to admit I'd been feeling naughtier than usual since she had pegged me. I was still buzzing from it and hoping that it was going to happen again soon. Until it did, I was going to make my own fun.

I was sipping my drink when she returned and dropped her panties onto my lap before sliding into her seat. I could see her face was flushed.

"How was that? Still thinking about the project?"

She grinned, and I could see a little fire in her smile.

"No, not so much. Now I'm thinking about getting you back to the bedroom and letting you use that wonderful cock of yours on me in any way that you want to."

I balled the panties in my hand and slipped them into my pocket.

"Then let's get out of here."

"No, wait," she said, reaching out and lightly touching my hand to stop me. "First, we pay for the meal."

"He said it was free," I replied.

"He did. But if we let him pay for it, then we're in his debt. When we negotiate, we don't want to be in his debt, no matter how small."

A few minutes and a sizable tip later, we were outside and heading for the gondola.

"It looks like we timed it perfectly." We walked straight into the car without having to wait in the line. Faith sat down beside me and snuggled in.

"Good, I don't have to share you." She sighed and moved her head to kiss me on the cheek.

For a moment, I thought about the trip up as she held onto me. She must've been really frightened. Otherwise, she would never have held Jeremy's hand, too.

I wasn't sure what to make of him. Ruggedly handsome, and with some charm, but quick to temper and overprotective from what I could see. Maybe I could find a way to put a smile on that face of his. My mind briefly flitted to thoughts of a more sexual encounter, but I knew from experience how poorly that could go for the deal. Jasmine, an executive at our company, fucked up a deal last year by sleeping with someone she shouldn't have.

We needed to keep Jeremy on our side, and not get tangled up in complications. He would be a treasure trove of information and a valuable asset if he could be persuaded to go into business with us.

I was pulled back to the moment as the car moved off and Faith tugged on my arm.

"Tristan," she said in that cutesy girl voice she put on when she really wanted me to give her something.

"Yes, love?" I said, brushing her hair with my hand.

"You got me all worked up. In the restaurant. I want you in me."

She looked at me hungrily and almost licked her lips.

I could feel myself getting hard. I knew she could feel it, too, with her hand resting on my lap. If we hadn't been hanging in the middle of the air, I might have done something about it.

"Perhaps during a gondola ride is not the best place for what you have in mind?" I enjoyed the desperate look on her face.

"Not even a quick blowjob?" she pleaded.

I looked out of the window, estimating how much time we had. "Well..."

Before I had a chance to finish, she was pulling me free, her hurried desperation making me harder. She wanted it and she would not stop till she got it. Faith was like that in business and the bedroom.

"Get down on the floor. I want you on your knees." I fully expected the look she gave me.

"It's filthy and wet. I'll ruin my clothes," she moaned.

"Do you want to suck my cock?" I asked.

She thought for a moment and then got down on her knees in front of me.

"Besides, if you ruin your clothing, you can always use it as an excuse to go shopping."

She almost purred as she put the tip of my cock against her lips and then sank down on it, taking it all the way in. Her warm mouth seemed to heat my entire body, and I could feel myself reacting as she desperately sucked on me.

Her head came up and my cock sprang from her lips.

"I know you like taking your time," she said. "But I want you to come for me before we get to the bottom."

She started jerking my cock in her hand and sucking me slowly, her tongue swirling and flicking and driving me crazy.

Normally I would tell her to slow down, make her take her time so I could feel every single dip of her head. But I desperately wanted to come, to show her how turned on she had got me.

My hands rested briefly on the back of her head before I pushed her down. Faith took as much into her mouth as she could for a few seconds of pleasure. I watched her head bounce back up, enjoying the look she gave me.

"Yes. Be rough," she commanded.

I grabbed her head and pushed it down again, thrusting up into her throat and giving her what she wanted. I love my wife, but when she tells me she wants it rough, I give it to her roughly.

With a moan escaping my lips, I let go and came, three spurts while holding her head down. Then I pulled her back up and kissed her neck while she gasped for air. For a moment, I wondered what Jeremy would say if he knew what we had done in his gondola.

After a moment, she turned and kissed me, letting me taste myself on her lips. Then she stood up and straightened herself.

"Best get yourself tucked away. We're nearly at the bottom. You're supposed to be a serious businessman."

I smiled and pointed at the cum on the corner of her lip.

We spent most of the rest of the evening in bed, exhausting each other and making up for our time apart, sometimes with me in charge, sometimes with her. That was how it worked in our marriage, both in and out of the bedroom. We both knew when to take control or to let the other person take charge.

Eventually we snuggled up and Faith drifted off to sleep. The wind had picked up outside, and I wondered if we would still have our snowboarding lesson. I was looking forward to it, getting out into the open air and doing some exercise. If it could be used as an opportunity to learn more about the resort, then so much the better.

I let my hand drift up to Faith's hair and started playing with it, giving her a light kiss on her nose.

The afternoon had been spent having sex with my wife and tomorrow we were moving to the next step in acquiring the resort.

Everything was going perfectly.

CHAPTER 6

Faith

"Fine, you go snowboarding. I'll just be here alone!" I hollered towards Tristan as he left the condo.

My morning sucked.

I hadn't slept well. I'd awoken in the middle of night and thought about Jeremy's offer of snowboarding lessons and decided it was a bad idea. We don't need to know how to snowboard to run a ski resort, especially since we don't plan on managing it ourselves. What we needed to do was look at the data again and try to find Jeremy's most vulnerable spot and hit him there. Tristan didn't agree with me, so we had a minor debate about it, and then did our own thing — at high volume.

Tristan was always more of a people person than me. Where I was awkward and put my foot in my mouth, he knew how to smooth people over and make them agreeable. Then I would come in with the cold hard facts and we'd tag team them. He knew how to calm me and get me out of my head, and helped me see the big picture whenever I got stuck on details. At the end of the deal, he was usually the one everyone loved. I was okay with it, though, since his people skills had made me fall in love with him as well.

His day with Jeremy would go better without me. Maybe he'd soften him up while I dug into the numbers and found the weak spot. I wish we hadn't fought about it. I didn't realize how intent he was on learning about the ski resort. If Tristan came back to the room, I'd climb into his lap and tell him I was sorry for being a brat.

I sighed as I made coffee and wandered over to the desk. The surface was littered with file folders scattered around my laptop. I itched to dig in and pick everything apart again. I needed to find details I missed. There had to be something, right?

I booted up the laptop and sipped my coffee, trying to find some Zen while I wondered how long Tristan planned to be gone. A folder on my laptop's main screen contained pictures of the resort from a recon mission in the fall. We'd hired a photographer for a couple of days to take general photos of the resort so we could see how it looked on a normal day when they didn't know they had visitors.

I clicked open the folder, scanning the thumbnail pictures, when one photo caught my eye. I opened it and enlarged it so I could inspect it. In the photo, a group of teenagers stood by the ski lift, laughing and enjoying themselves. I recognized Lucy, and I could tell by the wide grin on her face that she had a fun-loving streak inside her. The photographer had caught her in a couple of other photos as well, and in each one she looked happy and slightly mischievous.

My coffee mug was empty, so I went and filled it. When I sat back at the desk, I stared out of the nearest window, appreciating the mountain view but also thinking back to my childhood.

I used to be fun loving and incredibly devious. I was the friend who pulled pranks on everyone and made people laugh. My favorite thing to do to a friend on their birthday had been to wrap their gift in layers upon layers of newspaper before a last layer of birthday paper wrapping. What started out as this tiny item turned into this huge mound and no one knew what they were getting. The first time it happened to each friend was hilarious because they weren't expecting to take several minutes to open a gift. Eventually, my friends caught on to my shenanigans and it wasn't as much fun, but I always did stuff like that to get a laugh.

Where did that girl go? I'm convinced my parents are to blame. They persuaded me to go into business by saying that creative pursuits had little value in the "real world." The woman I am now is smart, capable, and successful. I have a wonderful life, but I lost my impulse to have fun somewhere along the way. My chief entertainment as an adult is passionate sex with my husband — which is fabulous, don't get me wrong. Sometimes, though, I wish I had more in my life purely for my enjoyment, like a hobby. Something I wanted to do for the fun of it.

As much as Lucy annoyed me yesterday, I hope she keeps that zest for life as she grows older. I doubted Jeremy would try to change her like my parents did me, since it seemed like she got the trait from him. He's practically a man-child who doesn't understand he'll lose the ski resort if he keeps on his current path.

My phone chirped with a notification which jolted me out of my stupor. It was an acquaintance's birthday, and shit, I needed to get busy. I opened up more files about the resort on my computer and hunkered down.

Several hours later, I relaxed in my chair and rubbed the back of my neck. I didn't know whether to be pissed or proud of myself. I couldn't find anything I'd missed, and all the reports were thorough and accurate. Fuck. I didn't think we were going to convince Jeremy to sell unless he wanted to sell. This deal was really not the slam dunk I thought it would be. A ball of tension lodged in my stomach because we were this close to any deal blowing up. I hoped Tristan was having more luck with Jeremy.

I stood up, stretched, and nibbled on a granola bar as I wandered into the bathroom. The massive two-person tub called to me, and I hoped a nice long soak would ease the stress that ramped up the longer I looked at the numbers. Ugh, why wasn't Tristan back? We could take a bath together and slow fuck my anxiety away.

While the bathtub filled with water, I searched my phone for some porn. I didn't plan on coming during my bath, but nothing said I couldn't touch myself a little to relax, right? As I perched on the counter and perused my favorite porn site, a video caught my eye. It wasn't my usual thing at all, but the longer I watched it, the more turned on I became.

By the time I lowered myself into the bath, I was wet and needy. I let the warm water relax me as I closed my eyes and sighed as my fingers eased between my legs. I imagined myself in the video with Tristan in it as well and worked myself up to a nice frenzy.

Where the fuck was he when I needed him?

CHAPTER 7

Jeremy

"Seriously, Dad. I could miss this one day of school. For entertainment purposes." Lucy tilted her head, clearly rethinking her words. "I meant educational purposes. To learn about business stuff."

"Watching two uptight rich people try to snowboard is not a reason to miss school, Luce," I said, pulling some bowls and a box of cereal out of the cabinet and pouring it for us. She settled at the kitchen counter, setting her phone down and reaching for a spoon.

It had been just the two of us forever, and this was our morning routine, even though she had become more independent since she'd entered middle school.

"But Dad." She widened her eyes. "Think of the learning opportunities."

"Your bus comes in fifteen minutes. Eat, brush your teeth, and get to the bus stop."

She folded her hands around her spoon and tilted her face up, giving me her most angelic expression. I wasn't fooled. Her dark eyes sparkled with mischief. "Plan B: we mount the GoPro to your helmet and film it for the learning opportunities."

"Eat, brush your teeth, and get to the bus stop," I repeated, laughing. "There will be no learning opportunities that involve making fun of Tristan and Faith. I'm not even sure they're coming, anyway."

Lucy pouted for a moment, trying the puppy dog eyes, before she gave up and dug into her food. Maybe I would shoot a little video of Tristan and Faith wiping out for Lucy's entertainment. She really was a good kid and I couldn't resist making her laugh. I finished my coffee and cereal and ruffled her hair, heading into my bedroom to get dressed. I hadn't heard from them again, so it was entirely possible they weren't planning on showing up. Perhaps they were on a plane back to Seattle, done with Tahoe.

I should have been delighted to realize I might have successfully sent them packing. Instead, the thought gave me an uneasy feeling in my gut, like there was unfinished business between us. And I was a little jittery as I waved to Lucy at the bus stop and climbed into my truck.

I headed to my office at the mountain first, parking in my usual spot and going inside to touch base with my staff before heading onto the snow. Tristan was there already. He was standing in the lobby, speaking to the receptionist, who was clearly charmed, either by his sexy British accent or his good looks. She was giggling in a flirty way, and her cheeks were pinker than I'd ever seen them.

Certainly, it wasn't his outfit that had charmed her, though, because he was dressed like a giant dork. My assistant, Carly, came in behind me and crashed into my back. "Jeremy, why are you standing there like an idiot?" she asked, then peeked around my shoulder. "Oh, right, the hot guy."

"What is he wearing?" I whispered.

"I think he opted for the most high-end gear shop in town. At least it looks waterproof." She snickered. "A bit on the tight side, but waterproof."

"How will he even bend over? And why is the jacket so short?" I rolled my eyes, picturing Tristan's outfit tearing apart during a wipeout, and waved Carly towards her office. "Go. Do some of the work I pay you for. I'll handle Mr. Tight Pants."

"I wouldn't mind handling him a little myself," Carly muttered, but she turned and headed for the suite of offices with a regretful sigh.

Tristan looked my way and adjusted his jacket. Yeah, it was way too short. It was from a ski brand I recognized and was the sort of outerwear designed to appeal to someone with a more upscale urban fashion sense. In this case, it seemed like perhaps they had overlooked the practical things, like staying warm and comfortable.

"Hi! Jeremy!" he said, picking up the bag by his feet. "Ready to show me how to snowboard?"

"Yes, but let's change your clothes before anyone else sees you." His eyes widened when I took his hand and dragged him back to my office. I realized as he yelped in surprise I shouldn't have been so forceful. "Sorry. I'm not pulling you back here to have my way with you. Not that you aren't attractive."

"Right," he said, staring at me. Realizing what I had just said, I blew out a breath and turned to a row of shelves next to my desk, pulling out a bin of outerwear.

"Forget I said it. Anyway, if you want to learn to snowboard, you need to wear something..." I hesitated, this time trying to think through my words. "More comfortable to move in." Tristan was a little taller than me, though not as broad in the shoulders. I was sure I could find something to fit him, and I dug through my jackets and pants.

"You have a lot of outerwear," he said.

"Yep. I wear it every day. Somehow, I never thought to buy a pair of pants as snug as yours, though."

"The woman at the shop said these are better than Gore-Tex." Tristan looked down at himself, brushing his hands over his ski pants, which were made of a strange tweed fabric. Were they stretchy, too? "I'm dressed ridiculously, aren't I? She insisted I wasn't."

I tried to be complimentary. "No, you're sexy." Right, so maybe tactful was a better approach. I cleared my throat before trying again.

"You can save that outfit for the streets of London. For snowboarding, it doesn't seem very practical to be wearing pants that'll bust a seam when you bend over to strap in." In the bins on my shelf, I finally found a pair of snowboard pants were a bit long on me and held them out. "These are a little roomier."

He smiled a little, setting down his bag and reaching for them. "I want to go back to that store and have a talk with the salesperson. It's entirely possible she spotted me as an easy mark and pulled one over on me." Tristan seemed more easygoing than I would have expected, and his smile was bemused as he unzipped his jacket. I chuckled, suddenly wanting him to feel better about his mistake.

"That kind of outfit is popular with wealthy skiers, but we're snowboarding. She probably didn't get what you were looking for."

I tried not to watch as he undressed. With a little effort, he peeled off his too-tight pants, revealing a snug pair of leggings and a form-fitting shirt underneath, which was almost as bad as finding him naked. The fabric hugged his thickly muscled thighs, flat stomach, and the bulge between his legs I definitely shouldn't have been looking at.

Tristan was muscular in a lean way that wasn't obvious when he was dressed. His fitness level was good news for our lesson, because nothing was worse than teaching an out of shape person to snowboard. There were other, more inappropriate things running through my mind as he turned to pick up his gear, and my eyes darted over the round, firm muscles of his ass. I wondered what it would be like to touch him, and felt my body respond, heating as blood rushed to my core.

I reminded myself that he was married, probably straight, and definitely not interested in me. I flushed and looked away, reaching for my boots and pulling them on.

"So, where's Faith?" I was desperate to turn the conversation towards anything other than my thoughts.

Tristan sighed. "I couldn't convince her to join us. She's trying to prove she can run a resort purely on research, I think." I glanced towards him, then immediately regretted it, because fuck, he was sexy, and I still hadn't recovered from my close call with an inappropriate erection. I wished he wasn't putting on more clothes — my clothes.

"Understanding the passion people have for their sports is an important part of this business."

"I agree, though she has a point, too. I'm sure she'll come around, eventually." He reached into his bag and pulled out a pair of boots, sitting to lace them tightly, then searching for his helmet and goggles.

"Too bad. I was hoping for a threesome." Shit, that hadn't come out right. "I mean, not like a sex threesome, I mean, all of us together, snowboarding." I was painfully aware that clarifying the point had only made things worse, but Tristan was staring at me again, a little smile playing around his lips.

"Have you ever had a sex threesome?" He still looked like he was going to laugh, but somehow kept his words serious-sounding.

"Oh, hell no. I was twenty when Lucy was born, and her mother only stuck around for three or four months before she ditched us for college. My youthful experimentation phase was cut off before it even started."

"Ah, that makes sense. No wild college days?"

"Nope, just a baby and a lot of panicking. Come on, let's head out onto the snow before I say anything that implies something else awkward." I picked up a snowboard leaning against the back wall of my office and led him back through the building.

"I think lots of people have threesomes in their thirties and forties, too," Tristan said, earning us a startled gasp from the receptionist. She handed us a lift ticket for Tristan, and we pushed outside into the bright Tahoe sun.

Outside, Tristan picked up a shiny new snowboard from a rack that sat along the side of the office building. Fortunately, unlike his outerwear, he picked a good quality board, one that I often recommended for beginners.

"How did you get the board right and the outerwear so wrong?" I asked, befuddled.

"Oh, I went to different shops. Clearly, I should have purchased everything at the snowboard shop."

"Yep, although usually people rent gear for the first few lessons. In case they don't like it." I gestured towards the learning area, leading him a few hundred yards across the snow.

"Why wouldn't I like it? I've surfed before and I liked that."

"You never know. Learning can be a little painful."

"My wife insisted we buy a condo here, so we'll be spending a lot of time in Tahoe. I might as well have a snowboard. Hopefully, we'll even own a resort here." He shot me a look.

"Nice try. I'd be happy to snowboard with you anytime, but I'm not selling."

"I wouldn't be so sure." He winked, then spun his snowboard around and started fiddling with the bindings. "Shall we get started? You'll need to show me how these straps work. I'm not sure how I feel about being strapped down to this thing."

Why did the thought of Tristan strapped down sound so delicious? I forced myself to stop thinking about bondage and led him to a quiet spot, away from the hubbub of the bunny hill. I set my snowboard and helmet on the snow, telling him to sit down. Kneeling at his feet, I positioned his snowboard on the snow in front of him, showing him how to set his feet into the bindings and click them closed.

It was all a bit too close, considering how attracted I was to him, but I couldn't resist a hands-on approach. I glanced up, meeting his eyes, then took a slow breath and forced myself to go through technical instructions, explaining the edges and the flex of the snowboard. Fortunately, I'd filled in at the snowsports school enough that I had it memorized, because my mind certainly wasn't focused on what I was saying.

Tristan was a good-natured and attentive student. I was happy with his progress as I helped him stand and showed him the basics of how to stop and turn. He picked things up quickly, and his experience surfing helped. I couldn't resist touching him a little during the lesson, holding his hands down as he learned to stop and got the basics of turning.

"I think you're ready for the lift," I said, pointing towards the tiny chairlift that led to the top of the little bunny hill.

Tristan glanced over at the lift, then down at his feet, which were still strapped to the snowboard. "So I'm supposed to get there by taking one foot out?"

"Yep, just dig your edge in and push with your free foot, like a skateboard. It's called skating." I showed him the movement. He followed my instructions, wobbling a little, and we made our way over to the lift line, where he paused, staring at the chair.

"Doesn't it go a little high for a beginner?"

"Not really, no." I smirked at him, and he shrugged, but remained relaxed and chatty as we slid through the lift line on our snowboards. He was a little shaky skating up to the lift, but loaded up without an issue. Things took a turn when the lift rose higher into the air, though. He stared wide-eyed down at the ground and yanked the safety bar down, then slid over on the seat until he was close enough to me our thighs touched.

"This is safe, right?" He was staring straight down at the ground, which probably wasn't helping.

I laughed and patted his knee. "It's safe. This is the bunny hill, the easiest run on the mountain. I won't let anything happen to you." I moved my hand away, realizing that I probably shouldn't be touching another man like that, but he snatched my hand and put it back, resting it on his thigh.

"Just for safety," he muttered.

"Right." I squeezed the firm muscle of his leg a little. In a reassuring way, not a sexual way, or at least that was what I told myself. "Look! There's a toddler on the chair in front of you and she's fine."

"Are we sure she's not just a very brave toddler? Perhaps she doesn't understand risk."

"I'm pretty sure she's having fun. We're already almost at the top. See? Short lift." I reached out to raise the safety bar, but he had a firm hold on the metal rod, and fought my attempt to raise it. "Hey. Tristan, we can't get off the lift until the bar is up."

"I think we need to be a little closer."

"No, look. This is where we lift the bar. Once you master this, we can go higher, or take the gondola, since we know you do well in enclosed cars." I yanked again, but he wouldn't let go of the damn thing.

"Not yet," he growled. Our grappling over the bar escalated until our boards were dragging in the snow. I finally pried it from his death grip. The lift operator lunged for the emergency stop button, right as the chair slid across the ramp at the top. I stood and glared at Tristan, who gave me a sheepish grin and tried to stand, wobbling a little.

"Dude. Clear the unloading area," the liftie shouted. I kicked my snowboard forward, gliding down the snow-covered ramp, and Tristan followed. Halfway down, he tripped on the edge of his snowboard and frantically grabbed at the air as he went down, tumbling into me and taking us both down.

I grunted as he landed in a heap on top of me, then froze in place as the heat and weight of his body pressed into mine. "Just when I was thinking you were a good student."

"I am a good student," he muttered, shifting in a way that only seemed to press his body closer to mine. His face was inches away, but I couldn't see his eyes, only my reflection in his mirror lens goggles. His warm breath tickled against my lips, and I shuddered, a tingle of awareness passing through me.

"Damn, I wish you weren't married."

"What?" Tristan pushed onto his knees, then leaped up. I groaned and pushed into a sitting position, then stood and skated off to the side, ducking out of the crowd of onlookers that had watched our antics. Hopefully, they couldn't tell I was aroused. I shot an embarrassed glare at the liftie, who was laughing his ass off as he started the lift again. I led Tristan to the edge of the run, where we sat down to strap in. He wrapped his arms around his knees for a moment, staring out at the scenery.

"Sorry, I have a bit of a problem with blurting out inappropriate things. I didn't mean that. I like Faith."

"No, you don't."

"Okay, I might like Faith if she wasn't so uptight. If she wasn't married to a man that I'm attracted to." There went the blurting again.

Tristan studied me, the mirror lens of his goggles obscuring his expression. "Are you gay?"

"No, bisexual. I think. Lucy came along and killed all my mojo before I figured it out." I glanced at him and he smirked, shaking his head. "Yeah, you're right, I've never had mojo. I know what I'm doing with women, well enough to hook up with randos on dating apps. Hooking up with a guy online is too intimidating. I mean, I don't even know how to suck cock." Someone gasped behind us, and I turned to find a random soccer mom standing there on her skis. "Sorry ma'am."

"This is a family establishment," she huffed, stomping off as best she could on her skis, which slipped out from under her and kept her from moving forward for a moment. I tried to hold in my laughter.

Tristan flopped onto his back in the snow. With his eyes hidden, it took me a moment to realize he was laughing his ass off. "Seriously, the things you say." He lifted his goggles off of his face and wiped his eyes. "You must get into a lot of trouble."

"Yeah, it's a bit of a problem," I said. "Come on, let's snowboard."

"You want me to go down that hill? It's massive."

I sighed and stood up, hopping my snowboard forward. "We've been over this. It's the bunny hill. Look, the toddler we saw on the lift is already halfway down."

"Shit. I can't very well ask to walk down now that you've pointed that out."

I helped him to his feet and showed him a few turns. As I'd expected before we got on the lift, he picked it up quickly. He had a talent for it, and over the next few runs, it was fun to watch him get the hang of it, even the lift. Fortunately, we had no more issues with unloading.

On our last run of the day, I took him to the top of the gondola for a longer run. He looked a little terrified, but tried to hide it, asking questions about the area instead.

"What would you do with this place if you had an influx of cash? Perhaps you could find an investor?" Tristan asked this casually, looking out the window. My heart stopped. This was a question that I knew the answer to. I studied him, wondering if there was an alternative to an outright purchase that they'd be happy with.

"Are you saying that you'd be willing to become investors instead of owners?"

"I'm not sure. I was curious. We wouldn't want to lose your expertise in the sport or the local area. Perhaps there's a balanced approach." He might have been buttering me up, but it was working.

"I went to a resort in Austria once where you could take the lifts, then ski down to another town and stay there. I've been mapping out a way to do that here. It seems like an impossible dream, but it would make Emerald Bay one of the biggest resorts in the US, and it would give us something unique."

"Do you think it would be profitable?" Tristan asked.

I scratched the back of my head, thinking. "The profit would be in the real estate. There's not much to the town, but there's a big plot of land for sale a few miles down the road, land that could be developed into condos, shops, restaurants. A whole new base area."

"Ah, now we're getting somewhere."

"We're getting to the top of the gondola. Try not to cry like a baby when you see the run we're going to take. It's still a beginner run full of little kids." I stood up and climbed out of the car.

He chuckled, following me onto the snow. "So taking me up the gondola was an evil scheme to humiliate me?"

"Perhaps." I smiled and set my board down, ready to show him some real snowboarding.

CHAPTER 8

Tristan

After a few hours, I was utterly exhausted.

Jeremy was great company and a fantastic instructor, and I could already feel myself starting to improve, but I feared that one more run might make me collapse.

Although if it was into his arms then maybe that wouldn't have been too bad.

His revelations today had my mind spinning. I couldn't deny that he was both attractive and the sort of guy that I would go for. In fact, back in my college days I went with my own fair share of guys like him. But his plans for the resort also interested me; his enthusiasm and joy in the potential was infectious.

The fact he was super fit and had a great body certainly hadn't gone unnoticed. I felt a little bit guilty for letting my eyes linger on him, drinking in his sexiness. I'm faithful to my wife, but I'm sure she wouldn't mind me indulging in a little eye candy.

Before we went our separate ways, Jeremy asked if we were free tomorrow.

"I don't think that Faith has anything planned, so I'm sure we could be. Why?"

He flashed the smile that lights up his face.

"I want to show you the land I told you about. If, and I do mean if, I ever looked for investment, this would be where I would concentrate the money. It's about an hour away, pretty isolated, but it has real potential. I would like the two of you to see it and tell me what you think."

Interesting, I thought. Could this be a slight thawing in his exterior?

He said he would text over the details later. With a wave he was gone, off to do whatever it is that he actually does.

Things seemed to be progressing nicely. Now to get Faith on board.

When I walked through the door it was obvious she had other things on her mind.

"Let's get you out of those clothes and into a shower," she said, pulling at my clothing as she led me through to the bathroom.

"Ouch. Careful, I'm a little on the delicate side," I replied as she did her best to strip me where I stood.

"Oh, was the bad man nasty to you?" she said, putting on that cutesy voice she sometimes uses when she wants something. From her hand slipping between my legs, it was obvious she wanted sex, and sooner rather than later.

"No, not nasty. I'm just not used to so much strenuous exercise."

By now I was stripped down to my boxers and her hand was rubbing me through them. I was tired, but I still reacted, getting hard under her touch.

"You get pretty strenuous with me," she said, her fingers wrapping around me and slowly stroking.

It felt amazing, but my body was crying out in pain.

"Faith, I need to have a shower and then a rest. He worked me hard today."

She sighed and gave my cock another squeeze.

"I want to work you hard as well," she sighed.

"How about this, I have a shower and while you're waiting, you go to the bedroom and get ready to give me a massage. While you're doing that, you can edge yourself for me."

She let out a moan, half in frustration and half in need.

"Please, don't tease me. I really want you."

I kissed her on the forehead, pulled down my boxers, and stepped into the shower.

"Then be a good girl and get ready. I'll be through in a few minutes."

I felt better after the shower but my body was aching more than it has in years. A rub down from Faith sounded like the perfect end to the day.

When I walked into the bedroom she was laid out on the bed, stripped naked and playing with herself. She gave me a cheeky grin as she rubbed her pussy and tweaked her nipple, then rolled over on to all fours and crawled to the edge of the bed.

"How about we skip the massage and just go straight to the sex?" she purred.

I knelt down beside the bed, took her face in my hands, and gave her a long deep kiss. She looked beautiful and the throbbing between my legs made me want to agree with her.

"Now, Faith, we had an agreement. Massage first."

She pouted but I could see she was playful, for now.

"Can I at least suck it, just a bit?" she asked, and I was powerless to say no.

Her hand reached out and wrapped around my cock, gently stroking. She dipped her head down to engulf it, taking her time to enjoy it as I hardened in her mouth.

All the stress and aches in my body seem to flow out of me and I could feel my eyes shutting for a moment. My hands reached for her, resting on her head, fingers in her hair as I guided her.

She slipped me from her mouth and licked the underside of my cock, making sure to keep eye contact with me.

"Oh, we have plans for tomorrow now. I arranged with Jeremy..." I started but she raised her finger to her mouth and made a shushing sound.

"That's for tomorrow," she said, taking my hand and pulling me forward.

I got onto the bed, flat on my back as she straddled me, her hands on my shoulders, massaging away the aches of the day. When she kissed me I felt the heat behind it, the love and lust in her.

She moved and kissed my shoulder, then slowly kissed down over my chest. Her hand slowly stroked up and down, keeping me hard for her as her mouth got nearer and nearer.

Suddenly the room felt warm and I let my eyes close. I felt like I was floating and everything seemed very far away.

The feel of her hand and her mouth on me sent shivers of pleasure through my body and as I started to drift I thought that I had the greatest and most caring wife in the world.

———◆O◆———

I woke up with the sunshine in my eyes.

The bed was empty and the light was streaming in through the window. The door to the bedroom was open and the smell of coffee was floating into the room.

I struggled for a few minutes to remember what happened the night before and then it hit me. Faith had been in the middle of giving me a blowjob when I fell asleep.

I knew that she was going to be pissed at me, but how much?

I scrambled out of bed, put on some boxers, and went to find her.

She was sitting in the kitchen, looking out the window. Mug of coffee in her hand.

"Morning," I said, and tried to gauge her mood.

She didn't reply and just sipped her coffee. This was unfortunate and worrying.

I walked round and stood behind her, rubbing her shoulders and dipping my head down to her neck, kissing it gently.

"I'm sorry about last night. I was exhausted and you just got me so comfy."

I felt her body relax a little but she still didn't say anything.

"Maybe I could make it up to you?" I reached round, cupped her breasts with my mouth on her shoulder, and bit down gently.

This got a moan out of her and her head fell back against me. I knew that she was angry, but her anger normally faded quickly if she was given a little attention.

As I turned her around, her phone went off.

We looked at each other for a moment before she sighed and picked it up.

While she talked on the phone, I made myself some coffee. We have a rule: if the phone goes off, we stop what we're doing and answer. There are far too many business decisions that need to be made quickly for us to ignore them. At times like this it's annoying, but it's the right thing to do.

I heard the sound of a voice on the other end and assumed it was Jeremy. For a moment I wondered why he phoned Faith, then I realized I hadn't given him my number.

I sat as Faith put down the phone.

"That was Jeremy. Apparently he'll be here to pick us up in half an hour. We're going to see some plot that he talked to you about. I take it you made some headway with him?"

She had slipped back into business mode and her anger had vanished.

"Yes. We talked about the prospect of becoming investors, rather than buying the resort outright. He has some plans that would require a cash injection. I thought it might be worth pursuing."

Faith thought on it for a second, then nodded her head, got up, and walked around the table.

"Sounds like a good plan," she said, trailing her hand over my shoulder as she passed by. "But you're still not out of my bad books, not until you make it up to me."

I thought of the strap-on sitting next to the bed and decided that maybe we would see another session with it in the near future. I was sure that if I let her peg me again, I would get back into her good books.

Half an hour later, we were both showered, dressed, and ready when Jeremy turned up. Faith grabbed a bottle of Champagne from the fridge to take along. We figured that if we closed the deal, we could use it to celebrate; if not, then we could commiserate with a glass of it. Faith had an oversized purse with her and tucked it inside.

He pulled up in his truck and I started to climb in beside him, but Faith put her arm around mine and dragged me towards the back. I looked at Jeremy and shrugged. I wasn't going to argue with her, even if he looked a little irritated.

As we climbed into the back of his truck, I suddenly remembered I hadn't told Faith about Jeremy's confession the day before. I needed to tell her, both because it would give her a thrill, but also because we might use it to our advantage.

"Morning, sleep well?" he asked, and we both nodded a yes.

"Okay then. It's going to be about an hour's drive. I'll leave you folks to whatever's going on with you."

He'd obviously picked up on the tension between me and Faith. He must have thought we were fighting, but really it was regret that we didn't get more time together before he showed up. That morning, while Faith had been showering, I had slipped in behind her. I gently pushed her up against the wall and ate out her pussy. Unfortunately, we'd had to cut it short as we were running out of time before Jeremy was due to arrive, so there was a sexual tension in the air. I had a feeling that once this trip was over, we might not be leaving the condo for a day or two.

"Terribly sorry, we have a load of work to catch up on. You don't mind, do you?"

He shook his head and concentrated on driving.

We both pulled out our phones and got on with work. Just because we were in a winter wonderland didn't mean everything else stood still. As we passed through the landscape, we found time to send each other some filthy messages.

"How did my tongue feel on your pussy?" I texted her.

Her phone beeped next to me and I saw her check it, her face blushing red.

"It felt so good. But I really need your cock inside me. While you were out having fun yesterday, I got all needy for you," she texted back.

I leaned over and kissed the side of her neck, my hand momentarily sliding between her legs.

As I leaned back, I glanced forward and saw Jeremy watching us in the mirror, so I flashed him a smile. He blushed and quickly returned his attention to the road.

For the rest of the journey, Faith snuggled up against me. Eventually, she put down the phone and pulled out one of her notebooks. I was curious what she was writing, but she only added a few things before she put it back in her pocket and rested her eyes. It was a pleasant feeling, driving through the snow, as my wife cuddled up beside me.

The truck slowed down and veered onto a narrower side road that wound through the forest. I closed my eyes as well, for what only seemed like a moment, blinking when Jeremy turned off the engine.

"Wake up, you two, we're finally here," he said.

CHAPTER 9

Faith

I stumbled out of the car, bleary-eyed, and blinked in confusion. Where were we? Jeremy must have noticed my bewilderment because he gave me the answer to my unasked question in a snide tone.

"You probably didn't notice while you were napping, but there was bad ice on the road and the drive took twice as long. I need food."

I glanced around at the tiny shithole of a diner he stopped at, wholly unimpressed. He could have taken us somewhere better. A large group of people streamed out of the diner and greeted another sizable group climbing out of a truck. I watched the two groups mingle. Many of them obviously knew each other. There were rounds of "How the hell are ya," and loud backslaps. There was a fair amount of handshaking going on — new partners being introduced to the old group, I imagined. Clearly it was a family gathering, since I overheard someone named 'cousin Jimmy' being referred to a lot. I wouldn't have guessed this would be a big meeting spot based on its run-down appearance, but one crazy family loving the place made sense.

Jeremy caught my eye while I watched the crowd. When his eyes dropped to my lips, I fought the urge to lick them while a fluttery sensation in my stomach made me blush. Dang it, why did he have to be so attractive? My lack of an orgasm last night and this morning was making me uncomfortable when he looked at me. I told myself the blush was because he probably read my mind about the diner and had nothing to do with any sort of reaction to him.

Tristan announced, "I'm hungry too. Let's get some food before we go see the property." I was jolted out of my thoughts about hunky Jeremy.

Tristan led the way into the diner, and Jeremy followed him. If I hadn't been watching Jeremy so closely, I wouldn't have noticed him inspecting Tristan's ass as Tristan climbed the steps to get to the door. What was going on here? I wasn't getting gay vibes from Jeremy. In fact, it was quite the opposite, but there was no way he would look at an ass that intently if he wasn't checking it out. Tristan's butt was delicious. Maybe Jeremy appreciated any fine ass within his line of sight?

Inside was as busy as the outside. The only available table was a small, rounded corner booth that was going to be a tight fit for three people. No one made a move to sit. The middle person was going to get squished. We stood at the table awkwardly while the harried waitress placed three menus and promised to return with water.

Jeremy was the first to suggest a solution. "I vote the shortest person gets the middle spot."

"I agree." My traitorous husband was quick to chime in, and I watched the men share a smile.

Imagining bumping elbows with Jeremy sounded horrible, so I attempted to veto their decision.

"You guys spent all day together yesterday and are probably best buds by now, so you can squeeze together."

I took a step back from the table to show I was serious while Tristan and Jeremy both replied.

Tristan announced, "Nope, it's decided," right as Jeremy said, "I could be the meat of the sandwich."

Knowing I was going to end up elbow-to-elbow with Jeremy either way, I slid into the booth without another word and glared at the men.

"Well, don't stand there. Sit down."

They sat on either side of me. Thankfully, everyone was quiet as we reviewed the menus, which were surprisingly comprehensive. No matter how I shifted in the seat, my knees and part of the outside of my thighs touched both men's legs. Every time one of us shifted, my overheated pussy thought I was being caressed on purpose.

I flashed back to the porno I watched before my bath. It was a threesome, but this time it wasn't only Tristan I imagined in the porno with me. Jeremy was the other star. My panties become embarrassingly wet and I told myself to keep Jeremy out of my sexual fantasies. We were attempting to get him to agree to a business deal, for fuck's sake. He wasn't here for my hot threesome daydream.

The waitress brought us the water. Tristan ordered tea and a full English breakfast. Jeremy said that sounded good, so he ordered the same, along with coffee and a slice of pecan pie. When Jeremy handed the waitress his menu, his side brushed against mine. My pussy clenched while a thrill of awareness of how close he was ran through me. Holy shit, I needed a good fucking from Tristan. This was all his fault for falling asleep the night before.

I realized everyone was silent and looking at me, so I blurted out the first things I could think of.

"Three eggs and hot chocolate, please."

The waitress asked how I wanted my eggs cooked and I felt like an idiot. No one orders three eggs. I told her I liked them scrambled, and then quickly added on a side of bacon as well. She winked at me and headed off with our menus, leaving us alone again. Tristan reached under the table to squeeze my thigh. He used the opportunity to run his hand towards the inside of my leg, tickling me through my trousers. I had to bite my lip to keep from moaning. Worse, I couldn't move because it would alert Jeremy that something was going on under the table. It made Tristan's roaming hand exquisite torture.

Tristan and Jeremy talked about their day yesterday, laughing like they were old friends, but Tristan's hand distracted me too much to pay attention. Maybe I could entice him into a quickie in the bathroom?

When the waitress set our drinks down at the table, Jeremy questioned her. "Why is it so busy today?"

"Oh, you know, it's Jimmy's birthday. Every year he plans a big bash and a lot of his family come up for the party." She waved her hand in the air, indicating all the people in the diner, but didn't explain who Jimmy was. I guess we were supposed to know.

I held my hot chocolate mug to my lips and mumbled into it, "Oh yeah, that's right. It's Jimmy's birthday this weekend," and Jeremy snickered.

Tristan hummed contentedly next to me with the first sip of his tea, which told me he thought it was good. My first sample of the hot chocolate made me slow down to savor it. Wow, it was shockingly good—rich and thick with a dense bitterness.

The food was just as delicious as the hot chocolate, and I was hungrier than I realized. I stayed quiet while Jeremy and Tristan talked about various aspects of running a resort. Normally I would have joined in, but the warmth of both men being so close distracted me. Every slight brush against me sent tingles down my spine.

The waitress brought Jeremy his pie, and it looked amazing. My mouth watered looking at it, and he saw me eyeing the slice.

"Want a bite?"

He scooped up some pie on his fork and didn't give me time to reply before he shoved it towards my mouth. I opened my lips instinctually and let him feed me. Once in my mouth, I pressed my lips together firmly and kept eye contact with him while he slowly slid the fork out. I chewed the morsel and groaned in pleasure. Holy shit, the pie was amazing too. Jeremy didn't take another bite, but stuck the fork straight from my mouth into his to lick it clean, and a shock of desire hit me. Oh fuck, I just ate some dude's pie and groaned.

I glanced over at Tristan to gauge his reaction to his wife moaning at another man's pie. He had that eager glint in his eyes he got whenever he was turned on, but I realized he was looking at Jeremy and not me. What the hell was going on here?

A rush of heat moved from my core to my face. I needed to go before my pussy ignited from my lack of sex and being squished close together with two hunky men. "Uh, guys? Let's eat and get out of here. I want to see this land and get home. I have stuff to do tonight, you know?"

I didn't mention that my stuff included fucking my husband three ways to Sunday. His lustful look at Jeremy made me consider a double stuffing fantasy with a dildo in my cooch and Tristan in my ass. Maybe round two would be me pegging him again.

My words spurred everyone to finish quickly and we split the check. As we walked out, I realized that the folks at the family reunion weren't as crazy as I'd thought. The diner might not have looked great, but the pie and hot chocolate were delicious. I'd come back.

When we climbed back into the truck, Tristan avoided my glance. He got in the front seat so he could quiz Jeremy about the area as we drove to the property. I daydreamed about pegging Tristan some more and relaxed. I may have dozed off. It seemed like it took forever to get to the property, but the clock on the dashboard only showed about an hour.

The men got out and trudged around in the snow, talking about an overall vision, while I leaned against the side of the truck and contemplated the area. I could picture the plan, but I wanted to run some numbers. I didn't even need to be here, but I wanted to spend time with Tristan. If he thought this was a good idea, I trusted his business sense. If the numbers panned out in our favor, it would be something to consider seriously.

I scribbled some of my thoughts in my notebook while I waited for the men to get done. After half an hour, Tristan and Jeremy walked back to me.

As they got back into earshot, Jeremy said, "Well, that's it. Let's get Faith home so she can do her stuff."

I couldn't tell if he was mocking me, or if he really genuinely cared that I wanted to go home. Either way, it didn't matter. I was one step closer to having Tristan's cock inside of me. My pussy hummed to life as I realized we were only a few hours away from sexy, fun times.

This time I dragged Tristan into the back with me before he could get any ideas to sit up front. I intended to cop a feel and tease him on the drive home. By the time we got back to the condo, I wanted him nice and hard, ready to shove me against a wall and fuck my brains out.

Jeremy started the truck, totally focused on the snowy road, while I leaned over to kiss Tristan's neck and briefly rub his cock through his jeans. He was already rock solid before I touched him. I briefly wondered what got him hard while they were out traipsing in the snow, but pushed the thought aside.

We drove over an hour before we came to a stop. I wasn't expecting to stop, so I glanced around sharply, gawking out the window. What the heck was going on? There were three cars in front of us and someone was going car to car, and then each car was turning around. Oh fuck, what's this?

Jeremy rolled down his window when the guy approached.

"Sorry folks, avalanche on the pass. There's no getting through, probably for hours."

Jeremy thanked him, rolled up his window, and turned the truck around. As we headed back, I heard him swear softly underneath his breath. Tristan and I looked at each other, wide eyed. What did this mean?

"Uh, what happens now?" I finally dared to ask Jeremy.

"Nothing. We're stuck here until they clear the pass."

His answer didn't give me the information I needed, so I tried again. "But what are we going to do?"

Jeremy sighed at my second question. "There's a motel of sorts close to the diner. We can stay there overnight."

Oooh, this wasn't ideal, but my slutty side liked the idea of getting fucked in some sleazy motel. Jeremy would get his own room, so Tristan and I could fuck like rabbits all night long. I was one hundred percent on board with this new plan, and a gush of wetness hit my panties while I squirmed in my seat. Yeah, I needed Tristan's cock in me ASAP.

When we got back to the area of the diner, Jeremy stopped at a tiny grocery store. We all stocked up on munchies to get us through the night, ordered sandwiches from a small deli area inside the store, and ate them in the car. It was getting towards early evening and we needed to find our lodging.

The drive didn't take long, and before I knew it, Jeremy pulled up in front of a log cabin with a flashing "VACANCY" sign, but I was confused. Where was the motel?

"Come on, let's get some cabins." Jeremy didn't wait for us and hopped out of the truck, heading towards the building.

Oh, wait? A cabin? Even better! Tristan and I scrambled out and followed him.

When we stepped inside, Jeremy was talking to a woman at the counter and I heard her say, "I'm sorry, we only have one cabin still available tonight. It's Jimmy's birthday weekend, you know."

The woman looked at Tristan and me when we entered. "I'm sorry, no more vacancies," she called out. She obviously didn't realize we were all together.

"Oh, they're with me," Jeremy mumbled, and the woman turned back to him and brightened. "No problem then, but the room only has one bed. One of you will have to sleep on the couch."

Ugh. There went my plans to fuck Tristan all night. No way in hell was I doing it with Jeremy in the same cabin. When Jeremy reached for his wallet to pay for the room, Tristan pushed past me to lay his card on the counter.

"Let me pay for it."

Jeremy didn't stop reaching for his wallet.

"No, it's fine. I'll pay."

I wondered if I was watching a power struggle, though neither man seemed more dominant over the other, so it was a toss-up who would win. A brief flash of them naked, sweaty, and wrestling flitted through my brain. I'd watch that show and it didn't matter who won. Their continued banter forced me to pay attention to what was going on.

Tristan argued, "You drove us here. We'll get the room."

That logic worked. Jeremy put his wallet back into his trousers and grinned at Tristan.

"Right, while you slept. You can pay for the room."

We took the key and drove around the building and down a slight incline to our cabin. The other cabins were far enough away that we weren't up in everyone else's business, but I counted at least six other cabins in view, all of them occupied.

As Jeremy unlocked the cabin door, I realized we all had no other clothing to wear. My panties were wet enough I wanted to wash them in the tub and let them dry overnight. I'd sleep in my husband's shirt, sans panties. Maybe I'd have some fun flashing Tristan. I wanted to make him sore he missed out on shoving his cock inside me tonight.

When Jeremy flipped on the lights, I looked around the room and blinked. Uh, what the fuck? It was a one-room cabin with a queen-sized bed on the far wall and a couch in front of a fireplace. There was a small kitchenette with a wood table and chairs tucked in the corner. The place was clean but old. The couch did not look comfortable, nor was it anywhere near long enough for someone to sleep on. Well, someone was going to have a terrible night's rest, but it wouldn't be me. The married couple obviously had dibs on the bed.

"I'm going to grab something from the truck and call home to Lucy. She'll need to stay at a friend's tonight. I'll be right back."

Jeremy headed outside. Tristan and I looked at each other for a moment before I dropped my purse on the couch and pounced on him. I jumped up, forcing him to grab my thighs and ass, while I wrapped my legs around him and kissed him passionately.

Nibbling my way down his neck, I whispered in his ear. "Quick, take me to the bathroom and fuck me. I need you so bad, it won't take long."

"Love, we can't. He's going to come back any moment, you know that."

Tristan let go of my legs. I slid down the length of his body, noticing how hard he was. Right when my feet hit the floor, the door opened and Jeremy came in, stomping snow off his boots.

We were standing suspiciously close, and it was obvious we'd been kissing.

"Uh, don't mind me," Jeremy mumbled at us, and it almost looked like he was blushing.

His words prompted me to glance at his crotch, and his jeans outlined his obviously hard package. At this rate, it was going to be an awkward night, so I decided we all needed some champagne.

I snagged my purse from the couch and pulled out the bottle. "If we're stuck here, I vote we get tipsy."

Tristan laughed. "Sounds good to me."

Jeremy didn't look surprised I was carrying champagne around and busied himself building a fire in the fireplace. What did that say about me, if someone thought it was perfectly normal that I had a bottle in my purse? I tried not to dwell on it and focused on the immediate issue of how we're to drink it.

Tristan solved the problem by rummaging around in the kitchenette drawers until he found a corkscrew, while I pulled out three white mugs. Oh yeah, this was totally happening. We're going to drink expensive champagne out of chipped mugs, and maybe some of the annoying sexual tension would ease.

We removed our outer clothes before grabbing a mug, but the cabin didn't have many seating options. It was the two-cushion couch, which realistically was for two people, or some hard wooden dining chairs.

Jeremy sat down on the couch, and Tristan joined him. I took a big gulp of champagne and tried not to cough on bubbles before I ventured over and pushed open Tristan's knees. I sat on the floor between them with my back against the couch while I watched the fire.

We sat in silence for a while, sipping our bubbly, and I relaxed. This wasn't so bad, but I was still glad Jeremy was sleeping on the couch. Tristan played with my hair as we sat there, brushing his fingers through it, making me giggle when he tickled my neck. I could feel the effects of the alcohol hitting me, and I sighed as Tristan started massaging my neck and shoulders. Fuuuck, this felt good.

I realized too late that my grand plan with the alcohol was a horrible one. I'd wanted us to relax, but I didn't think about how alcohol revved my high sex drive even more. Tristan's hands on me only made me want to get up, climb into his lap, and grind against him.

I tipped my head down towards my shoulder so Tristan could tickle my exposed neck, and I moaned a little as he caressed circles on the most sensitive area below my ear. When he leaned over to nibble and kiss my neck, my louder moan made me realize we needed to stop because we weren't alone. I glanced over at Jeremy, and he was watching us with hooded, unreadable eyes. I couldn't tell which one of us he was watching more since we were so close together. From all our brief interactions today, I was thinking he found us both attractive.

Tristan sat back and played with my hair some more. I relaxed again, only to be shocked when a third hand touched my hair.

"Shit, sorry." Jeremy snatched his hand back and mumbled what sounded like, "Looked soft in the firelight." Oh yeah, he was feeling the effects of the alcohol as well. His reply made me giggle. I was oddly pleased that he couldn't help himself and had to touch it.

I should tell him he can touch it. I opened my mouth to speak, but out of the corner of my eye, I saw Tristan take Jeremy's hand and move it to my hair. He kept his hand on Jeremy's and moved it through my hair, as if showing it was okay for him to caress me. I looked back at the fire while both guys played with my hair. That Tristan wanted Jeremy to touch me made me impossibly wetter.

This was so fucking hot it was unbelievable, and I wasn't sure how I was going to fall asleep tonight without a cock inside of me. I thought about the threesome porno and how revved up I got from it, and wondered if two cocks were better than one. I really should have just masturbated in the bath. If I had known it would be two days before I had sex again, I would have.

My mind drifted when I closed my eyes, while three hands explored beyond my hair and down to my neck and ears, caressing me. I played back the porno in my head and an overwhelming desire consumed me. Fuck it. I moved out from between Tristan's legs, forcing their hands to fall away from me. I sat on my knees with the fire behind me and faced them.

"I want you two to kiss."

CHAPTER 10

Jeremy

"I'm sorry, what?" I asked, standing and looking from Faith to Tristan. "Are you fucking with me?" Between the champagne and the cozy warmth of the cabin, I had been lulled into an unexpected place, mentally, one where I was comfortable and close to them. Faith's words startled me out of that. Tristan stood, too, stepping closer to me.

"We're not." He met my eyes and smiled a little, and it seemed sincere. He was so close that I could taste him. My breath grew unsteady as I thought about what Faith had suggested and what I wanted.

"What, then?"

"I think I need to know," he said, continuing to hold that intense eye contact. The deep rumble of his voice was mesmerizing, and my breath caught in my throat.

"Know what?"

"What it's like. With you." He glanced at Faith. "And my wife wants to watch. So why the hell not?"

"Why the hell not?" I knew I should try to regain control, but the heady mixture of champagne and lust was taking over. My pulse pounded and my entire body was hot and restless. I held his eyes as I closed the few inches between us, brushing my lips tentatively against his. His mouth was soft and tasted of champagne, and I wanted more. I tilted my head and lifted a hand up to cup his jaw and deepened the kiss. His arms slipped around my waist, and he pulled my body against his. His heat and the sleek planes of muscle drew me in, made me press close and devour him. I wasn't sure how much time passed, but when I finally pulled away, we were both breathing hard.

"Holy shit," Faith said, drawing our attention to her. She was still sitting, but leaning towards us more, her bright green eyes wide and dilated. I shook my head and grinned, breaking the strange tension of the moment. This was a terrible idea.

"Thank you. I've always wondered if I'd like that." Meeting Tristan's eyes again, I gathered myself, silently repeating all the reasons that I needed to stop this. It was inappropriate. They were married. They were trying to buy me out of my family's business. There was only one thing to do, and that was to put a stop to things. "I think I'll go take a shower and give you a little time to take care of her."

We both glanced at Faith, who had the look of a woman who desperately needed to be taken care of. She had been needy all day, blushing and squirming and gasping at every brief touch, even from me. I wasn't sure what Tristan's game was with teasing her, but he likely hadn't planned to be stuck in a cabin with me at the end.

Neither of them said a word as I stalked off to the bathroom and slipped inside, yanking off my clothes and turning on the water. While I was waiting for it to heat, I did the thing I had been craving so intensely: closed my eyes and wrapped my hand around my cock. In my imagination, I hadn't walked away. I stroked myself, thinking about Faith and Tristan, about what they were doing in the other room, about joining them there.

I'd loved feeling his cock, thick against mine, as we were kissing. And now, I was sure that he was buried inside her, making her come. I reached over to adjust the shower, intent on drowning out the sounds they might make, but a noise at the door interrupted me. A soft knock.

"What?" I growled.

Faith peeked in, her eyes widening as she saw I was naked. I yelped, moving my hands to cover my erection, which only drew her attention. She licked her lips and took a slow breath, stepping all the way through the door, her eyes darting around nervously, but always landing back on my poorly covered cock. She was down to her panties and bra, a pretty black lace set that barely covered anything, showing off her smooth skin, flushed with arousal. When she lifted her eyes to meet mine, the connection seemed to infuse her with a sudden boldness, and she finally spoke.

"I'm yours to use."

"What?" Certainly that wasn't the sexy, flirtatious comeback she was expecting, but I was having a little trouble processing. The shower water pounded behind me, and hot steam filled the room. Perhaps I hadn't heard her correctly.

She cleared her throat. "My husband wants to watch me fuck you." Her eyes dropped to my dick and widened as she bit her lower lip. Her lips were a soft, light pink, and would look so pretty wrapped around me. My control, my rational side, was slipping away. I dropped my hands and let her see me.

"Or I might want to join in," Tristan said, coming up behind her. He was shirtless now, and he wrapped his arms around her waist and yanked her against his chest, kissing her neck and making her whimper.

"I want to, but I'm trying to do the right thing here." My heart was racing and I couldn't steady my breathing. I drank in her pale, smooth skin, the heaving curves of her breasts, her slim waist, the curve of her hips. I wanted those long, gorgeous legs wrapped around my waist.

"What if doing this is the right thing?" Tristan asked. I watched his fingers slowly trace up her body, skimming the lace that encased her breasts. He found the clip on the front of her bra and bared her to me with one quick flick of his fingers. She arched, whimpering, as his long fingers circled her nipples, making her shudder. The other hand trailed down her stomach towards her panties. I wanted to lick that nipple, to kiss my way down her stomach, following the path of his hand. "We could work together and make my wife scream."

"Tristan, please," she whispered. His other hand slipped under her panties, between her legs. She shuddered, lost in his touch, but still boldly meeting my eyes. I stroked myself idly, watching the show, as he brought her closer to orgasm, made her beg, then backed off, leaving her pleading with him. He glanced at my cock, and I wondered if he wanted to taste me. I certainly wanted to taste him.

"Jeremy looks like he could use some relief. Why don't you let him have your mouth, Faith," he said, smirking a little.

Gasping softly, Faith stepped out of Tristan's embrace and dropped to her knees in front of me, tentatively reaching out to touch my cock, where it bobbed inches from her lips. She skimmed her fingertips through the bead of pre-cum formed at the tip, and I wondered if they did this often.

There was a sweet mix of hesitancy and wildness in her, like her body and her mind were at war. A look of determination crossed her face as she wrapped her hand around the base of my cock and shifted forward, moaning as her soft lips closed around the head. Finally, I gave up my battle to remain controlled, and grabbed her head, thrusting my hips forward, taking her mouth, filling her. She sucked eagerly, moaning in pleasure.

Behind her, Tristan slipped off the last of his clothes, pausing for a moment to turn off the shower. I was so lost in her I had completely forgotten the shower was running, despite the warm steam that surrounded us. He moved to stand beside me, so close to me I could feel his heat and the soft brush of his shoulder against mine as he tapped his thick cock against her cheek.

Faith let out a pleased little moan, then turned, and took him into her mouth, still gripping me, stroking my length as she sucked her husband in deeper than I would have thought possible. He was big and beautiful, thicker than me, though not as long, and she looked gorgeous sucking his cock. She didn't forget about me, though, and began switching between us, taking turns eagerly sucking and stroking each of us.

Every time my orgasm grew close, she would move to him, skimming her soft hand over my length in a way that wasn't quite enough. I wanted to touch him, but I wasn't sure if that was acceptable, so I slipped my fingers into her silky, dark hair and coaxed her mouth forward as she sucked me again.

"Fuck, I'm close," Tristan groaned. Faith grew bolder, sitting back a little and pressing the heads of our cocks together, stroking us like that.

"Can you come together for me?" she asked, swirling her tongue around us, trying to fit us both into her mouth while her hands pumped our shafts. That was too much. I shouted a curse as my orgasm hit me intensely, my hips slamming forward, my cum pouring over her tongue and lips. A moment later, I watched Tristan's cock jolt, groaning at the sensual show as the head of my cock was drenched in his cum. Faith eagerly cleaned up what hadn't landed in her mouth, her tongue still circling around us.

"Good girl," Tristan murmured gruffly, pulling her to her feet and kissing her wildly. I couldn't do anything but groan as she turned to me and kissed me. I'd always loved kissing women after blow jobs, tasting myself on their lips, but this was something even more alluring, and I deepened the kiss, desperate for the taste of him.

Although I was standing in the rustic bathroom of an even more rustic cabin, I was surrounded by luxurious sensations; the silk of her skin, the softness of her mouth, and his hot, firm body pressed close. He nibbled his way down her neck, thanking her for what she had done for us. Everything about it seemed good and right. I never wanted it to end, and I reached over, bold now, and grabbed his chin and kissed him, loving the way he tasted, too.

"Faith deserves some fun for that." My voice was soft as I took her hand and led her out into the main room. Tristan laughed and agreed. In contrast to the bathroom, the air in the cabin was cool against my overheated skin, and I turned and kissed her again, then watched as Tristan led her to the bed.

She crawled to the middle and sprawled out for us, the thin slip of her black panties still covering the part of her I wanted most to taste.

"You're so fucking lovely," I murmured, and she moaned, sliding her fingers under her panties and circling her clit, writhing against the crisp white duvet.

"Let us take care of that," Tristan murmured, pulling her hand away as together we crawled across the bed to her, kissing and touching her. I grasped her chin and pressed my lips against hers, loving the way she tasted of Tristan's cock. Moving my mouth to trace the curve of her throat, I let her husband take a turn kissing her.

I swept my hands over her body, learning her shape, loving the way she squirmed for us. Finally, my fingertips met Tristan's between her legs as she shuddered. We traced the edge of her panties, teasing her, skimming soft touches against the juncture of her thighs. Together, we kissed our way down her neck to her breasts, each taking one rigid peak into our mouths.

"Fuck me," she whimpered, but Tristan seemed determined to keep teasing her, and I knew I needed to follow his lead. She reached for my cock, grazing her nails gently over me, then grabbing me and pulling me close. Her begging turned into breathless demands. We pulled her panties out of the way and dipped our fingers into her drenched pussy together, stroking her closer to orgasm as we sucked her nipples.

I lifted my head from her breast and watched for a moment as I fucked her with two fingers and Tristan circled her clit with his thumb. She was a beautiful, needy mess. Her mouth was open, and she was making soft, begging, whimpering sounds, pleading with us to let her come. A few drops of our cum still dotted her chin and cheeks, and her long, sleek thighs were splayed out on her back for us, her panties shoved partway down, still clinging to her thighs. How much time had passed since we had come? I was so damn hard for her that my cock ached.

"Move her to the edge of the bed," I murmured, and Tristan lifted his head and grinned, his eyes warm with wickedness. Tristan stood and yanked her so her hips sat at the edge of the bed, dragging his cock against her slit.

"Fuck me," Faith growled. Her frustrated begging had been growing a little angrier, and that only added to the sparkle in Tristan's eyes. I crawled across the bed and straddled her face, reaching down to drag my cock across her lips. She sucked me in eagerly, and I groaned at the pleasure of those soft pink lips wrapped around my cock again. I crawled forward, settling my mouth between her legs.

The jolt of her hips, her breathless moan around my cock, and the sweet wet taste of her drenched pussy was enough to make me forget about Tristan entirely for a moment, but then I heard movement, and glanced up, finding him kneeling between her legs, his mouth inches from mine. We kissed again, letting our tongues tangle together as we feasted on her pussy. I flicked my tongue against her clit while her husband lapped up her juices, thrusting his tongue deep inside her.

Her whole body was shaking, but Tristan waited, driving her crazy with me, until she pulled away from my cock and growled at him to fuck her. With a soft laugh, he stood and nudged his cock against her, only inches from my mouth. And that I couldn't resist.

Shifting forward a little, I licked him, then swirled my tongue around his cock. He groaned, muttering a curse that let me know he hadn't expected that, and I smiled, sucking him into my mouth for a moment. It was wild, feeling the pulsing heat of another man's cock in my mouth for the first time as his wife sucked me off. The way he twitched and swelled between my lips was addictive, and I wanted more, wanted to taste him, to drink him down, but Faith needed him more. Or needed both of us, maybe.

Stroking my fingers over the silky skin of his erection, I guided him to her entrance, kissing them both as the head of his cock penetrated her, then returning my attention to her clit. I was watching from only inches away as he thrust in deep, stretching her. It was so damn sexy.

He started moving, spreading her open with every jolt of his hips, then backing way out, giving me a chance to run my tongue along his length and taste both of them. She let my cock pop out of her mouth as her entire body exploded beneath us. It was a hard, wild orgasm that didn't seem to end for a long time, and I could feel the strength of it in the quivering muscles of her thighs against my cheeks. She whimpered, her hand still gripping the base of my cock as her husband fucked her through another orgasm, with the help of my tongue against her clit.

I licked at them where they were joined, then reached out and tugged on his balls, tracing the base of his cock as he groaned, his turn to shudder in pleasure. I wanted his cum in my mouth with hers, all over my face, and then I wanted to pin his wife to the bed and fuck her until she screamed.

She was shuddering now, making incoherent little noises, and I kept at it, pleasuring them both as they fucked. He didn't last long like this, and when he exploded inside her, I lapped up the cum that leaked out, too turned on to think much about what I was doing. She started sucking my cock again as he pulled away, but that wasn't what I needed anymore.

She cried out as I moved away, turning to position myself over her. I shook my head and smiled, tracing my fingers over her lips. "I need to fuck you," I said, shifting to the edge of the bed, between her legs. "Where do you want my cum?" Faith glanced at her husband, who was crawling across the bed to stretch out beside her, his hands roaming over her body.

"Inside me," she whispered. Then she took a deep breath and met my eyes, her voice growing stronger. "Fuck me, Jeremy. Come in me." That was all the invitation I needed.

I wanted to be inside her messy pussy, to feel the warmth and wetness of his cum inside her as I fucked her. She was soft and ready for me, and I thrust in easily. I lifted her legs up around my shoulders as I pushed forward and pinned her into a position where I could fuck her forcefully. She grunted as my cock hit her deep, and Tristan leaned in and kissed her.

"You love his cock, don't you?" he asked, reaching between us and skimming his fingers over her clit.

"Yes," she whispered.

I pulled back and slammed in deep. She was so wet, and the way her inner muscles shuddered around me drove me higher and higher as I thrust into her. Her pussy felt perfect, like home, and I gripped her thighs roughly as I railed her, luxuriating in the warmth of her, the slick wetness of his cum inside her, and the sweet little moans she was making. She arched her back and slammed her hips against mine, her inner walls milking my cock as another wild orgasm shook her body, and I let go, coming deep inside her with a shout.

For a moment, we were all quiet, only the sound of our ragged breathing echoing through the little cabin. I held her eyes, and she smiled, her face soft with contentment, and then I glanced at Tristan and found him watching me, smiling softly as well.

"Holy shit," I muttered. She laughed, a raw, hoarse sound, and I dropped her legs, wrapping them around my waist and leaned forward to kiss her. She slipped her arms around me, holding me inside her for another moment, her thighs still quivering.

CHAPTER 11

Tristan

When I woke up it was still dark. It took me a couple seconds to remember where I was, then I felt Jeremy's hand resting on my chest. Opening my eyes, I lifted my hand and saw Faith cuddled behind him, asleep, with a smile on her face. It felt weird for a moment, seeing my wife snuggled up to another man, but the feeling passed and somehow it felt natural.

The night before rushed back to me. The last thing I remembered was Jeremy fucking Faith and before letting me lick and suck him clean. Then the adrenaline from the experience left our bodies. All three of us crashed pretty quickly and we fell asleep curled up together.

I glanced at my watch and saw it was only three in the morning. Plenty of time before we had to get up and face the aftermath.

Faith moved her hand, and it slipped down onto Jeremy's lap, her fingers wrapping around his cock and squeezing. I couldn't tell if she was awake, but I heard her let out a little moan as her fingers played with him, a little noise of contentment.

Then Jeremy woke. I could tell by the sudden stiffening of his body, the sound of a swift intake of breath, and then him groaning "oh god," as he felt Faith play with him.

I lifted my head up so he could see I was awake, watching the surprise in his eyes. I kissed him deeply, lifting my arm and stroking his face. Then I reached down and slipped my hand over Faith's, the two of us stroking him as he grew harder.

"I would hate for you to think that we only did it because we were drunk," I said, kissing the tip of his nose. It was something I did to Faith often and doing it to Jeremy felt intimate in a way I couldn't describe.

Faith moved behind him and I could see she was fully awake. She looked at me, as if to check everything was okay. I gave her a brief nod and watched as she started kissing the side of his neck.

"You don't have to," he started, but my kiss cut him off. I released Faith's hand, lifted mine to take his face between my hands, and kissed him slowly, savoring his taste.

I could tell from Faith's movements that she was stroking him faster and faster, his body shaking under her touch. He groaned into my mouth. Knowing it was Faith making him do it sent a bolt of lust through me. My cock was steel hard and pressed up against him. I knew he could feel it, maybe even feel the pre-cum leaking out over his skin.

"Come," Faith whispered, and I only just heard it. And he did, hard, his groans cut off by my kisses.

His cum splashed over my chest, three loads hitting my cold skin, warm and sticky and making me kiss him harder. Only when he stopped shuddering did I let him go.

"Oh god that was... I mean..." He struggled to find the words.

Faith was already moving, slipping between his legs and resting her back against his chest. She reached for his hands and lifted them to her breasts.

"Tristan, fuck me, please," she begged.

With a quick shuffle, I was kneeling above her. Reaching for the headboard of the bed and gripping it hard, it was as if both of them were under me, both of them looking at me. Jeremy had recovered and was making her groan as he twisted and pulled her nipples.

"Don't make me wait," Faith pleaded. I pushed inside her.

Almost as one, Jeremy and I moved our heads, so we were kissing and nibbling Faith's neck on either side, giving her all the attention she wanted. With each thrust into her, I could feel her shake and give herself more to me.

For a moment I thought, "If I had planned this, Jeremy could have been inside her as well." The idea of us filling Faith at the same time tipped me over that edge and I came, hammering into her, giving her every inch of me. My moans as I came mixed with hers and became one, both of us coming and losing ourselves to the moment.

We rolled off each other, silent for a moment, all of us catching our breath. Then, like before, we cuddled in a tangle of arms and legs, and eventually fell asleep.

The next time I woke, it was light.

Opening my eyes, I watched as Jeremy, standing at the bottom of the bed, pulled on his underwear and tucked his thick manhood away.

"Morning." I tried to keep my voice steady.

"Oh, shit. Hi." He stumbled in his rush to get dressed and then nearly fell over.

Faith mumbled something under the covers that I guessed was also a good morning.

"I was, um, just going to go phone, you know, check everything was okay."

I sat up in the bed, the covers falling forward. I knew I was naked and he could see everything, but after the night before, I thought we were beyond acting shy.

"You don't need to go on our account. I hope it's not because of last night?" I drank in his body as he got dressed.

"Yes. No. I mean. I'm not sure what happened last night." He kept his eyes on the floor.

Faith flipped off the covers and sat up, resting her head on my shoulder.

"What happened last night was we realized there was some attraction there and had fun." She smiled at him, sounding confident, but I could feel her shaking a little against me.

Jeremy stopped and looked at us.

"This wasn't some weird power play?"

We both shook our heads.

"And it's not just something you two do, picking up guys?"

"First time. And we never discussed it beforehand." Faith leaned forward and kissed my cheek. "I didn't even know Tristan was into guys till last night."

He stood there for a few moments, looking at us, then with a "Wow" he put his hands on his hips.

"I can't figure you two out. But that was an amazing night. Thank you."

And after scratching his neck and shuffling nervously, he almost ran out of the room.

I turned to kiss Faith, and she fell into my arms, the kiss turning to hugs and deeper kisses.

"Are you okay with what happened?" I asked her.

"Are you?"

I thought for a moment.

"Yes. Yes, I am. It was pretty amazing. I never thought I would get so turned on watching you with another guy. If it was anyone else apart from Jeremy, I don't think I would have been. But it felt..."

"Right?" she sighed as I kissed her on the neck.

"Yeah. And you, are you good with this?"

"Yes. I don't know if it's going to mess up the plan to buy the resort. But it felt special, not like a one-night stand. Seeing you with him was something I didn't know I needed to see."

"Uh, guys."

We turned around to see Jeremy in the doorway.

"I just got word. The road is clear. We should be able to get back."

He turned to go, but Faith called his name.

"Are you okay with what happened last night?" Faith leaned forward as she asked.

He looked around the room, evading the question for a second, but a big grin broke on his handsome face.

"It was kind of surprising and not something I was really looking for, but yeah, I don't regret it. In fact, it was pretty fucking amazing. If you two are fine and don't have any regrets, then I'm fine. Just, you know, maybe keep it on the down low. Don't want too many people finding out about this, you know?"

"We understand," I reassured him.

Faith kneeled forward on the bed, naked as the day she was born.

"Come here." It was her command, and he slowly obeyed.

She kissed him on his cheek and then leaned across to kiss me.

"Thank you both." She got up and headed to the shower.

We watched her go, our eyes on the cute ass she was no doubt wiggling because she knew it was getting attention.

When the door shut, we looked at each other for a moment.

"Okay then. I'll leave you two to get ready. I already hit the shower before you woke, so I'll wait in the car for you."

I nodded and swung my legs out of the bed. Jeremy had one more question.

"Are you sure this was real? You both were attracted to me?" He sounded like he needed reassurance.

"I'm surprised one of us didn't jump you before." I smiled and headed off to join Faith in the shower, leaving Jeremy with a dazed smile on his face.

CHAPTER 12

Faith

My post-coital warm fuzziness from our wonderful night lasted about halfway through the drive back to the resort. Tristan took the front seat at my insistence so I could drift off if I wanted. None of us got a lot of sleep last night. All three of us chatted about our childhood. People love hearing Tristan tell stories about his childhood because growing up in a family as rich as his put his life on such a different level. My family was well-off, but nothing like Tristan's. So many things he took as normal were definitely not. Most of us didn't have a live-in nanny or a private plane.

Not that Tristan was stuck up—far from it. But it was fun to hear about his childhood because his experiences were so different. I remembered thinking as a kid, "If only my parents were mega-rich," whenever they gave me with a household chore I didn't want to do. Tristan may not have taken any bags of trash to the garbage, but he still had to work hard in school, do his homework, and struggle with wanting to play when he needed to work, like any normal kid.

The car was warm. I dozed a little, lulled by their deep voices, until I was awakened by the truck hitting a bump in the road.

I glanced around, groggy, uncertain how long I was asleep. "Are we there yet?"

They both laughed at me, and I had to smile as well, realizing how I sounded.

Jeremy's eyes briefly met mine in the rearview mirror before he responded. "Still about an hour away."

A soft tingle ran down my spine from meeting his gaze. I said, "Thanks," with a yawn and snuggled down in my seat, intending to doze, but my brain had woken up too much. What happened last night was amazingly hot, but it probably wasn't smart of us — no, it REALLY wasn't smart of us. Fucking the person you were trying to buy a resort from was a horrible idea.

I was startled even more awake when I remembered what happened with a top executive named Jasmine. Getting involved with a property owner fucked up a multi-million dollar deal last year. She had somehow ended up sleeping with the Malibu resort owner we were trying to purchase a property from. She had been in Malibu for a week to work on the deal, but she'd ended up working the guy's cock more than anything else. In the end, what Jasmine considered to be a vacation fling meant more to him. When he'd found out she wasn't interested in continuing after she left, the deal had completely blown up.

I'd questioned how a successful woman could be so distracted by dick. Now I was learning it was more likely than it appeared.

Oh fuckity, fuck, fuck, fuck. I tensed up the more I stewed. Tristan reached his hand back to me and rubbed my knee, almost as if he sensed I was getting wound up about something. Tristan and Jeremy both fell silent, and we all seemed lost in our thoughts, which didn't help. Listening to them was an excellent distraction.

The miles blurred past while I contemplated where to go from here. Last night didn't feel wrong, and none of us was trying to manipulate the others. Maybe Jeremy was trying to muddy the waters and make us give up on the resort, but I don't think any of us had devious plans. We were just horny, slightly tipsy, and curious.

I didn't know Tristan was interested in guys, so that was a surprise, a pleasant one. Despite my outward appearance of confidence, internally I'd always been too insecure to suggest a threesome. I was always afraid it would turn into Tristan and the other person ignoring me. Intellectually, I knew Tristan would never do that, but I couldn't silence the tiny voice on my shoulder telling me it would be an excuse for him to fuck someone else. In my fantasy life, I'd always assumed it would be another woman. Being with two men went beyond my expectations and my wet pussy hoped it happens again. But God, it was such a bad idea.

I was still warring with myself when Jeremy dropped us off at our condo. He stopped but didn't get out, and I noticed his hands gripping the steering wheel tightly.

The silence was too thick. It felt like someone needed to say something, so I blurted, "Thanks for the fun night!"

No one said anything about another potential hookup in the future, and I didn't want to assume he wanted to do it again. If I was being honest, I didn't know if we should. We needed to be smart about this. If we wanted to pursue the relationship to see where it would go, we should probably wait until after the deal closed.

Jeremy looked at us with unreadable eyes. "No problem. It was fun. Have a good night."

Tristan hugged me after Jeremy drove away. "That was great, yeah?"

Wait, does he not know how we might have fucked up the entire deal? I was silent until we entered the condo. As soon as he closed the door, I let it all out in a rush.

"Tristan, we are so fucked. We shouldn't have done that. Why did we do that? Remember Jasmine?"

"That's not the same—"

I cut him off. "Your family would flip if we messed up this deal. How are we going to explain we BOTH slept with the owner? This wasn't like Jasmine. This was both of us. Do you want your family knowing we fucking had a threesome with Jeremy?"

I couldn't stand still any longer and paced around the room. Tristan moved to the kitchen table and leaned against the edge. He folded his arms and watched me vent.

"Oh, God... did it have to be so hot? And why didn't you tell me you were interested in guys?"

Tristan stepped forward. "Love, you need to calm down. Come here. It's not like that."

"How do you know? It could end exactly like that."

"Well, for one thing, my parents probably aren't going to fire us." He chuckled, and I let out a growl of frustration. He never could understand how it was for me to be the outsider in the family business.

I stopped and turned towards him, seeing the warmth and worry in his eyes, and my frustration evaporated. He unfolded his arms and opened them for me, and I launched myself into them. I buried my head into his chest, inhaling his scent, and tried to calm down, though his words didn't do as much as he seemed to think.

"I can't say I didn't think of this, but what's done is done. We can't change it now." He kissed my head, rubbed my back, and murmured everything would be fine. I so wanted to trust him, but deep down, I really felt like we messed up big time. We needed to keep our cocks and pussy in check until the deal was complete.

Tristan's voice held a hint of amusement when he spoke. "Love, let's nap for a bit and then we can talk. Okay? I think we're both tired. We didn't sleep much last night."

I sighed and agreed. I was tired, but with my roving thoughts, I had no idea if I could get any sleep. Even if insomnia didn't strike, sleep wouldn't change my opinion. We'd made a mistake and now we needed to fix it.

CHAPTER 13

Jeremy

"Right, Dad?" Lucy's voice startled me, and I couldn't for the life of me figure out what she was asking.

For the past day and a half, since we'd gotten home from the trip, I'd been completely unfocused. I hadn't felt this unsure of the next step in a relationship since I was a teenager. Fuck, it wasn't even a relationship. Faith and Tristan had shot me a quick text to say they were overloaded and catching up with other work, and I hadn't heard from them since.

"Right, Dad?" Lucy poked me.

I had been lost in a slightly inappropriate daydream about Tristan and Faith when I should have been focused on my dining companions. Dazed, I glanced from Lucy to Tom as a waitress breezed by and slid a beer in front of me. Fuck, was I still this zoned out? I frowned at Tom, who had suggested I meet with Faith. Really, I could blame him for all of this.

We were seated at a colorful table. Behind them, our favorite Mexican restaurant was bustling with people, full of noise and laughter. There was a distant and surreal quality to it all, though, like I wasn't actually there. This was getting ridiculous. I needed to get a handle on myself.

"Sorry guys, I haven't been sleeping well." I massaged my temples to emphasize my lack of sleep.

"Are you still tired after being trapped in that snowstorm? I was telling Tom that I couldn't believe you got stuck overnight in a cabin with the crazy rich people! How did you survive without slapping them both?"

"Slapping them both might have been a little fun." I blinked, realizing what I said, and glanced at Tom, whose mouth was hanging open. Lucy had been told a heavily redacted version of the cabin story, and Tom knew nothing. From the knowing expression in his eyes, I suspected that had changed.

"What?" Lucy frowned, thankfully clearly completely confused.

"Sorry, I meant, like, for violence. Enjoying violence." Fuck, that was worse. I shook my head and rubbed my eyes. "Yeah, ignore me."

"You say the weirdest shit, Dad." Lucy, who was used to me, shook her head and opened her menu.

"Yep, it's a curse." I leaned back in my chair and chuckled. She grinned and tapped me with her menu, then flipped to a page of nachos, her favorite food.

"Nachos?" Lucy asked.

I wasn't that hungry, honestly. My stomach was a bit of a mess from the drama. "Sure. Let's pick something to share, squirt."

As Lucy went through the menu options, I glanced up and found Tom still studying me, his eyes curious. "Back up. I need this story. You got trapped over the pass with them? You don't seem as grumpy about it as I would have expected." He sipped his beer.

"He won't admit it, but I think he likes them," Lucy said. "He decided they're cool."

"They're definitely not cool. They're sort of dorks, all focused on spreadsheets and cash flow."

"But you like them," Lucy repeated.

I liked them, but not in the way Lucy was thinking, and I needed to get out of this conversation, stat. I glanced around the restaurant, wondering if I should flee to the bathroom, but then spotted the perfect escape. "Isn't that Veronica?" I pointed to a blonde girl standing by the door.

"Oh! Can I go say hi? I'll be right back." Lucy was nothing if not easily distracted. She leaped up, not waiting for an answer before she rushed over to greet her friend, as if she hadn't just spent all day with her at school. Tom waited until Lucy was out of earshot, then leaned forward, pinning me with a sharp look.

"You fucked the woman?"

"What? No." I could tell from Tom's brows-up expression my lie wasn't believed.

"You went from wanting to kick her out of the resort to showing her your dreams of the future and screwing her in a mountain cabin? How did that happen?" Tom's forehead wrinkled with confusion. Or concern. Probably both. I smiled a little as I thought about Faith and Tristan, who probably wouldn't like to know I was calling them dorks. As attractive as they were, they were both driven, focused on business. They should have been boring and not at all my type. Instead, I couldn't stop thinking about having them again.

I fiddled with my napkin as I considered my next words. "I think you were right, Tom. They may have something to offer. I have to figure out how to pitch it to them, so I was working on it. A partnership." I wanted to pitch a partnership of a more personal nature along with my business idea, but I didn't think that would go well at all.

I expected some kind of gleeful gloating from Tom. Instead, his eyes were worried. "I did some digging, asking around. And this company has a terrible reputation. They get involved with the resort owners, if you know what I mean."

"Wait, what?"

"Do you remember Duncan Hennessy?"

"The pro surfer?" I couldn't figure out where he was going, because there was no way Faith and Tristan knew Hennessy.

"Yeah, well, when he retired from competing, he and his buddies bought a resort in Malibu, to turn it into a destination surf resort, right? A few years back, this beautiful woman from the Vaughn Group shows up, has a fling with him, and then right when he fell for her, she vanished. The deal blew up, never heard from her or Vaughn Group again."

"It wasn't Faith, was it?" My heart pounded. Was this their usual thing? No, they'd said they'd done nothing like it before. Hadn't they? I wasn't sure if I remembered either of them saying it was truly their first time. They'd certainly been confident enough with me to make me wonder.

"Probably? How many hot women executives can this place have?" Tom said. "Anyway, I think you should drop it with them. The deal and whatever else you've been doing."

"I haven't been doing anything," I said, ducking my head and staring down at my beer, avoiding eye contact.

He chuckled. "I don't need details. Hell, I don't want details, but be careful. You know that. They're from some big city. They're not like us."

"Who isn't like us?" Lucy asked, slipping into her chair.

"Never mind, Luce. Let's order those nachos, then you can tell us about training camp." Tom was brilliant in more ways than one, effectively distracting my daughter from the awkward topic of my recently complicated love life. No, not love life, sex life.

Lucy rambled on about her new favorite conversation topic: her recent invitation to a camp at the Olympic training center in Utah. Tom asked her questions, sounding interested. I sat back and let my mind wander because I already knew the details. Lucy was leaving in a week, and she'd be gone for almost a month. We'd been planning it since she'd won the competition.

For the first time, I felt a little happy she'd be out of town for a bit. I'd miss Lucy like crazy, but her trip would give me four weeks to get my shit sorted. I would be back to normal by the time she returned.

My phone buzzed. I glanced at it, disappointed to find a text from someone on my staff. For fuck's sake, I should have known it wasn't the Vaughns. I got a lot of calls and texts, and I needed to stop hoping each one was from them. It was too much of a letdown. Like Tom said, I needed to call them and cut them off.

But I didn't want to do that. I wanted to invite them to go snowboarding again, maybe fuck them in the gondola. Maybe ask them to stay.

"Dad, what are you thinking?" Lucy's laughing voice cut through my musing, and I glanced up to find both Lucy and Tom staring at me.

"What? I mean, I know it's a bad idea."

Lucy tilted her head at me, her eyes sparkling with humor. "So you don't want to share nachos anymore?"

I rubbed my hands over my face and groaned. Fuck. I needed to stop daydreaming and be more mindful of the present before I said anything really inappropriate. "No, sorry. I was distracted. Nachos it is!" I closed my menu and handed it to Lucy, determined to focus on my daughter, just as the waitress reappeared, taking our orders and rushing back off.

Dinner went better, and when we got home from the restaurant, there was a FedEx package waiting on our front porch. I knew what it was, and it was a fun distraction. "This one's for me." I snagged it before she could even read the label, trying not to be awkward about it. "More protein powder. You go do your homework."

"Fine. I need to pack, too," she said, moping up the stairs.

I set the package on the counter, staring at it for a moment. Was I really going to do this? I looked at the stairs before reaching into the fridge and cracking open a beer. I had to be sure Lucy wasn't going to reappear. The package was a little embarrassing. I had sex toys, but not this kind of sex toy.

Once I heard music blasting from her computer's speakers, I gave in to temptation, grabbing the package and rushing to my bedroom. I locked the bedroom door before opening the package, my heart pounding with excitement.

It was bigger than expected, and I wondered if it would hurt. I bit my lip, running my fingers over the length of it, feeling the velvety silicone. It had a nice texture to it. It still wasn't anything like Tristan's cock, which I had loved to touch, but it would do. I walked into the bathroom and cleaned my new toy. I could explore my fantasy without Tristan and Faith.

What would they do if they walked in right then? If they found me in the shower, fingering myself as I stroked my cock, lubing up a big suction-cup dildo to ride like I wanted to ride Tristan?

I closed my eyes and imagined finding Tristan sprawled on the bed, at our mercy, his body ours to use. Faith would sit on his face, giving a delightful moan as his tongue lapped up her juices. And I would straddle his hips and lower myself down onto his cock. I wanted to fuck him, but I was even more desperate to know what it felt like to have a man inside me.

I turned on the shower, sighing as the steamy water made the big shower room nice and warm. I pushed the toy onto the far wall, away from the flow of the water. Lubing it up was a sensual joy, stroking my hands over it, closing my eyes and imagining it was real as the slick liquid dripped down over it. Embarrassment warred with arousal as I turned and pushed it against my entrance, feeling the slick head where my fingers had just been.

A moment of discomfort quickly turned to delight as I imagined Tristan's cock sinking into me, stretching me open the way this toy was. Would Faith lean forward and suck me off, or would she be satisfied to watch? I ran my slick fingers over my cock as I pressed harder onto the toy with a groan. The heavy, full feeling of the toy was so good. I let myself have a wild daydream about being surrounded by them, pleasured at both ends, as I leaned back and flipped a switch on the toy that made it move.

Fuck, that might just be my new favorite sensation. I groaned and leaned back, stroking my cock harder. The way the firm silicone pulsed deep inside me had me close to the edge of orgasm in seconds, and I tried not to make too much noise as I gave in to the wave of pleasure.

I really needed to find out what a real cock felt like.

CHAPTER 14

Tristan

The next few days passed in a blur.

Faith decided that although it was fun and hot, sleeping with Jeremy had been a mistake. She kept comparing it to the fiasco we had over Malibu, but I didn't see it the same way at all.

"We were up front with him. It was something that was fun, but we didn't expect it or plan it and he knows we don't mean to use it against him in negotiations."

Faith was sitting across from me, sipping her coffee. She thought we needed to throw ourselves into work, so she spent days running figures and researching the potential of the area Jeremy had shown us. This was the first time she had stopped for more than a few minutes and also the first time she would listen to me about it.

"If that's the case, why hasn't he contacted us in three days?" she asked.

For a moment, this caused a brief stab to my heart, and I didn't know what to say.

"Maybe he's busy?"

I knew she was trying to do what was best, but when she said we shouldn't contact him, I thought it was a step too far. Faith insisted, and I have learned to pick my fights.

Instead, I had sent him a text to say that we were overloaded with work and would catch up with him later.

Faith finished her coffee and stood, heading back to her laptop.

"I just don't think fucking the owner of the resort we're trying to buy is wise. It's not good for business."

"And what about us? Was it good for us? Can you tell me you wouldn't want to do it again?" I asked.

She paused and turned round, confusion on her face.

"If it wasn't this situation, then yes, I would love to do it again. I didn't realize how much I wanted that, and it was even better than I imagined. But we need to be smart here, not get all horny and fuck this up."

I reached over and pulled her close, gently kissing her as my hands rested on her cheeks.

"Well, maybe we can get a little horny?" I smiled. It was time to break her out of her work routine and give her a little fun.

"I should get back to work..." She sighed, but I could tell that her heart wasn't in it.

"What you should do is take a break with your husband and let him relax you."

She smiled, seeming a little more like her normal self.

"Oh yeah, and how are you going to do that?" She giggled.

I scooped her up in my arms and carried her to the bed, placing her down gently before pulling off my shirt.

"Strip," I commanded.

"Oh!" She squeaked, not expecting me to be so forceful, but she soon recovered and stripped for me.

"I want you to close your eyes and let me do all the work."

My hands moved up the inside of her thighs, nice and slow to make her moan.

For a moment, I thought of the last time I heard her moan like that, with Jeremy there beside us. I was sure if he were here with us, then we could clear all of this up. And maybe see if the three of us together was as enjoyable a second time.

My fingers reached her pussy and softly stroked, drawing more moans from her.

"No more work for the rest of the night." I growled as I lay down on the bed, my face close enough to her to feel the heat radiating from her need.

"No, no work," she sighed, her voice sounding far away.

"Tonight is for us."

I pushed thoughts of Jeremy from my mind. This was about us reconnecting and Faith taking a break.

My fingers slipped inside her, making her back arch.

"Just us."

"That's my good girl." I lowered my mouth over her pussy and tasted her.

"Your good girl." She lost herself in pleasure.

I slowly fucked her with my fingers, keeping her on edge. Every time it seemed she was about to come, I would slow down, kiss her hip and wait for her to relax, then work her up again.

"Please, I want you inside me," she moaned eventually, not able to take any more.

I slowly nibbled my way up to her lips and kissed her deeply. My fingers wrapped around hers as I pinned her down on the bed, thrusting into her as my teeth found the soft flesh of her shoulder.

She came hard, wrapping herself around me. It was the first of many times she came.

An hour later, we lay in bed, snuggled up and tangled in the covers.

"That was so good." Faith trailed her fingers through my chest hair. She loved playing with it and said it relaxed her.

"You needed to stop and take a break. You were getting obsessive again."

She sank her head to my shoulder and didn't say anything for a few minutes. I could tell she was thinking about something and didn't know how to say it, so I gave her the time she needed.

"I really enjoyed being with Jeremy, and I loved seeing you with him. It was a side of you that you have never shown me. Who would have thought my husband liked guys and never told me? I don't want you to think I'm not into that."

I leaned over and kissed her head.

"I know, darling. It never crossed my mind."

"And I want to see it again, but the timing with Jeremy is wrong. We can't mess up this deal."

She was talking out loud, but she was really talking to herself. Sometimes she did that when she was trying to decide if she was doing the right thing. There's no point interrupting. She wants me there as someone to hold her and listen.

"Yeah, it's the smart thing to do. We keep working on the figures, present him with an offer he can't refuse, and everyone can be happy."

She went quiet for a few minutes and then looked at me.

"I'm sorry. I went off on one of my rants again, didn't I?"

I nodded, but smiled to show her it was okay.

Her hand moved under the covers. I felt her fingers wrapping around my shaft, slowly stroking it back to full length.

"I think I can make it up to you." She kissed my chest and continued to kiss her way down until she took me in her mouth.

My eyes closed and my hand slipped onto the back of her head, guiding her.

Things were good. This whole Jeremy thing would be sorted out. Something we had all enjoyed shouldn't cause so much fuss.

And while Faith had decided it was going to be a one-and-done encounter, I still had hopes that before everything was over, we might do it again.

CHAPTER 15

Faith

I jolted awake in the middle of the night and wondered what woke me up. I lay there for a moment, listening to the sound of Tristan's soft breathing. Was there someone in the room with us? I tried to avoid sitting up in case there actually was an intruder, but I scanned the room in the dim light and didn't see anything from my vantage point.

A few moments passed. Once I was convinced I imagined the whole thing, I relaxed back into bed. Well, fuck, what the hell woke me up then? A ball of anxiety lodged in my gut and I could tell something was wrong, but I didn't know what yet.

I'm an anxious person on a good day, but this was different. Something felt off, and my brain was giving me tiny hints. Visions of our cabin adventure with Jeremy filtered through my mind. God, that was hot, and Tristan clearly wanted to continue seeing Jeremy despite all my warnings.

Was there any way to not make it a bad idea? I had focused on why we shouldn't, but maybe I needed to look at it from another direction. If I could make it work, it would be the cherry on the top of the resort-buying sundae.

The thought of the sundae distracted me for a moment. I imagined getting a can of whipped cream and coating Tristan and Jeremy's cocks with it while I licked them clean. Then I'd coat Tristan's again and demand Jeremy lick it off.

It made no sense, but I felt Jeremy was perfect for us. My brain kept bringing Jeremy into the picture. I tried to imagine us playing with someone else and failed. I sighed, knowing sleep wasn't going to happen, but something shimmered at the edge of my awareness. If I could just grasp the thought, I felt it was the key to solving our problem.

I tried counting sheep as I continued to lie there, but did that ever fucking work for anything? I always lost count at 20-something and sleep still wouldn't claim me. What the fuck was I not remembering? I hated it when I felt like there was a puzzle piece missing. My brain would just have to feed it to me when I was ready.

I gently tossed aside the covers and slid out of bed. I figured I might as well be productive. The clock flashed 4 a.m., but it was daytime hours at many of our corporate offices. I could connect with my team and talk strategies.

I took a quick shower, washed my hair, and lathered my body with a delicious strawberry-scented body wash. As I was doing my final rinse, I almost dropped the hand-held spray nozzle.

Motherfucker! I figured it out.

I flipped the water off, sketchily dried myself, and hurried to my laptop in my robe. I brushed my hair while the laptop booted up. As soon as I logged into all my programs, I typed out a quick message to my assistant, instructing her to get the ball rolling on the property Jeremy showed us. I hadn't fully run the numbers, but the preliminary figures were in our favor. More importantly, my gut told me this was the way to go, no, that this was the ONLY way to go to get the cherry on my sundae.

Once my assistant replied she was on it, I relaxed. A big yawn told me I should try to get a little more sleep, so I removed my robe and climbed into bed naked with Tristan. I would tell him in the morning we're going to contact Jeremy. That should make him happy.

I woke up to the smell of coffee, and my heart warmed when Tristan filled a mug and brought it to me.

"You're my hero." I blew him a kiss as he set it on my nightstand.

Tristan smiled at me. "You know it, and don't you forget it."

I took a sip of coffee and hummed in happiness. My grand thought from the night before bubbled up, and it was time.

"Hey, hon?" He looked at me before I continued. "I changed my mind. I think we should see Jeremy again. In fact, I told my assistant to start the paperwork on the property. I think it's a good idea."

Tristan's eyes lit up. He sat on the edge of the bed next to me, taking my hand and squeezing it.

"You're sure?" He searched my face, probably trying to make sure I wasn't just saying that.

"Yes, Love. I'm sure."

The playful glint in his eye told me I made the right choice. Now I didn't want to wait another moment before calling him.

I smiled at Tristan. "Bring me my phone and I'll call him."

He quickly snagged my phone from the table next to my computer and brought it to me. I dialed Jeremy's number and kept him on speakerphone.

His voice was hesitant when he answered. "Hello?"

"Hey, Jeremy, this is Faith. We were wondering if you wanted to do something with us today."

A slight pause on the line almost made me cringe. My gut churned. Was he going to say no?

"Uh, sure. What did you have in mind?"

I relaxed and glanced at Tristan. He had a shit-eating grin on his face.

Laughing, I stumbled on my words. "Oh, uh... I didn't get that far."

Well fuck, what sort of idiot calls without a plan?

Jeremy quickly piped up. "Want to go up the mountain? It's going to be a beautiful day."

I didn't care what we did, and a glance at Tristan's smile said he liked the idea.

"That sounds fine. Give us an hour to get ready?"

CHAPTER 16

Jeremy

"I might stop holding your hands," I said to Faith, helping her through a turn on her snowboard. We were on the bunny hill, and I had set my snowboard to the side as I jogged along with her, giving her a lesson.

"I don't know about that." She wobbled a little, then found her balance again.

"No, I'm serious. You take instruction really well." I squeezed her hands and tried to loosen the death grip she had on me. I frowned and stepped back. "Why did that sound sexual? I meant snowboarding. You're a natural."

Faith laughed and moved in close, her eyes sparkling, her lips only inches from mine. "I don't know. Sexy instructions from you? Sounds fun." The thought of Faith kneeling in front of me, waiting for my commands, made my snowboard pants uncomfortably tight. This woman took me from zero to sixty with a few choice words. Yep, I was that guy. I had an erection on the bunny hill in the middle of the family learning area. Thankfully, my jacket was long enough to hide things.

I couldn't even remember why I had suggested snowboarding as our activity for the day. Something about not wanting to leap straight into fucking them, I thought. But she was sexy, even wobbling around on the bunny hill.

She had taken to snowboarding quickly, listening attentively as I showed her how to do things and following me perfectly. Where Tristan had been enthusiastic but a little reckless, Faith was nervous but intensely focused, and I enjoyed having her focus directed at me. I glanced at her husband to find him watching us, softly smiling. He looked proud of her, and as turned on as I was.

I leaned in, letting my lips brush her skin. "Go to the gondola. We'll see how well you follow instruction in there."

She glanced up the hill, nervous again, but nodded, her cheeks flushing pink. "Okay."

Faith and Tristan didn't protest as we made our way to the gondola and climbed into a car. I seated Tristan next to me, and Faith across from us. As we pulled off our helmets and mittens, I watched her, worrying about her fear of heights. She was still wearing the eager-to-please expression she'd had during our lesson. I grinned, raising an eyebrow at Tristan as the gondola doors slid closed.

Tristan had spoken little during the exchange, but I was pretty sure he was as turned on as I was. Impulsively, I reached over and ran my hand up his thigh. When he didn't stop me from touching him, I went further, cupping him between the legs, feeling how hard he was. Tristan was fucking into this, and I wanted his snowboard pants out of the way.

"Can we…" Tristan trailed off, staring at my hand as I reached for his fly. "How much time do we have alone in here?"

"The ride is about 15 minutes each way, but we'll stay on for a few rounds." I smiled and flipped a hidden latch at the top of the door. "This will keep the door from opening when we pass through the buildings. Faith will still have to pretend she's not about to come, though. Just in case."

Tristan's smile turned wicked as he looked towards his wife. "I think we can make it happen."

I turned my attention to Faith, who was squirming a little. I wasn't sure if it was from nerves or arousal. "Strip for us."

She eyed the wraparound windows surrounding us. "Can people see us?"

"Not really. The windows are mirrored and have a dark tint for the sun. At most, they'll be able to see a shadow. Look at the car above us."

"But it feels so exposed," she whispered, studying the other gondola. You really couldn't see anything in the cars that passed us, though we were surrounded by glass and it felt like we were on display.

"What happened to my good girl, who was following instructions so well?" Fuck, what had gotten into me? I needed to put a stop to my impulsive horniness. I rubbed a hand over my eyes, embarrassed. "Sorry, I don't know why I said that. If you're not comfortable with this, we can go back to my office and find somewhere private to play."

Even as I was telling myself to back off, I couldn't resist touching Tristan again. I shoved the waistband of his snowboard pants out of the way and slipped my hand under his leggings beneath, grasping his cock more fully. We could always fool around a little, then snowboard down with Tristan all hot and bothered. Not as sexy as a good old-fashioned gondola fuck, but it'd be fun. There was no question he was into this. His expression was one of pure contentment, his eyes falling closed as I tugged his leggings out of the way and stroked him.

Faith was quiet for a moment, long enough to worry me a little. Then she smiled and spoke. "I like this side of you, Jeremy. The way you're getting all dominant. Tristan and I have safe words. We'll let you know if you need to stop."

Tristan's smile widened. He pressed his hips up into my hand. I stroked him, thanking him for being so compliant, and his cock leaked a little pre-cum on my fingers. Faith's eyes darted around, but she leaned forward, untied her boots, and toed them off, kicking them under the bench. Standing, she teetered a little as the car swayed, then unbuttoned her snowboard pants, slipping them down over her hips. The space was tiny and unstable, so undressing was more awkward than a typical striptease, but I loved it anyway. She was baring herself to us, and her husband's cock was in my hand. That was all I needed to get completely fired up.

She set her jacket and shirt carefully on the bench and turned back to us, clad only in knee-high snowboard socks, her smile a little shy. I barely restrained the urge to launch myself at her and bury myself inside her. Her eyes were on my hand, and my hand was having a lot of fun. Maybe she needed a little more watching. Tristan lifted his hips as I pushed his pants further out of the way and stroked his length, feeling his silky heat, the bead of pre-cum at his tip.

"Do you want his cock, or mine?" I asked.

"Both." Faith blushed, ducking her head.

"Such a good little slut." I shifted a little and glanced down. "Maybe you can help me out. My hand is busy, but my pants are getting a little tight."

She kneeled between my legs, taking a slow breath, glancing up at Tristan as if waiting for permission. He nodded. Faith licked her lips and pushed the hem of my jacket out of the way, then reached for the button on my snowboard pants. She tugged at the zipper, pulling my pants and leggings down over my hips, gently freeing my cock. She reached for me, but I shook my head, stopping her before she touched me. I remembered from the car ride Tristan liked to deny her, and her adorable pouty expression as I told her to go sit was entirely worth it. "Show us how wet you are for us."

Faith whimpered as she took a seat on the bench across from us, tucking her jacket under her. Bold now, she spread her legs, bracing her feet on the sides of the gondola and running her index and middle fingers through her slick folds. She was taunting us, drawing us in. In my hand, Tristan's cock twitched. "Fuck, I want her," he groaned.

But he didn't make a move, still waiting for my commands. I was so into that.

Through the window behind Faith, I could see that we were about halfway to the top. We had seven minutes to tease her before we passed through the gondola building. I glanced down at Tristan, at the thick, pulsing erection in my hand, and I licked my lips, wondering what he would taste like. And I went for it. After all, they had turned the decision over to me.

I was nervous as I brushed my lips across the head of his cock, but Faith's gasp and Tristan's approving groan encouraged me. I stuck out my tongue and lapped up the bead of pre-cum that had formed just for me, enjoying his salty flavor. This scene had him leaking heavily and needy as hell. I slid my hand to the base of his erection and wrapped my lips around him, taking him deeper, loving the way he swelled against my tongue.

I knew this might simply be part of discovering my sexuality, part of admitting to something I'd always wanted to try, but I couldn't help but feel that my enjoyment of this moment was tied to Tristan and Faith specifically. How would I ever get enough of them?

I sucked him in deeper. His hands threaded through my hair, holding me where he wanted me. He whispered my name, and I tightened my lips around him, thinking I'd like to drink him down. I was lost in the taste and musky scent of him, until Faith made a noise that reminded me of our game, reminding me I could suck him off another day. Today, we needed to fuck his wife senseless. I lifted my head, smiling a little at the disappointed sound he made.

Faith looked so damn turned on. Her eyes were wide and dilated, her lips slightly parted, and her breasts were heaving from her panting. Her hands were tightly clasping the bench, and she was watching, not touching herself, which surprised me. "You don't want to make yourself come?"

"You didn't tell me to." She wiggled a little, like she desperately needed pressure between her legs.

My cock pulsed. I checked the window, clocking our location again. Three minutes from the top. "Do you want to watch your husband suck my dick?"

"Yes."

"Come here," I said, patting the bench next to me and scooting to the side. I didn't need to tell Tristan to kneel. Somehow he knew, shifting to the floor in front of me without a command. "I want you a little closer while he tastes me for the first time."

Her breath caught in her throat, but she stood and slipped onto the bench next to me. She pressed against my side, and I looped an arm around her waist, stroking her silky skin. I liked her naked and vulnerable, our little toy to fuck. I wondered how much Tristan would enjoy being in the same position, naked in a risky situation, while we were fully clothed. From his eager, slightly submissive expression, maybe quite a lot. I nodded to him and he leaned forward breathlessly, like he was desperate to taste me. He kissed his way up my shaft and encircled the head of my cock with his lips. I groaned and reached for Faith, pulling her mouth to mine as her husband took my cock deeper.

"He likes to be pegged," she whispered against my lips.

I groaned at the thought of truly fucking him, of burying myself inside him while his wife watched. I gripped the back of his head and pushed him deeper until he gagged. Instead of pulling away, he grabbed my ass, pulling me deeper. Maybe he had been fantasizing about this moment as much as I had. My hips jolted up, the pleasure of him engulfing me. I wanted more of the soft, wet warmth of his mouth, of that delicious tightness at the entrance to his throat. I glanced up and realized we were about to enter the building at the summit of the gondola. Usually, this would be time to get out, but I'd already decided we'd be riding back down... and maybe back up again.

"Shit," I laughed, pulling him away. He frowned and pushed back towards me, sucking me back into his mouth, and I fought for control. "Tristan. Sit down and cover up that beautiful cock. Hand me her coat."

Sighing, he stood and moved to the seat across from us, his eyes hungry and a little dazed. I lifted Faith into his lap, grinning a little as I positioned her so he could thrust into her, stroking my fingers over his length as I pushed the head of his cock against her entrance. They both groaned, and I eyed the rapidly approaching building as I tugged her jacket over her shoulders, covering her almost completely. He pulled her close, and she wrapped her legs around his waist, hiding what she could. She whimpered and writhed against him.

"Fuck, I can't stop her." Faith started bouncing on Tristan's cock and Tristan groaned, grabbing her ass, just as the gondola slowed, pulling into the building.

"Faith. Did I tell you to move?" The order came out a little harsh, but she stilled. "Try not to look like you're fucking. I'll tell the lift operator that Faith got scared and we're looping back around."

I sat back down, grabbed my helmet off of the seat and set it in my lap, covering my dick. The windows were dark enough no one could really see us, but I pushed the latch. I slid the window open enough to tell the lift operator we were heading back down, instructing him to radio the base and let them know we were riding through. The liftie gave me a sketchy salute, his eyes dropping to Faith for an instant before I slammed the window shut and blocked his view of her.

They were beautiful like this, wild and uninhibited, and I decided right then to enjoy them for as long as they were in town. Lucy left that morning for her camp, and I had the freedom to have some fun for once.

"Do you think they bought it?" Tristan asked, chuckling, pulling his wife tighter against him. I shrugged, lifting the helmet off my lap and giving my cock a slow stroke as we burst into the sun, heading down the hill. Tristan tossed Faith's jacket aside so I could see everything. They were beautiful, joined like that, with his cock buried deep inside her. He was thrusting his hips gently, and she was pushing against him with every thrust.

"Doesn't matter, as long as they pretended to buy it and let the guys at the base know not to open the doors." Faith looked up at me, her eyes landing on my cock, then whispered something in Tristan's ear. He nodded, and she lifted off him with a whimper and came to stand in front of me.

"I need you," she said. "I missed you."

Heart pounding, I reached for her and tugged her towards me. I slid my hips forward a little on the bench and guided her to turn, coaxing her to straddle me, facing Tristan. "We have 15 minutes to get her all hot before we need to hide what we're doing again." I slid my hands up her waist and cupped her breasts. She shivered a little at my touch. Maybe my hands were a little cold, because her skin felt like fire. "You like to be bared to us, sweet girl?" I stroked one hand down between her legs and slipped my fingers into her folds.

She was drenched, her clit already slick with her arousal, and she bucked against my hand as I circled, drawing her moisture over the tight little bud of nerves. With my other hand, I tugged at her nipple, making her writhe for us. Reaching back, she gripped my cock, pulling it against her entrance.

"Jeremy, please," she whimpered.

I groaned, pushing my hips up a little, and she moved, spreading her legs open more and bracing her arms on the walls of the gondola. Tristan was watching, his mouth ajar, his hand shuttling faster and faster on his cock. His eyes were focused on my cock as it stretched her open.

"Come closer. She's so damn wet and feels so good." Tristan didn't need to be asked twice. He dropped to the floor, kneeling between my legs, his face only inches from his wife's pussy as she bounced on top of me. "Do you want to lick her while I fuck her?" I asked. I shifted my hands again, gripping her hips and holding her still as I took over the movements, slamming my cock up into her again and again.

Tristan leaned forward, at first tentatively, as he tried to lick only her clit. Then he gave in to the wildness of the moment, kissing my balls and shaft, tracing his tongue along my length as I moved. He captured the head of my cock in his mouth for a moment as I slipped out of her, then pushed me back inside when she protested. The combined sensations were almost too much, but I wasn't ready for it to end. Faith was close, and I could feel her muscles quivering with her coming orgasm.

"Make her come for us, Tristan," I growled, fucking her harder and feeling her body arch as he returned his attention to her clit.

"Oh god," she whimpered.

I held her tightly, loving the way she convulsed around me as she came, her pussy milking the length of my cock as her hands grappled for purchase, shifting from the gondola walls to Tristan's hair. It was so fucking good I lost track of time, and I cursed as I realized that the shadowed entrance to the base gondola building was looming behind us. The slight jolt of the car entering the building let me know we were about to be exposed, fucking in the gondola.

"Tristan, move in front of the door, just in case."

I lifted Faith and laid her on the floor, nestling her in our discarded clothing and hiding her from the people in the building. Tristan shifted, blocking the doors with his back, kneeling on the floor by her head. When I'd given the order, I had fully intended to move back onto the bench after setting her down and try to look normal, but they were just too tempting like that. I dropped to the floor between Faith's legs and covered her with my body before I slammed my cock back into her, holding her with one hand and bracing myself on the bench above her with the other.

Tristan's cock was bobbing temptingly in front of me, and I lunged forward, wrapping my lips around him, sucking him in deep as I fucked her. I needed them too much to care about getting caught anymore. When I felt Faith's soft lips against mine, kissing me around her husband's cock, I lost it, fucking her roughly into the floor of the little car. Luckily, we slipped through the building without being caught, and we emerged into the sun without incident. It was beautiful, being with them like this, so lost in each other I couldn't bring myself to think about anything but them. I wanted to cover her with our cum, to mark her as ours.

"Fuck her tits," I hissed, barely restraining myself. Tristan crawled forward, his back to me, and straddled her waist, slipping his cock between his wife's breasts. I ran a hand down over the muscles of his back and ass. He was so close, his round bottom flexing, still half covered in his leggings and snowboard pants, and I remembered what she had said about him liking to be pegged. I slammed into his wife one last time, then pulled out and came all over her stomach with a groan, shooting hot strings of cum across her pale skin and splattering a little on the back of his pants.

Hopefully, no one but me would notice it.

I still wanted him, and I pressed against his back, gripping the base of his cock with one hand and pulling his mouth around to mine with the other. I could feel the rising throb of his orgasm and I loved it, loved jerking his cum out all over his wife's breasts while he trembled in my arms.

We stayed like that for a moment, catching our breath, until I spotted the top of the lift approaching again and realized we really needed to get Faith dressed. She was gorgeous painted with our cum, her expression happy and a little dazed. I lifted her, telling her we were in a rush as I stuffed her bra and shirt into my pocket. I helped her into her coat and Tristan slipped her feet into her snowboard pants. She was still shaky from her orgasm, and we were gentle with her as we got her ready, praising her and kissing her.

I was tying her boots as we slid into the building at the summit, and I flipped the lever that let the gondola door slide open. The liftie whistled at us, but I rolled my eyes and shot him a stern look as we walked out onto the snow. We found a spot amongst the people milling about at the top of the gondola to help Faith strap into her snowboard. She sat down, still looking a little dazed.

"You okay?" Tristan asked, meeting her eyes and giving her a quick kiss. "You look a little out of it. Are you sure you want to snowboard down?"

"I think so," Faith said, looking around. "Wow, the lake from here is so blue. It's incredible."

"We'll help you if you need it," I said, stroking a little hair out of her eyes as I knelt in front of her and helped her position her feet in her bindings.

Faith frowned and shook her head. "It's weird. I came so hard, but I need more. I need you both to fuck me again." That hadn't been at all what I expected her to say, and I burst out in a surprised laugh, leaning forward to lick a stray drop of Tristan's cum off of her chin, then sharing it with her, kissing her deeply.

"You'll have fun on this run, I promise. I'll hold your hands the whole way down, if you want me to. Then we can go have some more fun in that conference room we first met in."

"Was that what you were thinking about while we talked on that first day?" Faith asked, tilting her head.

I shrugged, grinning, then impulsively kissed her again. "A little." I had kissed her in front of my staff and guests, right at the top of my mountain, and I knew the small town rumor mill would go wild, but I realized I didn't care, and I leaned to the side and reached for Tristan, kissing him as well. He groaned and returned the kiss, then pulled back with a frown.

"You don't want to be discreet about this?" He looked around.

"I'm not a very discreet person, if you hadn't noticed." I fastened the last buckle on Faith's bindings, then standing and helping her to her feet. "Kind of impulsive, really."

"I like your brand of impulsive." Faith teetered a little as she tried her first turn by herself, then another, a big smile curving her lips. I looked at Tristan, standing next to me. We both watched her for a moment as she got the hang of her turns, before leaning forward to strap in our own bindings.

"She's doing so well."

"She's like that with everything," he said with a note of pride in his voice.

"I hope she keeps it up after you guys leave Tahoe." As soon as those words were out of my mouth, I wanted to pull them back in. Why was I talking about them leaving after that epic gondola ride? But they would leave, and acknowledging it was killing my good mood.

Tristan glanced at me, frowning. "We're not going anywhere until we figure this out."

"You guys live in Seattle. This is fun, but how is it going to last?" I tried to play it off casually, but if Lucy's mom had taught me anything, it was that people always left.

CHAPTER 17

Tristan

I finished tying the cord around Jeremy's hands and stood back, happy with my work. He looked so cute tied to the chair, naked except for some black boxers.

"Not feeling so in control now, are you?" I asked.

His face flushed, and that beautiful smile of his crept onto the edge of his lips.

"No, not so much."

Faith stepped forward, completely naked, and sank down to her knees in front of him, her hands on his legs, spreading them.

"I think you should call him Sir. And you should call me Miss," she purred.

Jeremy looked between us, a little dazed, and then nodded his head.

"Not so in control, Sir."

After our encounter in the gondola, we had spent some time on the hill, but the need in all of us had been fanned. We had a taste of what we wanted, but like a taste of a fine wine, now we wanted more. We invited him back to our condo rather than go to the conference room. This way, we didn't have to worry about anyone walking in on us. What we didn't say to him was that we were feeling a little more controlling now.

Faith reached out and stroked her hand along his boxers, her fingers rubbing along the hardness clearly visible through the thin material.

"Is that for me?" she asked.

"Yes."

She gave his cock a little playful slap, making him moan.

"What did you say?" she asked, her fingers slipping into the waistband and pulling his boxers down, causing his fully erect cock to spring up in front of her face.

"Yes, Miss. It's for you."

The need in his voice made my cock twitch as much as Faith taking the lead. He hadn't seen her like this yet, in control in the bedroom. I smiled at how much he was going to enjoy it.

My hand reached down and stroked my erection as I watched her kiss slowly along his length, from the bottom all the way to the top, and then take the tip between her lips. Jeremy's eyes were glazing over and I knew I needed to step in.

"Jeremy. Look at me."

I moved forward and put my hand on his cheek as he slowly turned his head. His eyes focused on me and I saw the blissed out look on his face.

"Open your mouth." I reached down and pulled my cock out of my boxers.

His mouth fell open, and I had an overwhelming urge to call him a good boy. I struggled for a second with it, wondering if it was too intimate, then laughed to myself. I would think that when my wife was between his legs, giving him a throat deep blowjob.

"Good boy. Now, you are going to suck me and make me come. Understand?"

He nodded his head, fuzzy but understanding.

As I guided my cock towards his lips, my phone in the other room went off. I recognized the ring straight away and knew who it was. The fun would have to wait.

"Should I stop?" asked Faith, her hand wrapped round Jeremy's hardness and still slowly stroking him up and down.

"No, you have your fun. Enjoy your plaything."

She nodded and stood up, kissing me hard. Then she straddled Jeremy and kissed him on the neck.

"I am going to ride you nice and slow. Let you fill me with that delicious cock of yours. And you will not come until I allow you. Understand?"

As I walked away, I was once again struck by how lucky I was to have such a perfect wife.

Half an hour later, I walked back into the room and smiled gently at the sight that greeted me.

Jeremy was on the bed, face down, and fast asleep. For a moment, the thought of going over and biting that sweet ass of his crossed my mind.

Next to him lay Faith. His arm was draped over her chest and I could see she was luxuriating in the afterglow of her fun.

She rolled to face me and giggled. Jeremy's hand slipped down and came to rest on her ass.

"How did it go?" she asked.

I lifted the chair and moved it to the side of the bed next to her.

"Not great. That was my mother. She wants to know how things are going, as you can imagine."

Faith pulled herself to a sitting position.

"What did you tell her?" she asked, concern in her voice.

"I told her that things are moving. That we are making progress, we're getting to know and like the owner, and we should be able to get a deal done soon."

"I guess she wasn't happy with that?" Faith replied.

"She said there was no reason for us to like him. We should either get the deal over with or give it up as a poor investment. And there are plenty of other things we should deal with instead of having a holiday and skiing."

Faith swung her legs off the bed and reached forward, taking my hands in hers and holding them. She knows how much of a force of nature my mother can be and how arguing with her is never really a good idea.

"And then I told her that maybe we LIKE liked him." I sighed.

"Oh." Faith gasped before leaning forward and kissing my forehead. She knows that my mother, my whole family, really, is conservative and old-fashioned. Practically Victorian.

"The conversation had gone badly from that point. Why did I need to be thinking about anyone else when I had a wife? Why did my wife need to be thinking about anyone else? Did I not realize the company had a reputation to uphold? Not to mention the family's reputation as well. And I was jeopardizing the deal. I listened without speaking, letting her go on and on. In the end, I said I would think about it and hung up the phone." I told Faith all this as she sat next to me.

When I finished, she kissed me again and told me to get into bed. Jeremy made a grumbling noise as I climbed in, but he didn't wake, just rolled over.

"It'll be okay." Faith as she kissed my neck.

Soon she was asleep, cuddled into me with her head on my shoulder.

I was lying in bed with the two people I most wanted to be with in the world, but it still took me a long time to get to sleep.

CHAPTER 18

Faith

The next morning I woke up snuggled between both men. Jeremy was half on his stomach, with his face smashed into the pillow and one leg hooked around mine. Tristan was on my other side, cuddled against me as close as he could get, with his arm stretched across my chest. Tristan's hand cupped the breast farthest from him, and my nipple hardened as soon as I woke up and noticed the warmth of his palm.

Both men were fast asleep, and I stared at the ceiling and daydreamed about how it would feel waking up like this every morning. I know so little about the poly lifestyle; is something like this called a throuple? I don't think having watched Shameless and laughing at the crazy antics of Veronica, Kev, and Svetlana counted as understanding the lifestyle.

The real question was, would I even want this to be full time? I loved Tristan with all my heart, but every time we were with Jeremy, something about him in the mix felt... perfect. But after being married so long, I'm a realist as well. The chances of meeting a third person and it working out was incredibly unlikely. Relationships were hard enough between two people. Wouldn't a third person make it twice as difficult? I needed to do research on the poly lifestyle before I spun myself crazy.

And yet.

I couldn't deny the deep sense of satisfaction that washed over me the longer I lay there with my men. Even feeling like they were both "my men" told me something. Fuck. I needed to make sure this deal happened. It felt like the only chance we had for a happy ending.

When Tristan started playing with my nipple, I knew he was awake. A nice, soft tingle spread to my pussy, and she hummed to life. I guess sex was another consideration I hadn't really contemplated in a threesome. Tristan and I already had a ton of sex and always had throughout our marriage. Would adding a third person mean we were having sex all the time? So far, it seemed whenever we were around Jeremy, we ended up in bed. Would that be our life: fucking, eating, and working? Oooh. Maybe that was a benefit, since one person wasn't necessarily always in the mood and maybe the third person would be? Like when Tristan took a phone call last night while I played with Jeremy.

Shit, that was hot. My pussy clenched at the thought of how fun it was to ride a tied-to-the-chair Jeremy last night. I faced him so I could see the arousal in his eyes, and when I came all over his cock, his eyes rolled back into his head and he came with me. Yeah. The sex in a throuple was probably an enormous benefit.

Tristan was still pulling at my nipple, but I could tell he wasn't trying to start something. His touch was more like he was warm and comfy, messing with whatever was under his hand while he floated, relaxed and half-asleep.

When I turned my head towards him, he opened his eyes and smiled at me.

He whispered, "Good morning, Love," as if he was trying to not wake Jeremy up.

I giggled quietly. "Good morning. I'd kiss you, but I seem to be hooked on something." I glanced down at Jeremy's leg, and Tristan did as well.

"It does seem you're trapped."

Tristan's eyes glinted mischievously, and his finger plucked at my nipple with more purpose. Oh jeez, he was about to prove my point that everything turned into sex when we were around Jeremy, but I still moaned at the sensation as my pussy became wet. Tristan kissed my shoulder. I could tell he was about to make a move on me, but Jeremy woke up.

Jeremy stretched and mumbled "morning" to both of us, and it stopped Tristan from continuing with his plan. I almost laughed at the timing. I needed to do some research today and not spend all day in bed with my two horny men.

"I need coffee," I announced to the room, and waited for them to untangle themselves from me.

Jeremy agreed. "Mmmm, coffee sounds good." I got a pleasant zing from his sexy morning voice. A little more gravelly than normal, and I wouldn't mind hearing it every day.

Once they released me, I scooted off the bed, slipped on a robe, and went to start the coffee. While the coffeemaker was doing its thing, I glanced through the open bedroom door and saw Tristan and Jeremy kissing. I was happy to see we weren't as awkward waking up today as we were before.

As I brought them mugs in bed, I questioned them. "So guys, what's the plan today? I have work I need to do. Non-negotiable."

Jeremy took a sip and hummed as if he approved, but then his eyes widened and he looked slightly panicked. "Oh shit, I have a meeting this morning. What time is it?"

When Tristan told him it was almost 8:30 a.m., Jeremy relaxed. "Good. The meeting is at ten. I better get showered and head to the office."

When he said he was going back to the resort, a stab of disappointment hit me. It seemed silly, but I wanted to be with them both today, just not fucking. I needed proof we could do something other than fall into bed.

Almost as if he was reading my mind, Tristan suggested, "We could take our laptops. If we work in the conference room, we can all have lunch together?"

I smiled at Tristan and told him that sounded good while Jeremy echoed my sentiments. What an ideal solution.

Two hours later, Tristan and I were ensconced in the conference room while Jeremy was down the hall in his office on Zoom. He didn't say what the meeting was for. I was curious, but I knew it wasn't any of my business... yet. That's what I was working on: acquiring the empty property so we could purchase the ski resort, so it would eventually be my business.

My assistant did a fabulous job of getting everything started after my instructions yesterday, and she had several other people helping her. That my assistant had an assistant sometimes made me giggle. Her assistant does a lot of the grunt work, freeing my assistant to work on complex issues. They both worked hard for me. I considered them an integral part of my team and always gave them gifts on the holidays to show my appreciation.

Tristan was standing by a window, looking outside, wearing a headset and talking to someone about a minor issue at another site. We still had the Japan deal going, but it was almost wrapped up. Then he'd focus one hundred percent on the negotiations for the Emerald Bay Mountain Resort.

We worked companionably for a while, each doing our own thing. It warmed my heart to know Jeremy was down the hall and would join us shortly. He'd talked about us getting sandwiches for lunch at a nearby deli. He swore they had the most amazing bread selection, and I wasn't one to turn down bread of any kind.

I hit a lull in my work and stared blankly at a picture of the mountain on the wall, daydreaming. In my daydream, I imagined all three of us having a big joint office at the resort, so that we'd be in the same room when we were all here. I loved open-office work environments, and it always helped me stay motivated. Something about everyone focusing together, even if it wasn't on a shared project, kept me on task.

By the time Jeremy was done with his meeting, my stomach was growling. We happily headed to the proposed deli. Right before we left, my assistant messaged me with fantastic news about the property. I was dying to spill it to the men, but I held back. I wanted to finalize everything before surprising them: we were officially purchasing the other property, just in case something happened and the deal didn't close.

It looked as if it wouldn't be a problem, though. The owners were more than willing to sell, and they indicated the offer we sent over was acceptable. They were having their lawyer review the paperwork and would get back to us within a couple of days. My assistant said they sounded ecstatic over the phone at the idea of a quick closing, so she assumed it was a done deal since we offered them a fair price. I wasn't willing to risk pissing off the owners by trying to undercut the value. This property was the key to changing Jeremy's mind. I wanted to show him that selling the resort didn't mean giving up his dreams for it. Maybe it could move things forward for all three of us outside of business.

But what to do with Jeremy? I was still undecided. If Tristan was telling his family we liked him, that meant he was serious and wanted this. Part of me wished I heard what his mother said, so I could gauge her reaction to all of this. Tristan's relationship with his mother might have clouded his judgment about her tone of voice and choice of words. She didn't seem like she was a horrible mother, but everyone I knew had issues stemming from their childhood, even in the most loving households. I firmly believed there was no such thing as the perfect parent, and Tristan's were no better or worse than any other family, even with all their money.

Jeremy was right. The deli sandwiches were delicious, and we sat at a small round corner table and chatted while we munched. The table was small enough that our knees touched. Today I had no problem with being this close to both of them. The excited butterflies in my stomach made me want to blurt out the awesome news about the property, but I stayed quiet while I fantasized about a happily ever after for all of us.

What if all this could work? I hadn't felt anything was missing in my life, but I now I thought that if this deal fell through and Jeremy walked away from us, there might be a small hole. I snickered into my sandwich as I thought back to how fast this all happened, considering I didn't even like Jeremy at first.

Laughing to myself made the guys stop talking and look at me.

"What are you giggling about, Love?" Tristan asked.

I glanced at both of them, reached my hands under the table, and rubbed each of their knees closest to me.

I smiled wistfully and replied, "Oh, nothing. Just feeling happy."

CHAPTER 19

Jeremy

My phone vibrating on the nightstand woke me the next morning, and I extracted myself from Tristan and Faith's arms to answer it quietly, glancing back at their sleeping forms. Sleeping with them was addictive. It wasn't only the sex, but the warm comfort of being all tangled up in the bed with two people I cared for. I looked down at the phone, seeing Lucy's name on the screen. I picked up the jeans I had discarded on the floor the night before and walked into the living room, pulling them on as I answered the phone.

Lucy hadn't been able to talk the day before. I had been busy with Tristan and Faith, and she had been busy with her coaches and friends. I was eager to hear from her, and the sudden tightness in my chest made me realize how much I missed her. We'd been just the two of us for so long it felt weird not having her around, and she would be at her snowboard camp for the rest of the month.

"Hey Luce, how's the camp going?" I tried to sound cheerful and relaxed. Lucy had a caregiving streak a mile wide, and I knew that if she sensed I was lonely without her, she'd start suggesting she cut the camp short.

"It's so great, Dad! I finally landed my backside rodeo. Can you believe it? The coaches are amazing."

"On the first day of camp? They must be good."

"Right? I hope you haven't been too lonely without me." She was wide awake and cheerful, telling me about all the tricks she'd learned. Lucy had always been a morning person, and I smiled as I imagined how crazy that would make Faith. Not that I expected Faith to be around Lucy much, since this was just a fling. I cleared my throat, focusing back on what Lucy was saying. "I miss you, though." She sounded a little homesick, and my heart flip-flopped.

I looked back towards the bedroom door and shook my head, smiling. I couldn't tell my daughter I'd spent the night with Tristan and Faith. Again. "I miss you too, Squirt. I bet the time will fly by at camp, and I'll see you in a few weeks. Tell me more about your coaches."

I walked to the coffeemaker and tucked my phone under my ear as I prepped coffee. First, I poured a cup for Faith, knowing now she loved to start her morning with coffee. I listened to Lucy as she raved about her coaches and the friends she was spending time with at the Olympic training facility. "I wish I could be there with you, Lucy," I said, shaking my head. "Sounds amazing."

"Ugh, Dad, no one's parents are here. But it'd be fun for you to see all of it."

"One of these days, I'll do that. Come along for one of your things and be the annoying soccer dad."

"No, you won't. How's your new boyfriend and girlfriend?" she asked.

I laughed.

"They're not..." I didn't know how to answer that question. What were they? They were nothing I could explain to a pre-teen girl. "Great, they're great. But they live in Seattle, so..."

"Never get attached to a tourist, they always leave," Lucy said dutifully. There had been a few years when Lucy was little, where she would meet a tourist kid at the playground and think she'd found a new best friend for life. When those new best friends went home from their vacations and the kids or the parents had never attempted to continue the friendship? Lucy had been left devastated. It was a hard lesson, but she understood now. Tourists were fun to meet and play with, but they weren't for attachments.

Irrationally, knowing everything I knew, I still wanted to insist that Tristan, Faith, and I could make long distance work.

Sighing, I signed off with Lucy and grabbed the coffee, planning to give it to Faith, but my phone buzzed again, and I answered it, thinking Lucy had forgotten something. Instead, it was my realtor with some bad news. Terrible news. I stared down at the phone for a long minute after hanging up with him, trying to figure out what the fuck was going on.

"Hey," Faith said, leaning against the door frame. "How is Lucy liking her camp?"

"Did you buy the property I showed you out from under me?" I asked, trying to control my temper. Surely there was an explanation, but what could it be? Why would she have kept it a secret?

"Oh." Faith looked around nervously, and her nerves told me more than her words. "I did, but I can explain."

A groggy Tristan stepped up behind her. "Explain what?"

"You're going to pretend you don't know that your wife just undermined my plans for my resort?" I asked.

"She what?" Tristan frowned, looking genuinely confused. Did that mean it was all Faith's doing? I was so fucking confused.

"I made it clear I will not sell Emerald Bay," I snapped. "What's the plan? Make it impossible for me to grow the resort, or to build a competing resort of your own right in my backyard?"

"That's not it," Faith said, stepping forward, her hands clasped together. "There's another option."

I brushed past them, back into the bedroom. I needed to get my things and go, and my heart pounded in my ears as I grabbed my shirt from the floor and my car keys from the nightstand. How had I fallen for their bullshit? I had been warned about their underhanded tactics. "I think we're done here. This is how you guys do business, right? Like what happened in Malibu? I should never have let myself fall for it. Emerald Bay Resort is not for sale."

"What the hell is he talking about, Faith?" Tristan asked.

"Jeremy, stop and listen," Faith said, grabbing for my arm, but I shook her off, turning to meet her eyes.

"You went behind my back and did this. There's nothing to listen to."

"It wasn't behind your back," Faith insisted, following me to the door. "Let me explain."

"Really? Wasn't it? Because I didn't know about it. This is a family business, and you are not my family. I don't want to hear from you, and I definitely don't want to see you on my property again." I turned and stalked out of their condo, climbing into my truck without another word, though I could hear Faith's protests. Taking a deep breath, I started the engine with jerky motions, slammed the truck into reverse and peeled out of the driveway, not looking back. It was best to never look back, and I needed to get as far away from them as possible.

CHAPTER 20

Tristan

The sound of Jeremy's car pulling away faded into the distance, and silence filled the room.

I stood there, staring at the door and then at Faith. Both of us were at a loss for words.

"What the hell happened?" I eventually asked.

Faith was already on the phone and trying to call Jeremy, but I could see he wasn't answering. After a few moments, she threw the phone down in frustration and started pacing.

"Faith, stop. Tell me what's going on."

It took a while, but she explained it all to me. How she bought the land, intending to show we were serious about helping Jeremy develop and improve the resort, and bringing us together even more.

I also saw how Jeremy could have taken it the wrong way.

"We need to let him calm down. Give him time. Then he will listen and realize this was all a misunderstanding." I tried to sound in control..

Faith shook her head.

"You saw how angry he was. He might never speak to us again."

I could tell this was hurting her. I also knew if she kept thinking about it, she would go round and round in circles.

"Faith, I want you to have a shower. I'll have coffee ready for you when you get out, and in the meantime, I'll try calling him again."

She was about to argue, but I gave her a stern look.

"Faith, go."

She headed to the shower, and I pulled out my phone, scrolling until I found Jeremy's number. This was all a stupid misunderstanding. If I could just get him to answer, I was sure that we could get this all sorted out.

I called his number. When it rang, I hoped he might answer, but after a few moments it disconnected. He was obviously not letting it go to voicemail, which meant he didn't want to listen to a message. He didn't want to hear our voices.

There was a heavy feeling in my heart. We had messed things up badly.

When Faith came back, she looked at me hopefully. All I could do was shake my head.

The gray sky loomed as our car pulled up outside the house in Seattle. Faith didn't wait for me, throwing open the door and sprinting for the front door.

We weren't exactly fighting, but we weren't exactly getting on either.

After two days of trying to contact Jeremy, we eventually headed home. Every call had been ignored, every text unread. When we called his office, we were repeatedly told he was out for the rest of the week and couldn't be reached.

Faith went from distraught to angry.

"If he would take one call, we could sort everything out. Why does he have to be such a pigheaded idiot? Sixty seconds and we could get this straightened out. It's this stupid behavior that put me off him when we met."

I tried to counsel waiting, letting him calm down, but Faith was having none of it.

"No. We tried. We were doing this for him. If he can't see it, then it's his loss."

And that was that; she had decided we weren't going to waste any more time on him and should go home to Seattle.

I followed her in. I immediately heard Faith on the phone, catching up on other business. It was like we had never been away, the way she was back in the flow of things. We had been putting other work off for too long. I knew there was no point in interrupting her. She needed to throw herself into this to take her mind off Jeremy.

I headed for the kitchen and started making an omelet. I had my method of distraction and cooking was good for that. As a bonus, I could ensure Faith didn't forget to eat, like she often did.

A few minutes later, I put a plate down in front of her, pointing to it and getting a nod. She indicated she would get to it in a minute, but I knew it would be cold by the time she did.

I took my plate and headed to the bedroom for some silence. As I ate, my thoughts turned to Jeremy.

It wasn't just the sex. Something about him seemed to work well with us. He was funny, intelligent, honest, and said what he thought without thinking. Now it looked like we had lost all that.

Of course, my mother would be pleased. She would take this as her being proven right, both on the purchase and in how I should run things.

I checked emails on my phone and quickly scanned them for a message from Jeremy, but there was nothing. I knew in my heart of hearts that if he hadn't contacted us by now, there was little chance he would. But I missed him, and I knew when Faith got a quiet moment, she would miss him, too.

I wondered what Jeremy was doing and if he was missing us.

CHAPTER 21

Faith

Coming back to Seattle was a good idea, but the quiet in the house depressed me. We came home a week ago and since then, I'd been restless and mentally unsettled. I'm the type of woman whose mind continually spun with thoughts, and it was exhausting. Whenever Tristan, Jeremy, and I were together, I found I could relax easier. I'd let my mind drift peacefully while I listened to them discuss plans and joke around. I was always welcome to talk if I wanted, but I spent a significant portion of my time daydreaming about the future and what needed to happen for us to buy the resort. Later, it turned into contemplating life with Jeremy after we closed on the resort deal.

I had been this way since childhood, and my teachers affectionately said my head was in the clouds. Since I didn't get in trouble at school and got good grades, no one cared if I daydreamed. When I reached high school age, my parents pressured me to become a neurosurgeon. They kept insisting I had the brains for it, but my older brother was already in med school, and I decided the family only needed one doctor. I didn't have any other plans for my future, but I knew I didn't want to be a doctor.

For the longest time, my primary goal was to find happiness in life. A significant portion of my childhood and teenage years were unhappy as I struggled to find my place in the world. I had tons of ideas and interests, but nothing stuck. I went to business school, telling myself it was the practical thing to do. Funny how things sometimes work. I don't think I would have taken my European trip after graduation if I had done a different degree, and it led me to Tristan.

Meeting him the summer after graduation changed everything and propelled my life in an amazing direction. I was successful without him and had a couple of job offers I was considering. I would be naïve if I didn't admit that having the financial backing of his family allowed me to take risks I wouldn't have otherwise. They gave me the platform to learn more quickly about business matters, since I didn't have to work my way up the chain of command. I would always be grateful for the opportunities provided by his family.

I'd grown up emotionally in the time since I met Tristan: learning my likes and dislikes, how to treat a partner the way they deserved, what it meant to be genuinely there for someone. We were happy together for years before Jeremy, which was why the pang in my heart when I thought about never seeing him again was more than uncomfortable. It forced me to question my choices and examine my life in a new way. Was this yearning for more than Tristan specific to Jeremy, or did it say something about my marriage? If we could get things back to normal, I wouldn't be so unsettled.

The helpless frustration of Jeremy not answering his phone or contacting us hurt me deeply. I was the fixer type of person, but it didn't appear there would be any resolution. How could we make it right if he never took our calls?

Tristan brooded for days, taking this harder than I expected. We tried having sex one night to feel better, but my climax was lackluster. I thought about Jeremy through most of it, wishing he was with us. Tristan was subdued while we made love, and I could tell his orgasm wasn't great, either. We'd lost our mojo, and I longed for it to come back. Sex was an important part of our marriage, and now things felt broken.

I sighed and figured to give it another couple days. It was probably too soon to expect everything to be normal.

A week later it wasn't entirely better, but I could see us headed in that direction. I had a hard time not going round and round and picking apart what I could have done differently. I should have laid my cards out on the table and told Jeremy what I was doing. It felt too soon after meeting him to admit I was buying the property so we could work towards a relationship.

What also dismayed me was imagining Jeremy at home, thinking the worst about us. He didn't know the full story, and he was probably shutting his heart off to us right now. Building a wall around it and painting us as the bad guys. All of this was my fault because I was too impulsive... and there was nothing I could do about it.

Deep down, I knew I needed to find acceptance of everything. What was the saying? Accept the things you cannot change, have the courage to change the things you can, and the wisdom to know the difference. Yeah, I wasn't there yet.

When we first got home, I'd hoped that Jeremy would contact us and we'd fly back immediately, so I didn't unpack. I had enough clothes that I didn't need the ones in my luggage. The fuchsia suitcase stood in the corner, mocking me, for two weeks as the days ran together with no contact from him. Resolved, I decided it was time to put my stuff away and bury the suitcase in the far corner of my closet. I was sure having a visual reminder in my bedroom didn't help me move past what happened.

As I put away my clothes, I came across several of the tiny notebooks I carried with me whenever I left the condo. I bought ones small enough to stuff in my coat pocket. If I didn't write ideas down when they hit, I was likely to forget it within a few minutes.

I resisted the urge to flip through the notes, since I'd included cute little things about the guys while I was out with them. I planned to keep them. Maybe one day I would want to read them. If we couldn't have Jeremy, the next-best outcome would be someday Tristan and I would reminisce about how much fun we had when we almost bought a third person into our relationship for more than one night.

We hadn't yet told his parents the deal fell through. That would make it all too real. We told them we were giving Jeremy a couple of weeks to think everything over and have his lawyers look at the paperwork. That kept them off our backs for now, but we were going to have to admit everything soon. I knew they'd ask what happened, and I still didn't know what to tell them. They won't fire us, but it won't be a comfortable discussion.

Unless we lied to them. I was pretty sure that wasn't the right answer.

Tristan and I needed to have a conversation about what happened, and finding the notebooks gave me the courage to seek him out. If we wanted things to get better, it was critical we talk about it instead of suffering silently on our own. I found him in our home office playing with his Newton's cradle, staring unseeingly through it, while the swinging silver orbs clicked rhythmically.

He glanced up when I came in and smiled tenderly at me. I came over and climbed into his lap. He circled his arms around me while I leaned my head against his shoulder. Sighing, I caressed his neck with my hand, enjoying the strong, steady pulse of his heartbeat under my fingertips.

Neither of us spoke for a bit. The woodsy smell of his cologne enveloped me, reminding me of that first summer with him and falling head over heels. He rubbed my shoulder and arm, and a rush of warmth flooded my heart. I still loved Tristan deeply, but it was impossible to say nothing had changed. The longer Jeremy was out of our lives, the more I came to realize how much it sucked.

I finally broke the silence and asked him softly, "Tristan, did you love Jeremy?"

He stilled his hand on my arm and was quiet.

When he answered, his voice was strained. "We didn't know him terribly long. Wouldn't it be crazy to say we loved him?"

His non-answer spoke volumes. I snuggled closer to him and kissed his neck.

"Not crazy. Remember when we met? I loved you from the first moment, and you said it only took you two days."

A visible shiver ran through Tristan, and he sighed.

"I remember. Can lightning strike twice like that?"

I played with the edge of his shirt collar while a heavy ball settled in my stomach. Since he seemed unwilling to admit it first, I was going to have to be the one to say it.

"Hon, it did for both of us."

Tristan let out a sad-sounding chuckle. "There's nothing to do about it now. If he felt the same way, he would've taken our calls."

I nodded my head against his shoulder and kissed his neck again. Tristan looked down at me, and his eyes shimmered with a film of tears. When he cried, it punched me in the gut worse than anything because I knew it took powerful feelings to bring them out. He wasn't afraid to show emotions, but he also didn't want to cry with me over the Budweiser Superbowl commercials.

He brushed his lips against mine, and I deepened the kiss by slanting my mouth against his, pouring all my passion into him. I needed him to understand I still loved him and we were in this together. I kept expecting Tristan to push for sex the longer we kissed, but for a change, neither of us showed any move to take it further. It was satisfying to make out, his powerful arms around me, loved and safe. We didn't stop until my stomach growled loud enough both of us heard it.

He broke his lips from mine and laughed breathlessly. "We better stop for food."

Before I could agree, he lifted me up and set my ass on the edge of the desk. I squeaked in surprise.

He gave my hand a squeeze as he asked, "Want to keep me company while I start dinner?"

"Sure. I'll be down in a couple of minutes." My pussy hummed angrily at me, while my soul remained dispirited. It was an annoying combination, and I needed to compose myself before joining him downstairs.

He kissed my nose and left. God, I loved Tristan, but the situation seemed almost worse now that we both admitted our deeper attachment to Jeremy. Our talk was good, necessary, but something wonderful better be at the other end of this dark tunnel we were in.

CHAPTER 22

Jeremy

Going through a traumatic breakup while Lucy wasn't home had been a terrible error in judgment. If she had been home, I wouldn't have had time to wallow. I certainly wouldn't have accumulated a massive pile of half-eaten takeout boxes on the coffee table. I'd procrastinated cleaning until the very last minute, and now I was trying to pretend I hadn't lived like a slovenly, depressed shell of a man for the past few weeks.

Also, if she had been home, I wouldn't have attempted to subsist entirely on my favorite ice cream for three days to cheer myself up. That was fine until I'd been forcibly reminded how lactose intolerant I was.

Now Lucy was on a plane back to California, and I had been forced to transform our house back into a living environment suitable for a pre-teen girl again. I was determined to be fatherly and fun to be around. Standing in the baggage claim area, I forced a smile onto my face. It became genuine as I saw her rushing off the escalator. I'd missed the hell out of her, and when she flung herself at me in a massive hug, I felt my heart lighten.

As we gathered her bags and headed out to the car, I was cheered by her nonstop talk about snowboard camp. The coaches, the things she'd learned, the cute boy she'd... Wait a minute.

"Love sucks, Luce. Don't fall for this guy. He's probably an idiot."

"Dad, I'm not in love. I'm not even going to date until I'm in high school." She shook her head. What? Had we decided that? I turned and frowned at her as we reached the truck. She was smiling, laughter in her eyes. "Oh, the look on your face when I mentioned dating!"

"I'm only preparing you for the reality of things. One day he's a cute snowboarder interested in talking shop. The next day, you're finding out he's snatched an important piece of property right out from under you." I hauled her board bag up into the truck with a grunt. Had her bags gotten heavier, or had I gotten weaker? Maybe all that takeout had failed me.

"I don't think Mason is into real estate. He's only twelve," Lucy said with a curious note.

I blinked. "Good point. I seem to have gotten sidetracked. Load up, let's get home and order a treat to celebrate your accomplishments. Your pick."

"Salted caramel swirl ice cream!" she squealed, slipping into the passenger seat.

My stomach revolted. "Your pick of anything non-dairy."

She stared hard at me. "You tried eating ice cream for every meal while I was gone, didn't you?"

"No. I would never do a thing like that." I tried not to look like I was lying, but Lucy's hard stare told me she didn't buy it.

Lucy yanked her door closed, pulled out her phone, and promptly fumbled it. It bounced off of her left hand, then her right, then hit the armrest and went flying into the back seat.

"How are you coordinated enough to train at an Olympic snowboard camp?" I asked, starting the engine. She laughed, swatting at my arm.

"Different coordination. I need my phone, though. I was going to plan my welcome home feast. Chinese from Chan's!" She unbuckled her seatbelt and crawled over the center console, ducking under the seat, feeling around for her phone.

"Already ordered your favorites. It should be there a bit after we get home."

"Huh, cute notebook." She resurfaced, tripping on the seatbelt and kicking me in the face as she climbed over the center console, settled into her seat, and buckled back in. She had her phone in one hand, and a little spiral-bound notepad in the other. "Doesn't seem your style, Dad. Can I have it?"

"Sure. Go for it." It was probably hers anyway. I backed out of the parking lot, and she flipped open the notebook.

"Crap. Most of the pages are used." She flipped some more and snickered at what she found. "Who IS this person? It's full of weird random notes. Look, this entry says 'Find out why people enjoy snowboarding. It looks painful.'"

"What?" I glanced down at the little notebook. It looked familiar somehow.

"Must be a friend of yours. All of my friends know why snowboarding is fun." She kept flipping, reading random things. "'Research winter driving courses. Call jacuzzi cleaning service.' Ooh, 'book a flight to Kauai.' I want to go! Melissa went there surfing. She says the breaks are epic. I have to find out what that means."

"Lucy, I'm sure these are someone's private notes." I tried to grab it out of her hand, but she kept reading.

"Holy crap. 'Talk to Jeremy about birth control.' DAD!" Lucy squealed, and I finally remembered where I'd seen the notebook. It was Faith's.

"Fuck. Please stop reading." At a stoplight, I tried to grab it again, but she was laughing too hard, frantically flipping through pages, and holding it where I couldn't reach it. Someone behind me honked their horn, and I had to focus on driving again. "What do you know about birth control, anyway?"

"Health class. But I don't want to think about health class and my dad. Gross. You should not date." She shuddered, then flipped again. "Huh."

"Huh?"

"There's a bunch of notes here. Phone number for Bombardier and Poma. She doesn't know if snowboarding is fun, but she was researching chairlifts?"

I sighed. Honesty time. Some of it, anyway. "These people were trying to buy the back property and prevent me from expanding the resort. Probably hoping I wouldn't be able to make it profitable and would be forced to sell." I glanced at her, watching her flip through a few more pages as I turned into our neighborhood.

"I don't think that's what this says, Dad," Lucy said.

"What do you mean?"

"It's like a bunch of numbers. I don't know. Ownership shares, it says? There are different percentages, and a bunch of math."

Startled, I pulled to a hard stop in our driveway, and Lucy slammed forward against her seatbelt with an "oof." She glanced at me, her eyes wide, then slowly handed me the notebook. "Whatever it is you're freaking out about, I'm sure it's fine." She used the slow voice you use with crazy people.

I took a deep breath, looking down at the page Lucy had been reading. It was full of Faith's random notes. She had been making phone calls. Running numbers. And there, on the next page, was her last note, the one that made me feel like I was going to throw up.

'Can we spend more time in Tahoe to be near Jeremy? Remote work more often? Long weekends?'

"I really fucked up," I whispered.

"What?" Lucy asked, stealing the notebook back. She frowned. "Are you and this chick in love, Dad?"

I leaned back against my headrest and closed my eyes, trying to figure out how to explain Faith and Tristan to Lucy. How do you tell a twelve-year-old about polyamory? "I might have been falling for them. But I messed it up. I thought they weren't what they said they were."

"They? Like two people or one nonbinary person?"

I frowned. "Two people. I was sort of dating Faith and Tristan. After I got stuck in that cabin with them."

"Oh my god, you did not fall for the dorky rich people." She nudged me with her elbow. I opened my eyes and grinned wryly at her, and she gasped. "You did! But, like both of them? I didn't even know you were bisexual. That's cool."

"You're okay with that?" I asked. "With me dating two people?"

She shrugged. "If it makes you happy, Dad. I don't judge. I mean, you know my friends." I knew I shouldn't have worried. This was the same girl who had given me an intense series of lectures about acceptance when her best friend had changed their pronouns, after all.

My need to figure out what had happened with Faith was intense. Somewhere, probably in my trash folder, there was an email she'd sent me. As I unloaded Lucy's bags and hauled them inside, I kept replaying my last conversation with Tristan and Faith. The one where I'd jumped to conclusions, and she'd tried to tell me I was jumping to conclusions. I wondered, not for the first time, if I'd been single for so long because of my issues, not my bad luck. Why did I sabotage everything good?

"I'm an asshole," I muttered. "And I might need therapy for it. I keep sabotaging everything good."

"Mason sees a therapist," Lucy said. "Want me to ask for his number?"

"No. I am not taking my therapist recommendations from a cute 12-year-old boy."

"Nothing wrong with seeing a therapist, and you've been through a lot, Dad, between grandpa dying and mom leaving."

I sighed. "I know. I know that."

"So, Tristan and Faith. Are you going to fix it?" Lucy was setting plates and chopsticks out on the kitchen island staring at me eagerly, which made me wonder how long she had been standing there like that.

"I don't think I can fix it."

She tilted her head, studying me. "You're the one always telling me I need to fight for my dreams. If these dorks make you happy, fight for them. You can do it. Win back the dorks!" Lucy pumped her first in the air, and I laughed.

I shook my head and gave her a big hug. "I missed you Luce. You have a way about you. You make the heavy stuff lighter."

"I know. It's a talent." She hugged me back. "Love you, Dad. Now we need a plan for the dorks." The doorbell rang, and I went to collect our takeout.

"Can you please stop calling them dorks?" I shouted back over my shoulder. "I think I'm in love with them."

"Awww. Dad! That's so adorable. Adorkable?"

"Lucy."

"Don't worry, I'll help you win them back. People find me charming." For the first time in weeks, I felt like things might actually turn out okay.

"Holy crap, these people are loaded," Lucy said, staring wide-eyed at Vaughn Resort Group's sleek office space. My stomach flip-flopped as I realized I was so close to seeing Faith and Tristan again. Lucy had spent the entire plane flight and the ride from the airport grilling me on what I was going to say when I made my big apology, but at the moment, my mind felt blank and a little hazy. We stood for a minute, taking in the elegant reception space, until Lucy finally got impatient. "Now what?"

"I have no idea." I wasn't entirely sure how I was going to locate Faith and Tristan, and in retrospect, it may have made way more sense to return one of their phone calls. Lucy thought I needed a grand gesture and refused to let me even text them.

Before I could talk to the receptionist, they appeared, and for a panicked moment, I thought they somehow knew I was there and had come to kick me out. I spotted Faith first, walking briskly out of a corridor to my left. She looked like the badass businesswoman she was in a charcoal gray pencil skirt, spiky black heels, and a tailored green blouse that matched her eyes. Tristan was right behind her, and they were chatting about something as they walked, not looking our way at all.

This was a terrible idea. I looked around for somewhere to hide. I reached for Lucy to drag her behind the nearest potted plant and regroup. Only Lucy wasn't standing next to me anymore. She was standing by the reception desk, digging through a bowl of candy. When had that happened?

Then Faith glanced at me and it was too late for the plant. She stopped mid-stride, her arms dropping to her sides. Her phone slipped out of her hand, landing on the floor with a thud, but she didn't seem to notice.

"Jeremy?"

Behind her, Tristan stiffened, his shoulders straightening, his lips forming a thin line. They were not happy to see me, but I guess I hadn't expected that they would be.

"Um, hi. You left your notebook in my car?" Fuck, what even was that? It wasn't the speech Lucy and I had practiced. I stepped closer, wanting to touch her, but I knew it would be creepy. I pulled the little book out of my pocket and handed it to her. Our fingers brushed, sending a jolt of awareness up my arm. Her eyebrows pushed together in confusion as she took it and looked down.

"You flew to Seattle to return my notebook? Personally?" She flipped it open, frowning. I glanced at Tristan, noting the tick in his jaw. That usually meant he was irritated. I swallowed, trying to remember what I was going to say.

"Uh. Yep." I swallowed again. Was my throat closing up? That couldn't be good. I reminded myself to breathe.

"Dude, Dad, they have like the good candy in that bowl. It's not some boring hard candy or anything. You should snag some. Oh, hi dorks." Lucy had the worst timing of any human on Earth. I shot my daughter a wide-eyed look, trying to communicate she should stop talking. She didn't. "Did he give his big love speech yet? I missed it."

"Lucy," I hissed, panic rising. They were definitely not in love with me. Tristan still looked pissed off, and I was pretty sure Faith now thought I was a lunatic. "Abort mission."

"Oh my god, he didn't even give the speech yet?"

"He gave me my notebook," Faith said, turning to Lucy. "You and your dad flew here to give me my notebook? I'm a little confused."

Tristan's lips twitched, like he was trying to hold back a smile. Lucy jabbed my arm with her elbow.

"Dad. Talk."

Nope. Nothing would come out, only more awkward silence.

"Holy shit, he's terrible at this. No wonder he's been single for so long." Lucy laughed at her own joke for a minute before recovering with an exasperated sigh. "He's here to tell you he loves you and he's very sorry that he was an idiot and jumped to conclusions, because, like I said, he's an idiot. Tell me if you're going to do some kind of romantic kissing thing, because I might want to cover my eyes." She glanced back at the candy bowl. "Or, you know, occupy myself elsewhere."

"Wait, what?" Faith asked.

"You should have done the boom box outside their house thing. It's the only way they'd understand," Lucy said out of the corner of her mouth. She bent over and picked up Faith's phone and handed it to her. "Dropped this."

I rubbed my hands over my face, not sure how to meet either of their eyes. "I'm sorry. This was clearly a mistake. I couldn't leave things like I left them."

"What were you hoping would happen here?" Tristan asked. His intense focus on me was intimidating. It didn't help that he looked dead sexy in his bespoke suit, tailored to fit his beautiful body to perfection.

"Basically, we were picturing something like the end of a rom-com," Lucy volunteered. I shot her a glare. "You know what? I brought my Nintendo Switch. I'll go occupy myself," she said, smiling cheerfully. "Good to see you, dorks. I hope you become my new mom and dad. Second dad? We'll have to come up with a name for you." She walked halfway across the room and turned around again. "Pops, maybe? And we can deal with your questionable fashion choices at some point."

She shot a pointed look at Faith's shoes, then waved and headed to the other side of the room. We watched her as she fist-bumped the rather startled receptionist, then grabbed a giant handful of the candy. She curled up on one couch, where she yanked her handheld game out of her bag and settled down.

"Questionable fashion choices?" Faith asked. "These are Louboutins."

I pinched the bridge of my nose, trying to stem the rising panic. "Sorry. Clearly bringing a pre-teen with no filter to this was an insane choice."

Faith smiled a little, and I hoped maybe she was loosening up a bit. "Why did you bring her?" And fuck if I could think of an explanation.

"Because that's what he wants," Tristan said. "He wants us to be serious. To commit. And he wants us to understand what comes with it. Him."

I flushed and ducked my head, taking a deep breath. "Yeah, I'm a single dad. I come with baggage, and the baggage has a bit of an attitude problem. She's not wrong, though. I didn't know how much I had grown to love you both until I screwed the whole thing up. And over money? The business shouldn't be more important to me than the people I love."

Faith's eyes warmed, and she smiled, stepping forward a half step, before her eyes darted to Tristan and she paused, awaiting his reaction.

"I have two conditions," he said. "Kneel."

I glanced around the lobby, widening my eyes. The receptionist was typing on a computer, and Lucy was zoned out on her game, no longer paying attention at all. Still, anyone could walk in at any moment to find me kneeling on the floor for them. I did it anyway, my body responding to his instructions before I could think too hard about it.

I remembered what it had been like the last time they'd taken control of me, and I shuddered in anticipation. Tristan stepped closer, tilting my chin up and forcing eye contact. He didn't speak for a moment, studying me, the pad of his thumb tracing over my lips as his palm cupped my jaw. Faith moved next to him, pressed up against his side, and stroked a hand through my hair. Tristan's thumb slipped into my mouth, and I couldn't hold back the moan of pleasure as I sucked on it, trying to show him how much I wanted another part of his anatomy there.

The reception area faded away, and it was just the three of us, the things they were doing to me. Finally, he spoke. "Two conditions," he repeated. "One. You will read contract Faith has drafted and trust that we're doing our best to do the right thing for all of us."

I nodded, so happy to be touched by him it was difficult to focus on his words or what I was agreeing to. Weirdly, I didn't want him to remove his thumb from my mouth, and I didn't speak, just sucked his thumb deeper. He made an approving noise.

"Two. You show us your devotion by offering us free use of your body for the rest of your time in Seattle. I understand you're not always submissive. Faith and I are both switches as well. But you will submit to us until we are convinced you are remorseful." He pulled his thumb from my mouth, still touching my chin, awaiting my answer.

"Yes, Sir," I whispered, and he finally let a soft smile creep across his face.

"Good. Come, let's read and discuss the contracts and then we'll take your daughter to lunch," Tristan said, helping me to my feet and giving me a soft kiss. I wanted to melt into that kiss. I almost lost it when he turned my chin and offered my mouth to Faith, who was a little greedier when she kissed me.

They led me back to an office, closing the door behind them, and I shuddered in anticipation as Tristan pulled out the contract. I didn't bothering reading any of it, signing each place indicated for signature. I knew my complete disregard for the contents of the contract would likely give my lawyer an aneurysm if she heard about it, but Tristan was right. I trusted them to be fair, to understand the market value of the resort, and to give me what it was worth.

"You sure you don't want to read that?" Faith asked.

"I'm choosing to trust you," I said, and the slow smile that spread across her face let me know I'd made the right decision.

I felt lighter as I set the pen aside and closed the thick pile of documents. Tristan pulled me to my feet, praising me in that sexy way he had when he was feeling dominant. They surrounded me, taking turns kissing me passionately, their hands on my body, and mine on theirs. I had given them free use, and I shuddered at the thought of what they might do to me. Would Tristan finally fuck me?

"I didn't realize how much I missed you guys," I said.

"We feel the same. About everything," Tristan murmured. "We've talked about it quite a lot, and we've both fallen for you, too."

"You don't want to know what you signed?" Faith asked, interrupting our love declarations with a worried expression.

I grimaced, feeling the flush rise in my cheeks again. "I'm not sure I do. You gave me a good deal, though, right?"

She grinned. "Sort of. We will hold an 80% ownership of the resort, and you keep 20%."

I narrowed my eyes. "I thought you weren't interested in a partnership."

"We can compromise, too. There's also a stipulation that you stay on as the resort's general manager until you sell your shares or resign from the position. There's a salary, of course. A little more than what you were paying yourself."

"How did you convince your bosses of that?"

"Well, you didn't sell it to us for very much. The property I purchased, and the development of new terrain and new lodging, are listed as capital improvements offered by Vaughn Resort Group as part of the deal. I knew you cared most about the success of the resort and about how it was run, so to sell the deal to Tristan's family, I lowballed you on the price."

I laughed, shaking my head. "Then you gave me a higher salary?"

"Substantially higher. More in line with what we'd normally pay a GM of one of our properties. They wouldn't question the salary, but they were questioning the wisdom of paying full price for a resort on top of the expansion budget, so I needed to make the numbers work. Is that okay?" She looked nervous, but there was no reason for her to be. I pulled her close and kissed her roughly, trying to communicate how happy I was with her plan.

"It's perfect, really. My reservations were never about the money, and you knew it. I can't believe I doubted you."

"She's brilliant, isn't she? It's part of why we love her," Tristan said, and I couldn't disagree. "Now for our second demand."

CHAPTER 23

Faith

It was always a fun time when Tristan went dominant. I could tell Jeremy was already fuzzy and willing to obey whatever we commanded. Since this wasn't pre-planned, I didn't know where Tristan was going with everything. Chances were, he didn't either. When I looked at my to-do list this morning, fucking Jeremy in my office wasn't on there.

The shock and joy when I spotted him in the lobby made my hands tingle and my heart catch in my throat. Despite being confused at why he was there, I wanted to throw myself at him and cover his face with kisses. I held back while butterflies swirled in my stomach and made sure I didn't show my emotions while he explained himself.

Tristan taking immediate control surprised me, but it felt right. When Jeremy kneeled on the floor of the lobby and sucked on Tristan's thumb, I imagined watching the two of them play together in our bed. I wanted to relax on the lounge chair, rub my clit, and order them around. Since Jeremy agreed to be our toy for the weekend, I planned to make it happen.

But now it was time for Tristan's second demand.

"Faith, lock the door."

The steel in Tristan's voice made the butterflies jump in eagerness. I knew that voice. He only brought it out when he was feeling extra dominant, and it always meant I was about to have a good time. Wondering if the thumb sucking brought it out in Tristan, I locked the door and faced the room. Leaning against the door, I settled in and waited for the show to start. This should be good, and I hoped Tristan planned to make Jeremy suck his cock.

"Faith."

Tristan saying my name startled me and I met his eyes.

"Remove your skirt and bend over the desk."

The command was so unexpected I jolted from my slack position to stand straight while my pussy clenched in anticipation. I thought we were controlling Jeremy this weekend? When I hesitated, Tristan's eyes narrowed.

"Faith... NOW."

Oh shit.

I hurried over to the desk and fumbled with the zipper and inner button on my skirt. When I finally got them undone, I released my skirt, letting it pool on the carpet around my high heels. He didn't tell me to remove my panties, so I leaned over the desk, feeling the black satin and lace stretch across my ass.

Tristan moved behind me and rubbed my cheeks. I hummed with pleasure. My mind whirled with the possibilities of what might happen. Was he going to fuck me to torture Jeremy and make him watch?

Tristan sighed and rubbed my pussy through my panties, creating an inferno of need in my core. His voice held a tinge of regret in it. "We don't have a lot of time right now, so this will be fast."

I squirmed against his hand, and he rewarded me with a sharp slap on my ass. I gasped as he yanked down my panties.

"Jeremy, come over here and fuck Faith."

Jeremy replied, "Yes, Sir," while I moaned out a long, "Oooh," at the thought of Jeremy's cock inside me again after a month.

I gripped the edge of the desk with my hands. I heard Jeremy unbuckling his pants and the sound of his zipper. The tip of his cock probed my slick cave entrance, and I almost groaned.

Tristan called out as Jeremy was about to press in. "Jeremy?"

"Yes, Sir?" Jeremy's voice was soft and dazed.

Since the head of his cock sat right against my pussy, I rotated my hips in the hopes he'd press in further. Oh, my god. He needed to fuck me before I went crazy.

Tristan continued with what he was saying to Jeremy while I wiggled and squirmed my ass stealthily, hoping Tristan didn't notice what I was doing. I was getting a tingle from the tip of Jeremy's cock, but nowhere near enough to satisfy me.

"I want you to fuck her hard and fast until she climaxes, but you're not allowed to come. Consider it part of your punishment. Now fuck her."

As soon as Tristan gave Jeremy the green light, he plowed forward, plunging straight to my core. It happened faster than I expected, and I squealed while my pussy stretched and molded around him. My nerve endings zinged, and I repositioned myself to get better leverage so I could thrust against him.

Jeremy set a swift but steady pace. Each time he knocked against my ass, my nipples scraped against the surface of the desk through the fabric of my blouse and satin bra. My head swirled as the pleasure mounted in my core. I was almost lost in the bliss but I wanted to see how Tristan was doing. I peeked over my shoulder at him.

He was standing so he could see Jeremy's cock moving in and out of my pussy. He was intent on the action between us, and a quick glance at his pants showed an obvious bulge. Once I verified Tristan was fine, I closed my eyes and let the ecstasy wash over me.

I was so far gone in the pleasure, I barely heard Tristan bark out, "Fuck her faster," but my head spun when Jeremy started hammering against me. His harsh breathing filled the room, and when he started moaning loudly every time he bottomed out, I guessed he was close to coming.

I didn't know what Tristan would do to him if he came before I did, so I tried a slightly different position. As soon as I arched my back, forcing my ass to tilt up and changing the angle of entry, Jeremy's cock hit a delightful spot and I lost all thought other than coming.

I raced closer and closer to my orgasm while chanting out, "Oh, my god."

Desperate to come, I slid one hand down between me and the desk to probe my folds. As I rubbed circles around my clit, Jeremy hit the most perfect spot and I exploded around his cock.

"Ooooh, god!" I screamed loud enough that anyone passing would hear, but the waves of rapture overtook me and I didn't care. Jeremy groaned as I shuddered underneath him and my pussy clenched around his cock.

"Don't you dare come!" Tristan's hard demand forced Jeremy to pull out immediately.

Jeremy expelled a long, "Fuuuck." His ragged panting and my soft mewls as I came down from my high filled the room.

My core quivered from tiny aftershocks, and I couldn't raise my head.

"Good boy." Tristan praised Jeremy, and I smiled weakly. BDSM play was going to be fun with three people.

I felt my panties being pulled back up, and Tristan helped me stand.

"Come over here," Tristan murmured. I thought he was talking to me. When I felt the arms of both men wrap around me, I realized he was speaking to Jeremy. I turned to face him and kissed with all my pent-up passion from the last month. A pleasant warmth overtook me the longer our lips locked, and my pussy tried to sputter back to life. As our tongues twined together, I had an overwhelming sense of rightness. Having both men's arms around me, I realized I never gave up hope this would happen. I might have told myself it was over with Jeremy, but my heart never accepted it.

We still needed to take Lucy to lunch, so we couldn't cuddle together for long. Tristan and I shared a deep kiss and a quiet moment while Jeremy used the restroom to clean up, promising to meet us in the lobby in a few minutes.

"Are you happy, my Love?" Tristan whispered to me between kisses.

"Very. Are you?"

"Mmmhmmm," was all he could reply while my tongue plundered his mouth and I stroked the bulge in his pants. When we broke apart, Tristan was the one with a dazed expression and I hid my smirk.

I kept my tone light and flirty, but I needed to tell him something. "Oh, Tristan?"

"Yes, Love?"

He reached down to the floor, grabbed my skirt, and helped me close and adjust it. He was intent on his task, so I tipped his chin up, forcing him to look me in the eye just like he did with Jeremy in the lobby.

I rubbed my hand against the stiffness in his pants and switched my voice to Domme Faith. As I squeezed his cock just enough to produce the perfect amount of discomfort I knew Tristan enjoyed, I announced, "Tonight, I'm in charge. Got it?"

His eyes widened, and he grinned at me. "Yes, Mistress."

Satisfied, I released him and we both straightened our clothes before heading out to the lobby to gather Jeremy and Lucy for lunch.

CHAPTER 24

Tristan

Lunch went even better than I had hoped.

We gathered up Lucy and Jeremy, took them out to the car, and told them we would treat them to the finest lunch in Seattle.

"I'm not sure we are the fancy lunch types," grumbled Lucy, looking out of the window at the city passing by.

I smiled to myself, knowing where we were going. I had a feeling that Lucy might enjoy herself more than she expected.

"Lucy, be nice. They're kind enough to take us out somewhere nice," sighed Jeremy. I could tell his heart wasn't in it, still a little dazed from earlier.

"You would say that, you LOVE them," replied Lucy. I spotted Faith covering her mouth to hide the giggles. It was a habit she had picked up from me I found adorable.

We pulled up outside Diamond Dogs and got out, watching Lucy stare at the sign in confusion.

"Diamond Dogs?"

"The owner is a big David Bowie fan. And, as you can see, it's pretty near the baseball stadium."

"It's... a hot dog place?" she asked.

Faith smiled and took the lead, ruffling Lucy's hair as she walked past. I waited for Lucy to react, but she seemed confused and didn't notice.

"No, it's THE hot dog place. Best in the city. And there is no way you're going to be able to eat the hot chili dog. It's far too hot for you," I grinned.

I could see the smile on Jeremy's face and laughed when Lucy shouted, "Oh, you are ON."

Half an hour later, we were sitting in the booth, happily watching Lucy finish her third hot dog.

"Okay, I admit, this was pretty awesome. I thought we were going to go to some stuffy restaurant, but this place was great. Maybe you two aren't so bad after all."

She jumped up and headed for the restroom. Jeremy watched her go till she disappeared around the corner and then he turned back to us.

"Thank you for this. I know that she's a lot, especially when you weren't really expecting her to be, you know, suddenly part of your life."

Faith reached forward to rub his hand, at the same time leaning against me.

"We both like her. She's full of spirit and says what she thinks. And she's funny. It will do us good having her around."

"And you are sure you still want us around?" he asked.

I could feel Faith's hand slipping over my lap, finding my cock and squeezing through my trousers.

"Yes, very much so," I said, trying to keep my voice calm as Faith let her fingers play.

Abruptly her hand pulled back as Lucy walked up to the table.

"What's next?"

"You have got to be kidding me."

Lucy was running around the house, up the stairs, along the corridors and peeking in all the rooms. She returned every so often to drop a pithy comment.

"You guys live in a mansion."

She ran off again and Jeremy started after her.

"I'll try to calm her down," he promised.

"It's okay. Don't worry about it. Third door on the left is the best guest bedroom. You can get her settled in there. You can also show her the game room downstairs." Faith laughed. "It's full of old pinball machines and arcade games. Seems her type of thing."

Jeremy ran to catch up with her, while we headed to the bedroom to change into something a little less business and a lot more pleasure. By the time I had freshened up and put on fresh trousers and shirt, Faith had settled on the bed wearing a little black nightgown and nothing else.

"Why are you not dressed? I thought we were going to..."

Before I could finish, she pointed at the floor beside the bed. "Kneel."

I could feel my legs go weak at the command. I walked over and sank down, keeping my eyes on her.

"You thought we were going to hang out with Jeremy, talk for a while, then come back here later?"

I nodded my head.

"I told you earlier I'm in charge tonight. Remember?" I did, and I nodded again. "Good. There will be no talking, no catching up. You two will do exactly as I command."

I nodded my head a third time.

"Why did you let me get changed, then?" I asked.

She smiled and reached for me, running her fingers through my hair.

"Because, sweet boy, we now have a young girl wandering around our house and you should be dressed appropriately. I want you to go get Jeremy and bring him here. Then we can see about getting you out of those clothes."

With a wave of her hand, she dismissed me.

I stood and walked to the door, my legs feeling unsteady and my head spinning. Whenever Faith gets commanding, I always feel fuzzy. And extremely turned on.

I headed towards the guest room and thought about the events of the day. First Jeremy turning up and my heart leaping in my chest, wondering if perhaps there was still a way to save this. When it turned out that he was here to apologize, his vulnerability set off my Dom side and I needed him to submit to me, to kneel and show he accepted that sometimes we would be in charge. His resistance with the resort made me think he might never fully give up that control, but him sucking my thumb had dispelled those worries.

There was no one in the guest room, but they had obviously been there. Some cases and bags were thrown on the bed and Jeremy's jacket lay over one chair. We could collect his things later and move him into our room. I remembered the games room and headed off to look there.

Making him fuck Faith earlier had been a whim with a purpose. I knew he wanted me, and I had triggered a feeling in him he had been hiding away, but I was only half of the equation. I needed him to know we came as a package. Faith's enjoyment of him was as important to me as mine. From the way he fucked her, I had no worries that he was into only one of us.

As I reached the stairs, Jeremy appeared and waved, his beautiful smile breaking out and lighting up his face.

"Oh man, we are never getting Lucy out of that games room. When she saw the Space Harrier machine, she flipped."

Before he could say anything else, I pulled him over and thrust him against the wall, my mouth on his neck, kissing and licking as I rubbed him through his jeans.

"Oh, fuck." He groaned as I let go of him. "That was unexpected."

I could feel the love for this funny, sweet, charming man swelling in me.

"Faith wants me to bring you to her. I have a strong suspicion she wants me to fuck you." At this, he blushed bright red, and I had an almost overwhelming compulsion to kiss him again.

"But I want to tell you something before that happens. I love you. We both do. We both realized that without you, we had a hole in the center of our lives. To prevent any more misunderstandings in the future, we will both do everything we can to make you and Lucy happy."

His redness deepened a shade and I could see he was struggling to find the words. This man who always said what he thought, caught speechless?

"Is that okay?" I asked.

"Yeah," he laughed. "Yeah, that's pretty much perfect."

I took his hand and guided him towards the bedroom.

"Good. Now I hope you have plenty of energy, because Faith is in a commanding mood. I advise you to call her Mistress when she talks to you."

Jeremy laughed as we opened the door into the bedroom, then stopped when he glanced at me and saw I was serious.

Faith was kneeling on the bed as we walked in.

I noticed she had been busy while I was away. She'd lit candles around the room and laid out a selection of our toys and lube on the chest of drawers. It made me wonder what she had planned for the night.

"Best to have everything available, just in case," she said, noticing where I was looking.

Catching the look on Jeremy's face, I smiled. His mouth dropped open as he saw how Faith was dressed in her black nightdress and as she crawled across the covers towards us.

"Jeremy, the shower is through there. Go clean up and come back naked for my inspection," she purred.

He gulped, unable to take his eyes off her.

"Run along like a good boy." She laughed, but there was an edge of command in her words.

He seemed to wake up from a daze and nodded.

"Yes Mistress." He headed into the ensuite.

Faith rolled off the bed and walked up to me. She placed her fingers on my chest, slowly tracing them to my neck.

"Yes, Mistress? Someone has been training him well."

I leaned in to kiss her, feeling her body mold against me.

"You're in charge tonight. I thought I had better make sure he knew that."

Her hand slipped under my shirt and traced a little circle around my nipple.

"Strip."

She leaned against the bed and watched me take off my shirt. That wicked smile of hers appeared as I pulled the belt free from my trousers and pushed them down, along with my boxers.

"Now stroke your cock."

Behind the soft lilt of her voice, I could hear a cold steel. She knew what she wanted, and she was going to get it.

Wrapping my fingers round my quickly growing erection, I kept eye contact with her as I stroked myself to full length.

She walked over to the chest of drawers, selecting a bottle of lube. Flicking the cap open, she poured it all over my cock, her hand gripping me and rubbing the cool liquid all up and down my shaft.

"You know what I am going to make you do?" she asked.

I nodded, my head a little clouded from the feel of her hand working up and down.

"And you want it as much as I do?"

"Yes. I want it and I want you to watch."

She gave me a playful slap on the face. I was thankful she hadn't used the messy, lubed-up hand.

"It's just as well that's what I want, because I'm in charge."

A movement to the side of us made us both look round. Jeremy was standing there, naked, gazing shyly at us.

"Um, hi."

Faith walked straight over and took his hand, bringing him back over to me.

"Kiss Tristan," she commanded, stepping back to watch.

Jeremy turned to me, flashing me that gorgeous smile. He leaned forward and kissed me, softly at first, then with increased pressure. His tongue danced with mine before he suddenly sighed against my mouth.

I knew Faith had wrapped her hand around his cock and started stroking him, because she did the same to me.

"My good boys, playing together for their Mistress. Now I want you to pleasure me, Jeremy."

We broke off the kiss and watched as she made her way back to the bed, climbing up and kneeling at the end.

"Tristan, I want you to fuck Jeremy."

We all knew it was going to happen, but with the words out of her mouth there was suddenly a tension in the room, a need.

I made Jeremy put his hands on the edge of the bed, facing away from me and looking into Faith's eyes, and I spread his legs out while making sure he was well braced.

"Tell me you want this," I said to Jeremy.

"Oh, fuck yes. So much."

The tip of my cock pressed against him, enough to make him groan. I knew I had to be gentle, but the need in me was building, making me want to take him and fill him and have my way with him.

Luckily, Faith was still very much in charge.

"Bend forward, Jeremy, time to show what you can do with that mouth of yours."

While Jeremy did, she pulled off her nightgown, stunning in her nakedness. As always, I was enthralled by the way her confidence in her own skin shone through, especially when she took control.

Climbing forward onto the bed, she lay down and guided his head down to her pussy, and sighed as he licked.

Not being able to control myself any more, I pushed slowly inside him.

And oh god did it feel good. His tightness engulfed me, making my entire body buzz. Moans escaped his lips and floated up to me like the most rapturous music. With each thrust, he gave more of himself, his body relaxing, allowing me to use him as I wanted.

I was thinking how perfect the moment was, then I looked at Faith, saw her smile and then mouth, "I love you," to me.

The moans from Jeremy were getting louder, making me thrust deeper and harder each time. It was no longer about the sex; it was about claiming him, making him ours, and, in a way, him claiming us.

"Oh fuck, harder, fuck him harder. He's being such a good boy," groaned Faith.

I could see that Jeremy was resting on one hand. With his other he had pushed his fingers inside Faith and was doing an excellent job of bringing her to orgasm, considering how hard I was plowing into him.

Suddenly, everything seemed to slow down: Faith's cries as her orgasm hit, Jeremy's squirming under me, even my own thrusts. The world paused in a perfect second. I thought that this, this could be how things would be in the future. A perfect unit, each enjoying the other two as much as they were enjoyed. Sometimes in charge, sometimes controlled, but always wanted.

And then I came as hard as I ever remembered and time crashed back in on me, the sounds, the feelings, the whole build up to the act, all crashing down and I exploded inside Jeremy.

Each thrust made him shake, each one drawing more moans and shouts. But still I went on, emptying myself into him, weeks of need and wanting distilled into one act.

Then I felt a hand on my face and turned to see Faith. In my lust, I had not even noticed her slipping from the bed.

"Tristan, stop now. Any more and he might forget how to think."

I glanced down at Jeremy, who was now collapsed on the bed, a blissed out expression on his face, and I knew she was right.

Pulling out of him, I bent and kissed the back of his neck, then helped him stand.

"How was that for you?" I asked, guiding him to the bed.

"It was, well, indescribable," he laughed.

He slipped under the covers and Faith got in beside him, moving him over so I could get in, sandwiching her between us.

"That was amazing," Faith said before kissing Jeremy, my body pressing up against her. "I hope you still have plenty of energy, Jeremy, cause it's my time for some attention now."

As I watched Faith and Jeremy embrace, my cock tried to stir to life. I kissed her neck and her sexy little whimpers brought me back to hardness.

It was a long time before we got any sleep.

CHAPTER 25

Jeremy

The next morning, I awoke pinned between Tristan and Faith, with Faith nestled against my stomach. I was sore enough to remember exactly what I allowed to happen, and exactly how much I had enjoyed it. Tristan's cock felt incredible. The sensation of being owned, being filled like that, had been both pleasurable and emotionally loaded.

I wondered idly if Tristan would enjoy having me inside him as well, but I didn't know how to broach the subject, especially not with the distraction of Faith's soft skin pressed up against my cock. She shifted, and I felt my morning wood slip between her thighs. She must have been awake, because she was rubbing against my cock like she was trying to find the pressure she needed.

"You can always use me in the morning if you need me, Faith," I murmured. She moaned softly as she grabbed my cock and guided it inside her, letting me softly fuck her in a spooning position. I slipped my hand over her hip and dragged her closer.

"Even if you're asleep?" she asked.

"Mmm, yes, I'm into being fucked awake by my loves."

Behind me, Tristan stirred, pressing closer. This might be my new favorite: sleeping pinned between the couple, their warm bodies embracing me. His cock was soft. I reached back and stroked him as Faith bounced against me, her pussy slipping deliciously over the head of my erection. Tristan groaned and lifted onto his elbow, gripping my chin and twisting my face around so he could kiss me. I loved the way he kissed, warm and tender. Faith, on the other hand, was all-in and a little forceful with her kisses—the one time I didn't feel like she was overthinking anything.

He pulled back and ran a thumb over my lip, pressing his body closer to my back, and every nerve ending in my body fired up as their bare skin slid against every part of me. I sucked Tristan's thumb again, echoing the day before, letting him know where I wanted him. I hadn't tasted him yet, and I needed it desperately.

"You're still our free use toy?" he asked, guiding a disappointed Faith away from me and rolling me onto my back.

"Of course." I grinned. "Not all day. We'll eventually have to make sure Lucy hasn't eaten all of your food. But every moment we're alone, you have me, all of me, until tomorrow afternoon when our flight leaves. And you can do whatever you like with my body." I flushed, stunned at the offer I was making, not to mention how much I wanted them to take me up on it.

"I have an idea." Faith climbed to straddle me. I let her place me where she wanted me, acting every part of the toy. I groaned as she guided me back inside her warmth, dragging my hand to her clit, where I dipped my fingers through her wet folds and rubbed until she was shuddering in pleasure. She blew out a breath, like she was trying to focus, then stilled. "I propose every time we visit each other, a different one of us is the slave."

Faith grinned wickedly, her eyes sparkling with warmth, and I couldn't help but pull her down for a kiss, lifting my hips and slamming in deep. She felt like home, soft and warm and full of pleasure. The sweet whimpering noises she made as she writhed on top of me drove me to move faster, thrusting up into her. Tristan wasn't to be forgotten. I turned my head to look for him; he was kneeling near the head of the bed and his cock was only inches from my lips.

I groaned, lifting my head and tasting him, gripping his ass to pull him close. Never in a million years had I imagined I would take pleasure from sucking cock, from the way he grabbed my face and thrust deep into my mouth, taking what he needed from me as Faith did the same on top of me. Her lips met mine around Tristan, and I backed off, kissing her around his cock for a while, then giving her a turn while I took a breather.

I didn't let her have him for long, though. I'd missed his taste, and I wanted him back. He seemed to know it, shoving into my mouth and thrusting hard. Faith stroked my face while her husband fucked my mouth, whispering dirty words of encouragement as she bounced on my cock and ground her hips against mine. I tried to remember to play with her clit, but being fucked at both ends wrecked my focus. It didn't seem to matter, because she was close enough that she came hard, with a wild, quivering orgasm that milked my cock in the most pleasurable way.

Despite the intense pressure building, I tried to hold on, not wanting to come until both of my lovers had had their fill of my body. Tristan's thrusts were growing faster and wilder, Faith was still bouncing on my cock, and the sensations were intense enough to make my eyes roll back. I whimpered, shaking, as I felt Tristan's cock swell in my mouth, throbbing as he thrust again and again, dumping a massive load of cum that reminded me of how he had come inside me the night before. I tried to swallow his cum, but it was too much and it dribbled out onto my chin. I punched my hips upward, and came deep inside Faith with a shout muffled by Tristan, still throbbing between my lips.

He pulled back and leaned down, gently kissing my messy face. "Good boy," he said, and his praise felt like everything.

"I agree." Faith shifted to lie on my stomach, breathing hard. After a moment of recovery, she kissed me too, taking her time to get a healthy taste of her husband's cum. "Mm, you taste so good with Tristan on your lips."

We settled together for a bit, but soon the sticky, sweaty, after-sex feeling made me feel a little squirmy.

"Okay, shower?" I asked. I was a mess, and I didn't really mind it, but there was an eleven-year-old out in their house somewhere. "Next time, I'll have Lucy stay with a friend, and you can fuck me on every surface of this house."

Faith grinned. "That sounds fun. But we don't mind that she's here. It'll be fun to hang out with her, too."

"She'll leave for another snowboard training camp in a few months. Maybe we can do something special then."

"That's a lot of camps," Tristan said.

"She wants a shot at the Winter Olympics in four years. There's an amazing coaching facility in Utah, so I get her there as much as I can. Anyway, we'll have to arrange something for the three of us while Lucy is gone. Perhaps a trip to a hedonistic resort? There's one I heard about called Temptation in Paradise."

I stood and stretched, noting both of their eyes on my body and smiling. It felt good to be admired by my lovers. I took each of them by the hand and led them into the bathroom, happy to find a massive, luxurious shower inside. Maybe we spent a little too long in the shower, and a little too much time soaping each other, but we came out of it squeaky clean and well satisfied, if a bit later than expected.

Lucy was sitting on a stool at Tristan and Faith's big kitchen island. The kitchen was a bit of a mess, but we couldn't yell at Lucy as she waved her hands with a flourish over a pile of pancakes, bacon, and eggs.

"I made breakfast!" Lucy said. Faith went straight for the coffee machine, grabbing a slice of bacon on the way, and moaning in pleasure as she bit into it. "You guys were being lame and sleeping in, so I searched Seattle for fun activities. Did you know there's a science museum?"

I settled down with my plate of food, resting a hand on Tristan's thigh to remind myself he was real and he was mine. We both ate and listened as Lucy and Faith chatted about fun things to do in Seattle. I didn't have much time to spend with them, and I made the most of the next twenty-four hours. We toured the city with Lucy in the afternoon, and I spent the night pinned between Faith and Tristan, used in every way possible. This time, when I left, we had plans for a visit in Tahoe in a week, and for lots of video chat hijinks in the meantime.

I was exhausted as I fell into a seat on our plane, but I hadn't felt this happy in a very long time. I glanced at Lucy, wondering what she thought of it all, and found her studying me.

"I didn't realize how lonely you were, Dad. You should have said something."

"I wasn't lonely; I had my favorite sidekick." I ruffled her hair. "You needed me, squirt. And I knew I'd have my time one day. I didn't want to miss a moment of your childhood."

"Well, now that I'm all grown up, there's no reason for you to put your life on hold anymore."

"You're eleven," I said, rolling my eyes.

"Do you think maybe we should work on teaching me to drive? My sixteenth birthday is just around the corner." She tilted her head, pondering. "I could drive you to the airport, stay home alone, invite a few friends over. It'd be nothing like the parties you see in movies."

"Why do I not trust that?"

"Come on, Dad. You said it yourself, I'm twelve."

"Almost."

"Almost, fine, whatevs. I don't even know where to buy a keg. But I'm sure I'll find out by the time I'm in high school. Your love life is going to make me so popular."

"Lucy," I admonished.

She cracked up. "I'm kidding, Dad. I'm happy for you. You and the dorks are good together."

"You gonna stop calling them dorks?" I elbowed her gently.

"Nope. It's my nickname for them."

"But you like them."

"I do like them," Lucy said. "Tristan is so chill, and Faith is fun, which, like, totally surprised me. And most of all, you look so happy."

"That's good, because Faith is coming out next weekend," I said. "Tristan has to go to London, and I think she wants to visit and have some bonding time with you."

"Oh god, she's going to get me to go to the Prada store or something, isn't she?" Lucy groaned.

"You could show her your favorite spots," I said, grinning.

Lucy gave a long-suffering sigh. "The things I do for you, Dad."

But I knew Lucy, and I knew she was excited. We'd always said we were fine as we were, but maybe she wanted a woman around sometimes.

CHAPTER 26

Faith

As the plane touched down on the runway at the Tahoe airport, the butterflies in my stomach swirled in excitement at seeing Jeremy. I'd vacillated between anxious and thrilled the entire flight. We were about to see how Jeremy and I got along when it was the two of us. I knew this was an important test for our new relationship.

I'd been oddly ecstatic when I pulled my fuchsia suitcase from the depths of the closet so I could pack for the trip. The suitcase that just a month ago made me miserable now revved me up, and I couldn't wait to spend time with Jeremy.

When I realized how excited I was to be going on the trip by myself, I wondered if I should be guilty. My parents raised me with the belief I would get married and that was the only person I would ever sleep with or love for the rest of my life. Navigating a new polyamorous relationship was going to take some adjustments. I didn't know what was right or wrong anymore, and I had to trust my gut instincts to lead me down the correct path.

After a couple of days, I couldn't put my concern aside. Maybe I shouldn't want to spend time with only Jeremy. So I rolled up my sleeves and dug into some online research. Every website and article I found stressed how important open communication was, and that told me I needed to talk to Tristan.

Tristan was just so... Tristan. When I told him I was excited to see Jeremy but wasn't sure it was okay, he pulled me into his lap and wrapped his arms around me. Then he told me he wanted this to work. We discussed how we can't always be together. He was right, and it was silly to expect any different. He also pointed out that not being excited to see Jeremy would be an actual problem. I felt so much better after talking with him. I allowed myself to express my excitement about the trip. He'd grin at me and kiss my nose whenever I chatted enthusiastically about my plans.

When I met Tristan, I wasn't seeking a partner that soothed my overthinking brain, but the universe must have known I needed it. Tristan always explained things, so I realized everything was going to be okay, and this time was no different. When he dropped me off for my flight, I gave him a long soulful kiss and promised I'd message him multiple times per day, take lots of pictures. We also made plans to video chat like we normally did when we're apart. This time would be interesting, because I was going to get Jeremy in on the video fun. My pussy hummed her approval at the thought of all the ways Jeremy and I could "torture" Tristan long distance.

Stepping off the plane, I smiled at the few people I passed on my way through the airport's small terminal for private aircraft. Jeremy said he'd meet me in the lounge. When I turned my phone back on, I saw I had a text message from him saying he was there. It was late at night and a Thursday, so I didn't know if Lucy would be with him. She probably had school in the morning. When I spotted him, he was alone, leaning against a railing, and shifting from foot to foot. Even from a distance, I could tell he was nervous.

At first, he wasn't looking in my direction. Then he turned to me and gave me an adorable, shy smile. My heart fluttered, and I sped up, dragging my wheeled suitcase and dodging around a slower-moving couple. He stopped leaning on the railing and straightened up as I got closer. When I was a couple feet from him, I let go of the handle of my suitcase, squealed, and launched myself into his arms just like I do with Tristan when I haven't seen him for a few days.

Even though we hadn't spent a lot of one-on-one time together, greeting him this way felt natural. I wrapped my legs around his waist and mashed my lips to his, not caring about technique. He kissed me back with enthusiasm, our tongues twining. The longer we stayed locked together, the more aware I was of his strength, his hands cupping my ass so I didn't slide down. I wanted to grind against him, but we were in public, so I held back. When we finally broke apart, we were both breathless. He held me until I lowered my legs to the ground and could stand on my own.

I giggled out, "Hi," and he laughed, "Hello," back to me.

Suddenly bashful, I didn't know what else to say to him. He took the handle of my luggage and we walked out to the parking lot in silence. I figured he probably felt awkward like I did, but we kept peeking at each other and smiling, so I knew he was happy.

Once we were in his truck and driving towards the resort, we loosened up and chatted about our weekend plans. Sitting close to him was making it hard to concentrate. I probably sounded like an idiot. His hands on the steering wheel kept distracting me. I imagined them on my breasts instead. I was tempted to unbuckle my seat belt and slide over to him. How long would it take for me to get him hard if I rubbed him through his jeans? The rational part of my brain kept my slutty side in check.

Barely.

I didn't want us to end up in a ditch since I planned to jump him as soon as we set foot inside his front door. Waiting for a tow truck to help us out of a ditch would ruin my plans to get his cock in me.

When we got to his place, he seemed as eager as I was to get inside. I had texted Tristan on the drive I landed safely and he replied, telling me to have fun and ending it with a smiley face. The only thing left on the agenda for tonight was to get Jeremy naked and into bed.

He wheeled my luggage inside. As soon as the front door closed, he turned to me. "Are you hungry?"

I whispered, "No," and it was true. I might have been hungry on the plane, but now that we were alone, all desire for food was gone. My skin tingled, and I had the urge to lie on the bed with both of us naked and rub my legs against his. My pussy ached for his cock, and I let the slutty part of my brain finally take over.

I slipped my hand into his and pulled him towards me for another kiss. He didn't resist, and I plastered myself against his long, hard body. All my passion for him flowed through my lips. His hard cock pressed against me through his jeans and I bumped against him, hoping to drive him wild. He moaned against my mouth before switching to tiny pecks so he could say a few words between each one.

"Remember how... last weekend... you said... every time we visited... someone else... would be the slave?"

What's this?

I pulled back from his mouth and peered up at him. He grinned down at me with a naughty twinkle in his eyes. A warmth spread from my core and my panties dampened. I remembered coming up with the plan to switch off who was in charge, but I didn't think it would actually happen.

Deciding to have a little fun with it, I widened my eyes and gave him my best innocent look. "No, I don't recall saying anything like that."

He laughed and started unzipping my jacket. "Oh, I'm sure you do."

I stood still, pretending to be helpless while he finished removing my outer clothes. I wanted to be comfortable on the plane, so I wore jeans with a loose blouse tucked in. He pulled the top out of my jeans and over my head, forcing me to raise my arms. When he encountered a camisole underneath the blouse, he dropped my shirt to the floor and sighed as if my many layers of clothing frustrated him.

He stopped disrobing me, and his voice had a playful tone. "Here's what we're going to do. You're going to follow me to my bedroom and do everything I tell you tonight because I'm in charge. Okay?"

My pussy clenched, and a shiver ran down my spine from the newness of everything. It had been years since anyone but Tristan dominated me, and Jeremy's style differed from Tristan's. When he tagged on the "Okay" at the end of his command, I almost giggled despite how hot he sounded. No way in hell would Tristan have asked me if it was okay, but years of history made a difference. This power play felt more lighthearted with Jeremy. He brought out my bratty side, and I wanted to needle him and try to make him either laugh or fuck me hard. But I appreciated he was giving me an out if I wanted it.

I didn't.

I tilted my head to the side and quirked my lips at him. "And what should I call you tonight?"

He gave me a full grin and replied, "You can call me Your Liege, Your Majesty, or Commander. Your choice."

I almost snorted at him when he rattled off his list. I studied him for a moment before inspiration struck and my lips twitched from suppressed laughter. "No, I don't like any of those."

His eyes lit up with a twinkle of amusement. "No?"

I pulled my camisole over my head to reveal a pink lace bra and dropped it on the pile of clothes. I announced, "You're going to be Beast, or My Beast, if I'm in a good mood."

He didn't yet know my favorite movie was Beauty and the Beast, but he'd find out soon enough.

Giving Jeremy my most cutesy voice, I purred at him, "Okay, Beast. Lead me to your room and fuck me. I'm all yours tonight."

Instead of showing me the way, he scooped me in his arms while I squealed and threw my arms around his neck.

"I'll take you to my room, but I decide how and when I fuck you this weekend." His reply made me giggle because he lowered his voice into a mock growl. I knew this night would end with me being fucked, no matter how he threatened the "how and when."

"Yes, My Beast, whatever you want," I replied sweetly as he carried me down the hall. My heart thudded in my chest the closer we got to his room, and I knew I was going to enjoy this teasing dynamic with Jeremy.

Jeremy dropped me into the middle of his bed, and I giggled when I bounced. I was curious what his room looked like, but I didn't get time to scope it out. He immediately covered my body with his and crushed his lips to mine. Neediness swirled in my gut, and I ran my fingers through his hair while our tongues dueled.

The overthinking part of my brain piped up, and I briefly wondered if Jeremy found it odd that it was the two of us tonight, but I pushed it aside. I didn't want to dwell on my insecurities about Jeremy, and I wanted to enjoy my first night in his bed. Being in his arms was surreal, since I hadn't been with anyone but Tristan for years now. Every detail about Jeremy that differed from Tristan thrilled me. Jeremy, being more physically active than Tristan was, had more defined muscles — and I wouldn't hate on that.

As I slid my hands over his arms and up his shoulders, I wanted to lick every inch of him. It might take me days to explore all the differences. I wanted to learn all of Jeremy's secret erogenous zones that only a long-term lover would know. But I wasn't in charge tonight, and Jeremy seemed like a man on a mission.

He ran his hands underneath me, unhooked my bra, and slipped it off. With my breasts unbound, he focused his attention on them, licking and sucking my nipples to drive me wild. The longer he sucked on them, the wetter I got, and I assumed by now my panties were a mess.

My breasts had always been extra sensitive. Sometimes Tristan sucked on them so long he brought me to orgasm. Jeremy's attention was sending shivers of delight through my body. He played with them for a long time, and I wondered when he'd last had unfettered access to a pair of boobs. He acted like a man dying of thirst, and my tits were his oasis. When he sucked on a nipple extra hard, I closed my eyes, moaned, and arched against him. With no visual distraction, I immersed myself in the pleasure and let my body take over while my brain shut off.

My mind was fuzzy when he decided he had enough of my breasts and kissed his way down my stomach. When he encountered the band of my jeans, he unzipped them and sat up on his knees to pull them off. Opening my eyes, I reached down to help him, but he stopped me from helping and quickly did it himself.

"Don't. I want you to lie there."

Oh shit, fine. I closed my eyes again as he started at my foot and trailed his fingers up my leg. I adjusted slightly, opening my legs, and he caressed my inner thigh. My panties were still on, and when he reached the apex of my legs, he rubbed me through the thin pink satin.

My breath hitched, and I pushed my hips up towards his hand, wishing he would slip a finger inside me — or better yet, his cock. I moaned in relief when he pushed aside my flimsy panties and slipped his fingers between my folds. When he immediately rubbed circles around my clit, I bucked against his hand. I was already close to my orgasm from his sucking on my nipples.

"Ohhh god, Jeremy. I want you to fuck me," I groaned out when he sped up his fingers.

Until then, neither of us had said much as we filled the room with our heavy breathing and moans. My words broke the spell and Jeremy stilled his hand without removing it from between my legs.

"Hey!" I shimmied my hips, hoping he'd rub against my clit again.

Jeremy laughed. "You're forgetting that I decide what we're doing tonight."

Oops. He was the one in charge. In my mindless state, I wasn't thinking; I just needed him.

I was curious to see how easily I could get what I wanted from Jeremy, so I used my cutesy voice that would get Tristan to cave to my demands, adding a contrite tone. "Oh, I'm sorry, My Beast. I really wanted your cock and forgot."

To emphasize my point, I wiggled my hips and forced his hand to rub me again. It was going to be fun to learn the way Jeremy's mind worked. I felt both guys would keep me on my toes.

When Jeremy didn't give me what I wanted, even with my additional encouragement, I switched tactics. Lowering my voice to a deeper, sexier register, I exaggerated my response. "Beast, feel how wet I am for you? I need your cock. Will you please give it to me? Pretty please?"

"Maybe." He leaned over and nibbled on my stomach, grazed me with his teeth, and kissed the same spot. When his fingers gently swirled around my clit again, I sighed in relief as the swirls of pleasure ramped up in my core. Now, if I could get his cock inside me, I'd be a happy camper.

Jeremy lifted his hand from my pussy and unzipped his jeans. I admired his strong shoulders and toned stomach. As he removed his clothes, my pussy tingled. Once he was naked, he kissed his way up my stomach again, sucked on my nipple for a moment, giving me a zing of delight that went straight to my core, and continued up to my mouth. As he pressed his length against me, we kissed passionately. I rubbed my legs against his and enjoyed the contrast of the rough hair on his legs versus my shaved skin.

I smoothed my hands along his shoulders, enjoying his strength, and explored his chest as my hands moved down his sides. Mmm, yeah. His abs made me imagine licking his chest on my way to his cock. I brushed my hands along the path, caressing those wonderful abs before I continued down the path I wanted to travel with my mouth. When I reached his cock, I stroked him and he moaned.

Kissing me hard, he pumped his cock into my hand, encouraging me to rub him harder.

He groaned and mumbled against my lips. "I've decided I want to fuck you now."

My body tingled at his words and I wanted to tell him to come and get it, but I held my tongue this time. I didn't want to risk him stopping before I got his cock inside of me.

I spread my legs and pulled my knees up. He rolled on top of me and nestled between them. He propped himself up on one arm and used his other hand to guide his cock to my wet cave entrance. When he teased me by running the tip of his cock up and down my slippery folds, I couldn't stand the torture anymore.

I thrashed my head against the pillow and begged, "Oh god, please Jeremy, please fuck me. I can't wait any longer."

Too late, I realized I called him Jeremy and not Beast.

Jeremy chuckled at me. "Oh, Faith. You were doing so well. Now I'm going to have to punish you."

Ohhh.

My pussy clenched with need and I stared at him with round eyes, afraid of what he was going to say next. If this was Tristan, I wouldn't be coming tonight.

With one swift thrust, Jeremy slammed into me. I cried out from the exquisite pleasure of his shaft burrowing itself to my core. My head spun, and I was confused at how this was bad, but the pleasure was too intense. I couldn't ask.

Jeremy leaned close and whispered in my ear, "Your punishment is being fucked hard."

While he drilled into me, I whimpered, "Ooooh, fuck," as he rocked against me vigorously. Spikes of pleasure shot from my core, and I almost wished this moment would slow down so I could enjoy it more, but I was too worked up to stop the impending orgasm.

When his bed frame knocked against the wall, the faint, fleeting voice of reason said I should warn him to temper his enthusiasm, but I was too far gone and chanted for him to fuck me. My words made Jeremy even more frantic, and he whacked against me so hard it felt like he was slapping my pussy with each thrust. Everything felt amazing, and Jeremy and I moaned in unison as we lost ourselves in each other.

When he hooked his arm around my thigh and pressed one of my knees up towards my chest while he continued to drill into me, I shattered. The friction from the new position shot me over the abyss. I locked eyes with him and cried out, waves of rapture rippling along my body.

I kept my eyes open because I wanted to watch him come. When he finally exploded, the intimacy of seeing his eyes glaze over from ecstasy gave me a warm glow. At that moment, I knew for sure that I loved him. This. I wanted this for the rest of my life, him and Tristan.

Jeremy bucked against me a couple more times, unloading the last few drops of his cum, before he rolled onto his side and snuggled against me.

I wanted to tell him I loved him, but I held back, uncertain if the timing was right. I didn't want to mess anything up with him or scare him off before we had our fun weekend together.

He kissed my shoulder softly and murmured, "I might need to get Tristan to show me how to punish you."

Shifting to my side, I cuddled against his full length and kissed him before replying. "No, I think I like your method of punishment just fine."

"Uh huh," was all he said. We lay in our embrace for several minutes, kissing and touching, until the sexual haze faded and I came back to my senses. Since he didn't say he loved me, my rational side was glad I didn't say it first.

Later, we had a midnight snack run and stood in the kitchen giggling like teenagers while we fed each other cheese, crackers and grapes. We came back to bed and cuddled. As we settled in, I knew he had deep feelings for me. The way he treated me tonight and his obvious joy with me told me this wasn't one sided.

Right before I fell asleep in his arms, I wondered if he loved me yet.

CHAPTER 27

Tristan

For the fourth time in as many minutes, I read the first line of the document on my laptop and didn't make it to the end. Every time I tried, my mind wandered to what Faith and Jeremy were doing.

I didn't mind being back here in London while they were having fun. Truthfully. First, I had work I needed to catch up on. The world would not slow down for me because I had a new person in my life.

But second, I thought it would be a nice bonding experience for them. With the way our lives worked, we wouldn't always be together, the three of us. Often it would be two of us. The sooner we tried this out to make sure it was the way forward, the better.

Besides, I thought Faith was looking forward to spending some time with Lucy. She'd really taken a shine to her, and it seemed the two of them were going to get along well. Lucy had something of the spark her dad has about her, and I thought it appealed to Faith.

I looked back at the document and tried to read it again. Halfway through the sentence, I gave up.

It was late anyway, and I needed to take a break. At least I was in the apartment instead of in the office, so I could sit back and relax.

The real problem was I was horny and had been the entire trip. All this wondering about Faith and Jeremy together had me thinking about sex rather than thinking about business. I kept catching myself wondering what they were doing. Kissing, fucking, who was taking charge? Who was being a willing sub?

I pushed the laptop away across the table and stood up, grabbed my whisky glass, and wandered over to the window.

Much had changed since the last time I had been in London, but some things stayed the same. Whenever Faith wasn't with me, I always seemed to think about her and fantasize about the things I wanted to do to her. Now I had the bonus of Jeremy being in those fantasies.

I sipped at the whisky and thought of kissing them, one after the other, the taste of them both mixing.

As my mind wandered to the two of them, I suddenly realized my hand had wandered as well, resting on the bulge in my trousers and rubbing gently at the hardness trapped inside.

I smiled to myself and thought of someone in the darkness seeing me and taking a picture. It was the sort of thing my family would go crazy about, me oblivious to the reputation of the company.

I walked back to the sofa and sat down, placing the glass on the table.

I pulled my trousers open and reached inside, my fingers tracing along my boxers and the length of my shaft. I could have just pulled it out, but I wanted to tease myself.

I closed my eyes and imagined Jeremy and Faith before me, on their knees and looking up at me, both of them eager to please. I imagined offering them my hardness, the two of them competing to get me in their mouths, both licking and kissing my shaft, trying to be the one I choose to use.

My hand slipped under my boxers and I grabbed my shaft tightly, enjoying the throb as I squeezed it. There is a certain joy to a hard cock pulsing between your fingers, whether that cock is yours or someone else's.

I glanced at the clock. It was nearly time for our Zoom call.

As I worked myself to full length, I used my other hand to pull down my trousers and boxers. My balls were full and looked huge. Faith had told me once that she never really found balls attractive until she met me. Now she found the potential of them, the fullness of them, gave her a buzz and had her heart thumping. She said her joy in it was vulgar, but she loved it all the same.

When the alarm went off, I leaned forward and pressed connect on the laptop. With a flicker, the picture filled the screen and I could see both Jeremy and Faith.

They obviously had the laptop set up at the end of the bed as Faith was on all fours, her face near the screen. Jeremy knelt behind her, slowly fucking her with a determined look on his face.

The sight of them made me stroke a little faster. I leaned back in the chair and relaxed, finding a steady rhythm.

"Oh fuck," said Faith, seeing what I was doing. I saw Jeremy glance at the screen and smile, but most of his concentration was on fucking my wife. The deep, hard thrusts seemed to answer my earlier wonderings about who was in charge.

"I see the two of you are getting on well."

Faith was struggling to speak, with Jeremy slamming into her so hard, but she tried.

"Sorry, we lost track of time. Was going to dress up all pretty for you," she gasped.

I rubbed the pre-cum leaking from my cock and spread it over the tip. Each movement was done slowly so she could see what I was doing.

"Oh, you look pretty enough to me. Wouldn't you agree, Jeremy?"

He nodded, a grin on his face. Then he reached out and put his hand on Faith's shoulder, steadying himself as he increased his pace.

I matched him with my strokes, going faster and faster.

"Fuck, Tristan, he feels so good. You should be here. I wish you were using my mouth," moaned Faith between gasps.

I sat forward and made sure I had her attention.

"FAITH. You may not come yet, not until I tell you. Understand? If you come, Jeremy will punish you."

The idea of Jeremy punishing her, perhaps with a spanking session, made her whimper, like I knew it would, but she tried her hardest to follow my instructions.

"Jeremy." I moved my gaze to him.

"Yeah?"

"Come for me. Fill Faith with your cum."

With one last thrust, he plunged into her and exploded. I saw the ecstatic look on his face and saw Faith collapsing onto the bed, lost in her own orgasm, and it overwhelmed me, my cock spurting and splashing cum all over me. It felt so intense I had to struggle not to lose myself in it and forget the other two were there.

Jeremy pulled Faith to him, wrapping her in his arms. She looked happy and exhausted, and I wanted to kiss her. I wanted to kiss both of them.

"You made quite the mess of yourself." Jeremy laughed as he looked at me.

Faith snuggled her head against him and looked directly into the camera.

"Please, can you come here soon? We both miss you."

There were still things I needed to do in London, but I knew no matter what, I would be back in the arms of those two again soon.

CHAPTER 28

Jeremy

"I want to take Lucy shopping." Faith made her announcement as she pulled on her jeans. I was leaning over the bed frame, trying to figure out the source of the banging noise it kept making. Stupid bed. We'd just had a shower, and I kind of wanted to lounge in bed and send Tristan naughty photos of his wife's tits. Seeing him come for us on video had been hot as hell.

Faith, unfortunately, had been energized by our morning shower sex, and was cheerfully planning the rest of our day. I glanced at her as she fastened her bra and started buttoning a white cotton blouse over her breasts. *No! No shirt, come back, breasts.*

"Shopping? Why?"

"I want to do something with her. If we're..." She looked at the wall for a moment, then took a deep breath. "If we're in this for the long haul, whatever this is, I want Lucy to like me. What better way to win over a pre-teen girl than a shopping spree?" I wondered at that pause. Maybe she was missing Tristan.

"But shopping?" I winked at her. "That's your idea?"

"It'll be fun, and I can get to know her better. She can pick the stores. You can come along and, you know, make me look cool."

"I kind of figured I'd spend the day naked with my slave."

"Getting out and doing something will take my mind off of missing Tristan."

I was pleased I'd read her right. Faith wandered over to me, tracing a finger over the muscles of my bare chest and giving me a sweet, pouty expression that made me pull her into my lap. The touching wasn't convincing if she wanted me to get dressed, but I wouldn't point that out.

I gave her ass a slap and lifted her to straddle me, nuzzling her lace-covered breasts through the opening in her half-buttoned shirt. She squealed and giggled. Faith's body was enough of a distraction for me, though I missed Tristan, too. I wanted more of him inside me. The small taste he'd given me of that new pleasure was definitely not enough.

She whimpered and squirmed in my lap as I pushed her shirt out of the way and licked her nipples through her silky bra. I was going to take advantage of the whole slave thing, and...

Lucy knocked. My daughter had impeccable timing.

"Are we going shopping, still?" Lucy yelled through the locked door. Faith gave me a wide-eyed look, and I sighed and lifted her out of my lap.

"We're coming, just getting dressed." Faith adjusted her bra. I stood and scooped her close, kissing her roughly. "We will continue this later. Ooh. Or you guys can go without me. I'll nap. Or call Tristan and see what time it is in the UK." I wrapped my hand around my cock, thinking about the possibilities.

"Jeremy, this is important. Come with us. Please?" Faith's sincerity was clear.

I glanced at her ass and considered ordering her to comply, but decided this was an important part of making our relationship about more than sex. I let them rush me out the door and into my truck.

We headed towards a coffee shop drive-through to buy muffins and drinks to fuel the shopping trip. Faith was staring at me oddly as we waited in line for our order.

"What?" I asked.

"You went along with me way too easily."

"Me? No. I love shopping."

In the back seat, Lucy cracked up. "That's a lie. He must want to spend time with you."

Faith flushed and ducked her head, looking rather adorable, and I reached over the center console and squeezed her thigh. I let my hand trail a little too high between her legs, making her shift in her seat. "Spend time with you, exactly. Wholesome, family activities." I winked.

"Yes, exactly what I think of when I think of you." Faith leaned back in her seat. She turned sideways and looked back at Lucy.

"Lucy, woman to woman, what can I help you shop for? Shopping with this guy can't always be fun." She poked my arm for emphasis, and I moved my hand even higher on her thigh, letting my pinkie trail somewhere I definitely wasn't supposed to be touching.

Lucy tilted her head, thinking for a moment. The coffee line finally moved forward a bit and I pulled my hand back and turned my focus back to driving. "Maybe you could show me how to shop for a bra?"

"A bra? You're just a kid. Are you sure you need a bra?" I was confused.

Faith slapped my shoulder, letting out a cackle. "She's going through puberty. I'm trying to picture you shopping for bras. It doesn't compute."

Lucy leaned forward, giggling. "I asked him for bras. He disappeared for two hours, came back, threw a pile of training bras at me, and ran. I don't think any of them even fit." Faith had discovered the best way to win over my daughter: teasing me.

"It wasn't that bad. Was it?" All right, it had been almost that bad. Being a single dad was much easier with the little girl stuff than the growing up stuff. The period talk had not gone according to plan. Faith smirked at me, her eyes sparkling with humor, reached over and rubbed my shoulder.

"Don't worry, Beast, I've got your back," she murmured, and I flushed, pulling up to the coffee shop window and collecting our food and drinks.

"All right, where do we go for bras? Do we have to drive into Reno and find a mall?" I asked as I distributed the coffees and pulled away, and Faith sipped her coffee, trailing a hand idly over my body.

"I think there's a shop in Emerald Bay, isn't there? In the cute little shopping area?"

Well, at least I'd avoid a long drive into the city. I turned towards the tiny touristy shopping district in our hometown. Lucy and Faith struck up a conversation about bra fit I didn't want to listen to. Faith's hand settled on my thigh, almost where I wanted it, but not quite. I shifted, trying to get her hand more on my dick, but she wouldn't comply.

It only took a few minutes to get to the four blocks of shops in the historic downtown. I parked right in front of a hot pink, girly shop that was clearly not going to be pleasant for me. Fortunately, the shop had a couch off to the side, and I settled down to wait. I shot Tristan a text as a woman measured Lucy and talked to her about cup size, while Faith chatted with both of them and perused the store's offerings.

Faith caught my attention, holding up a pretty sheer lace bra over her shirt and winking at me. She returned to shopping, but tucked it into a pile of lacy lingerie she was setting aside. I needed to touch her, and I fidgeted for a few minutes before giving in to the urge, standing and walking over. She was browsing a rack of corsets as I stepped up and wrapped my arms around her waist. I leaned down to brush my lips against her ear.

"Don't you need to try it on?" I whispered. "Preferably with me in the room."

"We're here to support Lucy." Faith turned towards me. She glanced at Lucy and the saleswoman, then held up a corset thing that didn't seem like it'd cover much of her breasts. "I also found this."

"Fuck." I felt all the blood in my body rush between my legs. "You need to put that on. Why are we shopping with my kid? I need to be railing you while you wear it and nothing else." I edged in closer, trying to figure out where we could go for what I needed.

"We need to focus on Lucy," Faith whispered.

Brushing my lips against her forehead, I leaned in, keeping my voice low. "I can't get enough of you, even when I know I'm being ridiculous. I've never felt like this with anyone but you and Tristan."

"Your daughter is beautiful." The saleswoman's voice surprised us, and we jumped guiltily apart, looking towards Lucy. She was digging through a rack of youth sports bras, looking for her size. In a moment she stopped and walked over, her arms loaded down with a lot more clothes than I would have expected.

"Ready to try some stuff on?"

"Yes, go try on the things you've picked out. Especially that one thing, Faith." Faith glanced at me, her eyes twinkling, then slipped into a dressing room next to Lucy's. I didn't follow them, because there was no way I could be around Faith as she tried on lingerie. Even having her ten yards away was going to kill me. As I repeated a mantra in my head about self-control, I could hear the women chatting and laughing, and the salesperson came back by.

"Your wife and daughter are lovely," she said, smiling. "Would you like some coffee while you wait? They might be a while."

My stomach flip-flopped at her innocent assumption, and yet, it didn't send me spiraling into panic. I could imagine sitting out here, joking with Tristan while Lucy and Faith shopped. I sat back and sipped my coffee, listening to the women talking and laughing.

My phone buzzed, and I found a message from Tristan. *Send me a photo of whatever you guys are up to today. Miss you both.*

I would, as soon as we got out of here.

"More stores?" I asked.

"Of course," Faith said, laughing, swinging a shopping bag. Both of them were rosy-cheeked and cheerful, and I couldn't figure out why they weren't exhausted. I was exhausted. Maybe it was because I was carrying most of the bags. Lucy's phone buzzed, and she piled more shopping bags on me as she dug through her pocket to pull it out. I hauled them all over to my truck and started loading them into the back seat.

"Are you sure you guys need more stuff?" I asked, surveying the damage. Lucy was frowning at her phone.

"Crap. Anna's birthday party! Dad, I forgot. It starts in twenty minutes. I can't miss it, it's like the social event of sixth grade. Can I go? Please?" She gave me her biggest puppy dog eyes. "It's at the arcade, so it's perfect, really. Right across the street!"

I glanced at Faith, and she winked. Bonding with my daughter was all well and good, but finding out my daughter had somewhere to be all afternoon while we continued our less family-friendly activities was even better.

I had never been so glad to hear about a nearby children's birthday party in my life. I had to put on a show of reluctance, though.

"I suppose you can go." Lucy bounced and wrapped herself around me, and Faith's eyes gleamed. "Let's go into Maria's store. We'll grab her a gift and walk you over." I led them to a friend's little shop, which carried an eclectic mix of gifts and knickknacks for tourists. Luckily, it included a little section of toys and books that made it popular with local kids.

"Thanks for all the shopping, Faith," Lucy said, grinning. "It was surprisingly non-dorky." I rolled my eyes, holding the door as the two of them rushed inside. Lucy darted to a section of toys, probably hoping to find a popular fidget toy for her friend. I pulled Faith behind a display of mugs with cute sayings on them, looking for somewhere with a little privacy.

"How was that corset you picked out? I can't stop thinking about it. Especially now we'll have some time alone," I said. She giggled softly, moving my hand to her waist, so I could feel the boning of the undergarment against my hand. Fuck. She had a sexy secret under her casual white blouse. It was killing me.

I needed to see it. "Unbutton a button," I whispered. "Give me a little peek. Or there will be a consequence."

I sucked at figuring out the consequences, but whatever. The threat added a thrill of excitement.

She glanced at me, her eyes widening in shock, but flushed and whispered, "Yes, Beast." She took my hand and moved us further into the corner, into a little alcove, glancing around to make sure no one was wandering past, before slipping her fingers up the front of her blouse and popping out one button.

"Not enough," I said. She grinned and opened another button. The tips of her fingers brushed across the edge of her blouse, pushing it aside as her breathing quickened. Faith quickly flashed me a little of the undergarment. It was beautiful, white lace with pink details, and cups that curved under her breasts, leaving her mostly on display.

"Fuck. I've never needed someone like I need you," I groaned, grabbing her chin and kissing her fiercely.

Kissing her was a mistake.

I was supposed to get hold of my rational mind before we got arrested, because right now, I was wondering if I could fuck her up against a stack of Lake Tahoe hoodies without anyone catching us. I deepened the kiss, and she whimpered, wrapping her arms around my shoulders. Maybe if I just slid her jeans down over her hips...

"Dad? Where did you go? I'm ready!" Lucy's voice called across the store. We jumped apart, adjusting our clothes. When had my hand gone up her shirt? Faith flushed and burst out in embarrassed laughter. She buttoned one open button, but left more of her cleavage exposed. I liked that. She reached up and brushed her thumb across my lip.

"You have lipstick all over your mouth," she muttered. "We're terrible at this."

"We need to find somewhere to fuck, stat," I said. "A bathroom? I don't care. We'll drop Lucy off and handle things."

We emerged from behind the display, probably looking like a couple of teenagers who had been caught behind the bleachers. Lucy stood with a shopping basket full of weird looking toy noodle things. She grinned and held it out.

"They have fidget ramen, now." I had no idea what fidget ramen was, but I was thrilled she seemed cheerfully oblivious to what happened between Faith and me. I piled her purchases into a gift bag at the register and paid as quickly as possible.

"I think I've had enough shopping. What's your favorite lunch spot around here?" Faith asked Lucy as we left the store. She glanced at me. "Preferably with clean bathrooms, because I could really use one of those right now." Subtle. I smirked at her, and she winked.

"Joe's Burgers is good," Lucy said. "Hey, Anna and her mom are over in front of the arcade. Can I just go? Please, Dad?" I nodded, and she was off, waving and jogging across a crosswalk to greet her friend with a squeal.

"Okay, so I'm thrilled you're bonding with her, but we need some privacy. Now."

I shook my head and led Faith towards the upscale burger joint Lucy had mentioned. Come to think of it, they had nice bathrooms; the spacious single stall kind with a deadbolt on the door. I led Faith inside, ducking past the hostess stand and heading towards the back hall where the bathrooms were.

"This is so wrong," Faith muttered. I locked the bathroom door and pushed her against it, kissing her desperately as my hands roamed over her body. I opened the buttons on her blouse, and she laughed as I took in the beautiful corset with a groan. "So much for my foray into being a responsible mother figure."

"Even responsible mothers have sex. How do you think they got pregnant? Shirt off."

Faith looked both ways, as if someone might hide somewhere in the locked single stall bathroom. She even blushed as she tossed her blouse onto a purse hook on the wall.

The corset from the lingerie shop had to be the hottest thing I'd ever seen her wear: lace and silk, with low cut cups that supported her tits but left them mostly on display. I reached out and tweaked her nipple, and she moaned. I loved how responsive her nipples were, the way she could go from zero to begging with nipple play.

"We can stop if you like." My lips moved against the soft skin of her breast. "I'm sure we can make it back to my house without completely losing it." It was easy to distract her from her worries about being responsible, but I wanted to be sure she was okay with what we were doing.

"No. Definitely don't stop. We'll just be quick and inconspicuous." Big vocabulary for a woman who had her nipple in my mouth. I could make her forget her big words. I backed up a step and pulled out my phone.

"What are you doing?"

"Tristan wants a photo of what we're up to." I shot a quick photo of the sexy corset, angling the camera to obscure her face. "He should see how gorgeous you are."

I sent the text, then turned her to face the mirror, coaxing her to lean over the counter and rest her hands on it. With the phone in video mode, I stepped up behind her, again careful not to include her face. I wouldn't want an identifiable video of her like this out in the world. It was for Tristan and Tristan alone. I recorded myself as I ran a hand down her back.

"Unbutton your jeans and push them down." She whimpered, lifting her hands off of the counter and following my command. "Do you like being on video for him?"

"Yes," she whispered.

"Panties off, too. Pose for me." As she complied, I slipped a hand between her legs. She curved her back to give me better access, and I followed my motions with the camera. I slipped my fingers inside her, feeling how wet she was, showing Tristan how wet she was.

"I'm about to use my little fucktoy in a restaurant bathroom. I can't spend a whole day with her and not need her so badly it hurts."

She whimpered, pressing into my hand, her body trembling with arousal. I let the video roll for a few more seconds as I played with her clit, then I sent the text and set the phone on the counter, shoving her forward.

I pushed my jeans and boxers out of the way in one quick motion, lined up with her entrance and slammed in deep. I murmured dirty words in her ear about how I was planning to use her body for my pleasure. She whimpered, shaking at the force of my thrusts. I knew being fucked like this drove her crazy, and I could sense she was already close. The teasing during our shopping excursion had her on edge.

"You want to walk around all messy with my cum?" I asked.

She looked over her shoulder at me. "Send him another video. Your cock in me." She shuddered as she spoke, and I groaned. I liked that idea. I picked up my phone, only to find a text from Tristan. He'd shot a photo of his lower body, and he was in bed, his hand wrapped around his big cock.

Fuck. I wanted him in my mouth, but I needed to focus on the shot that would make him come. I pulled back.

"Tilt your hips." I aimed the camera at where we were joined. Faith shifted, whimpering as she took me deeper. Her inner muscles twitched with pleasure, and I filmed, our hips as I pulled back, then thrust in again. She braced herself against the counter, and I watched on the screen as her pussy stretched around me. I pulled fully out, then slammed back in. My cock was wet with her juices, and she was making the most delightful sounds.

Satisfied, I sent another text, set the phone back down and focused on the task at hand. I grabbed her shoulders and whispered dirty words as I used her the way she liked to be used.

She slipped a hand between her legs, flicking her clit, making her pussy even more deliciously wet. I covered her mouth with my hand as she got louder, then came, her pussy milking an intense orgasm out of me. I finished deep inside her, biting back my shout of pleasure. We stood like that, breathing hard for a moment, before Faith reached for the phone. She gasped softly at the photo Tristan had sent back, one of his cock right as a stream of cum poured out. "He came with us," she said.

"I like that," I murmured, kissing her cheek.

I helped her pull her clothes back into place, checking in the mirror to make sure we both looked put together again. Or at least, not like she'd been used in the bathroom. In the hall, outside the bathroom, I couldn't resist one last kiss, as I thanked her for being such a good girl. As we pulled apart, I noticed a woman staring at us, and shot her a glare. Some people were so uptight.

CHAPTER 29

Faith

As soon as I walked into the house, I dropped my suitcase by the door and pulled my phone out to text Tristan I was home. I'd taken a late flight back to Seattle, so with the time zone difference, Tristan would start his workday in London soon.

The weekend had been amazing, and I was on cloud nine, despite not getting much sleep. I wanted to dance around the living room, but had no energy for that much activity. I wrapped my arms around my waist and hugged myself instead. If Tristan were here, I'd climb into his lap and recount every tiny detail of the trip. I wanted to tell him the weekend deepened my bond with Jeremy and I had zero doubts about our future together.

Knowing I should unpack before my lack of sleep hit me like a sledgehammer, I grabbed the handle of my suitcase, intending to drag it up upstairs. I'd managed the first stair when my phone trilled with Tristan's special ringtone. Oooo, I should give Jeremy his own as well. Maybe I could find a Beauty and the Beast one. I answered the phone while walking into the living room.

I barely greeted Tristan before I launched into an excited chatter. "Hi, Love. I have soooo many things to tell you. You were right. This weekend was exactly what I needed. I really think this is going to work out, and I hope you saved the bathroom video. I want to watch it again with you. We should recreate it and send it to Jeremy. Give him something to wank to before he sees us again."

When I paused, Tristan cut in. His subdued tone put me on edge. "Faith, we need to talk. Check your email."

A rock settled in my gut. "Okay. Give me a moment."

I wasn't sure what would make Tristan sound so serious, but it couldn't be good. As I sat on the couch, I brought up my email on my phone and saw one forwarded from Tristan's work account. I was confused when I opened it and it took my brain a moment to figure out what I was looking at. It was a picture of me and Jeremy kissing after we had our slutty bathroom sex. I hadn't known someone had photographed us. The shitty angle and grainy photo screamed nonprofessional. Despite the crappy picture, if anyone knew me, it was obviously me in the shot.

Mystified and slightly annoyed, I pondered, "Why in the hell did someone take our picture?"

That was stalker-level shit right there, and why did they use his work email?

"Someone recognized you and sent it to my family. Now there's a meeting scheduled tomorrow to discuss my adulterous wife."

That made me snort. Adulterous, my ass. His family needed to check themselves before they worried about us. But fuck, I wanted him home. Jeremy and I planned to video chat in the morning and I was going to talk to him about staging a surprise for Tristan tomorrow night.

Tristan was good at smoothing things over with his family, and would when he talked to them. I was more upset that some creepy-ass person took my picture and I couldn't let it go.

"Did they say who took the photo?"

He sighed, sounding tired. "No, they wouldn't tell me."

I wished I was there with him so I could give him a big hug and kiss him all over his face. Shit, I'd been so happy before he called. The more I thought about the photo, the more upset I got. Why can't people just worry about their own life?

I didn't even try to hide my crankiness. "Well, fuck them and fuck whoever took that stupid picture."

That got a tiny chuckle out of Tristan. "Faith, I have a work meeting in a few minutes and I need to go. Will you tell Jeremy what's going on?"

"Yes, love. I'll talk to Jeremy. Don't let your family get you down and try to have a good day at work."

We signed off with a quick exchange of loving words. As soon as I hung up the phone a weariness washed over me. I kicked off my shoes and curled up on the couch, pulling a soft blanket off the back, and snuggled in. Yawning widely, I picked up my phone, intending to make a quick call to Jeremy to explain the situation, but first I wanted to look at the picture again.

I studied the picture, and a warm fuzziness blossomed in my core. Jeremy and I looked happy. I yawned again, and as my eyes drifted closed, the phone slipped out of my hand and smacked me in the face. I jolted awake and set the phone on the floor, deciding to call Jeremy first thing in the morning.

CHAPTER 30

Tristan

More and more often, lately, I seemed to sit on the sofa in our London apartment and wondering about how swiftly things had changed in my life.

The whole thing with Jeremy had been unexpected, amazing, and not something either Faith or I had planned. When it happened, it was fast and became our new way of life.

I thought it was going to be like that forever, before my family told me they knew about Jeremy and Faith. Worse, they had a picture of the two of them together.

It was nothing major, just the two of them sitting in a booth in a restaurant, but they were kissing. They sent me the picture and I suppose they thought she was cheating on me.

Faith was upset, but we both knew it wasn't the end of the world. I needed to make my case and explain what was going on. She understood it meant me staying in London instead of coming back to her, but with something as big as this, flying back was a terrible idea.

Instead of heading home, I sat in the apartment, unable to sleep, waiting to plead my case in front of my family and the board in the morning.

Suddenly, my laptop sounded the familiar chime of someone trying to connect on a video call. It was Jeremy. I reached forward and pressed the connect button.

He was sitting there smiling, dressed in his boxers.

"Hey there, sad face, what's the matter?" A hint of concern creeped onto his face.

I rubbed my brow, trying to find the words to explain.

"Jeremy, you know I come from a traditional family. Quite proper, in fact."

He nodded, the smile fading now that he knew something was up.

"Somehow, they have found out about you. Or more accurately, they know about you and Faith. Someone saw the two of you together and reported it to the head office."

I could see the color drain from him. The whispered, "Oh shit," was nearly inaudible.

"I've been called into the office tomorrow. I let Faith know. She was going to let you know. Guess she hasn't had a chance yet."

I could see that Jeremy was struggling. Normally he would say anything that came to mind, but suddenly he didn't know what to think.

"After the meeting I'll fly back to Seattle to see Faith," I said, to break the silence.

"Tristan."

I glanced up, only then realizing that my head had dropped, and I had been looking at the floor without seeing it.

"Yes, Jeremy?"

"I would understand, you know? If our thing is too much. If it is going to get in the way of you and Faith's lives. I never want to cause you pain. I care far too much about both of you to want to make your lives harder."

I nodded, but his words set my head spinning. Thinking about a future without the three of us together was more than I could bear.

"I know," I said.

We sat in silence for a moment, both lost in our thoughts.

"Jeremy, I think I have to go now. I need to get some sleep before tomorrow."

I could tell he was taking it badly. The two of us sitting here not talking was not helping, so I disconnected.

For a moment, I tried to remember if I said I would get back to him with how it went. Surely I had? Either way, after the meeting, I would let him know Faith and I were going to come out and see him. Nothing my family said would change my mind.

Outside, it rained. I settled down on the sofa, closed my eyes and chased a sleep that wouldn't come.

I arrived for the meeting exactly at the chime of the hour.

Walking into the boardroom and seeing the faces of the directors of the company staring at me was bad enough. Spotting my mother at the head of the table, looking disapproving, brought a whole new level of anxiety.

As always, when she got especially angry, she didn't speak to me directly. She got one of her underlings to do it. Jackson was her right-hand man and as old-fashioned as they come. I often wondered what he thought about having a woman in charge.

"Tristan, you know why we have called you here. This is a potential scandal and something must be done about it."

On the table in front of me had been placed a folder. I flicked it open and stared at the picture.

How can a picture of two people so obviously happy cause so much trouble?

I had looked at the picture a hundred times since they sent it to me, but only now did I notice how normal it seemed. The two of them enjoying a moment together. I smiled at the thought we had so quickly become such a happy unit.

"Oh, do you think this is funny?" barked my mother, standing and leaning on the table. "Do you think this is something to smile about?"

I studied how happy they looked in the picture. And how I wished to be there with them.

All night I had been working out what I would say. How I would explain to them what the situation was, how they misunderstood. How things were not as they seemed. I would plead my case. But now, looking at the picture and realizing it represented the life I wanted for us, I suddenly knew what I was going to say.

"Mother. Sit down."

I glanced at her and saw outrage on her face. Jackson had turned red in the face and an indistinct murmur rose from the other directors. She found her voice first.

"How dare you—"

"I said sit down NOW."

With a gasp, she dropped into her seat.

"Is there a single person at this table that can say I don't do a good job?" I asked.

I was met with silence.

"And is there a single person here that can say Faith is not good at her job?"

I looked at each person in the room, ready to pounce on anyone that would say a single thing about my wife.

"No one here doubts your ability to do the job," mumbled Jackson, the fire taken out of him by me seizing control. "We are here to talk about your wife's infidelity and how it will affect the company."

I stood up, straightened my jacket, and stared him dead in the eye.

"No, that is what you are here to talk about, but you do not have all the facts. Faith is not cheating on me. I am fully aware she is with Jeremy. In fact, I encouraged it."

This drew a gasp from the gathered group.

"Moreover, we intend to include him in our marriage from now on," I said, looking directly at my mother.

"You are letting another man sleep with your wife?" she spluttered. "Have you lost control of her?"

I thought of how I got Faith and Jeremy down on their knees in front of me and grinned at the idea of me having lost control.

"No mother, I have not. It's not only Faith sleeping with him. I am also sleeping with him. We both love him dearly and have no intention of giving him up."

Jackson slammed his hand down on the table.

"The scandal will ruin our reputation," he growled.

"It didn't happen when you got your secretary pregnant," I answered. "It didn't happen when it was found out some of our dealings in Korea were morally questionable. And it didn't happen when my mother slept with a competitor."

I had never talked to my mother about that. It had come to light a few years after my father died, but occurred when he was still alive.

"The big difference," I continued, "is that when you were caught, it wasn't in public, so you hushed it all up. Do you want to know the other difference? There is nothing wrong with what we are doing. The three of us all know what it is. We are adults and we all give consent. However it affects the company's reputation is of no concern to me. We will continue to bring in profits and keep your pockets lined."

I stopped to catch my breath. I couldn't remember the last time I had been this worked up and needed to calm down.

"We can't have you carrying on in public..." Jackson started, but I looked at him and it took the wind out of his sails.

Screw calming down.

"You don't get a choice. Not unless you want to remove me and Faith from the company, and you know that would be more of a scandal. Either let us live our lives or try to get rid of us. What's it to be, Mother?"

Every head in the room turned to her. She was giving me her sternest glare, the one that I had grown up with, the one I knew meant she was about to give her opinion.

"Very well." The room breathed again.

"If that's all then," I replied, turning and walking towards the door. Her last words caught me with my hand on the handle.

"Just be discreet."

I spun round and went back to the table, putting both my hands on it and looking at her straight on.

"No. This is not negotiable. The three of us are in love and we will not hide it. We do what we want and if you or anyone else does not like it, then that's tough."

I looked at each of them, not one under the age of sixty.

"It's a new world now. It's not your world anymore. I don't need to hide the fact that I am bi. Faith does not need to hide that she is equally in love with two men. The world has changed and you have not changed with it. If anything, see this as a way of showing that our company is progressive and supports all lifestyles. Instead, you see a challenge to your old ways. Well, no more. I have been groomed to take over this company. That is exactly what I will do when the time comes, but I will make goddamn sure it's a company which welcomes everyone and never asks them to hide who they are."

I banged the table, making everyone jump.

"If we are finished here, I am going home to my wife. I don't want to hear another word about this."

Throwing open the boardroom doors and stalking down the corridor, I could hear the buzz of conversation behind me, but I didn't care. I had told them the truth and stuck up for my relationship.

Whatever happened next, I could be happy knowing I stood up for Faith and Jeremy.

I called the elevator and pulled out my phone, eager to let Faith know what had happened. My body shook as the enormity of what had occurred hit me. I had never expected I would stand up to my family like that, but knew I now had a much more important family to protect.

CHAPTER 31

Faith

My phone alarm woke me early the next morning. Disoriented, I glanced around. What was I doing in the living room? Then I remembered falling asleep after the phone call with Tristan. I had set my alarm to make sure I had plenty of time to shower and eat before my scheduled video call with Jeremy.

I had planned to call him first thing in the morning about the photo, but I chose to wait until I could see him on video. This deserved more than voice chat. I hoped the conversation about Tristan's family wouldn't kill the mood, but I bet once I explained Tristan was handling it and it wasn't that big of a deal, he'd relax and we could continue on with the fun.

If the timing felt right, I was going to tell Jeremy how special the weekend ended up being and how much he thrilled me. The sexual heat during our shopping trip was one of the hottest things that happened to me in a long time. Tristan's being turned on by it only made it better.

As I got up and stretched, my pussy twinged and a flush ran through my body. Reminiscing about the weekend made me wet, and I contemplated greeting Jeremy naked when I called him for our video chat. Since it was a weekday, I didn't think Lucy would be around, but the slight doubt made me discard the idea. A sexy nightgown would do the trick and save my dignity if Lucy was with him.

I was in my closet eying my drawer of lingerie when my phone trilled with Tristan's ringtone.

"Hi, hon!" I couldn't keep the happiness out of my voice. "How did it go with your family? Did you smooth things over with your mother, or is the dragon still huffing?"

That got a chuckle out of Tristan. "Oh, the dragon is going to be huffing for a long time about this, but I don't care."

When Tristan's voice trembled at the end of his sentence, I could tell something was up. "What happened?"

Tristan exclamation took me by surprise. "It was amazing, Faith!"

I smiled when I realized the quiver in his voice was because he was elated, not upset.

Tristan rushed out with the rest of it. "I stood up for you and Jeremy, told my family I was in love with you both and I was bisexual. I finished with this was MY family and we were going to be together."

"Wow." Goddammit, what I wouldn't have given to be a fly on the wall during that meeting.

"Faith, it was all true. This is the life I want, with both of you."

I thought about it for a moment and wished he were home. I wanted to kiss him deeply and tell him how delighted I was. After last weekend with Jeremy, I was right there with Tristan. This was what I wanted as well.

I must have been quiet too long because he broke into my thoughts. His voice was light and joking, but I could tell he was serious. "I hope I didn't come out to my mother prematurely."

"What? No, silly... I was wishing I could kiss you. It must have been some meeting. I can imagine the look on their faces. I'm so fucking proud of you and love you so much."

Tristan sighed happily. "It really was magnificent. Standing up for you both felt... powerful."

I was about to giggle and tell him not to let it go to his head. He was still going to be on his knees for me often, no matter how much he dominated in the boardroom, but he continued on.

"Did you talk to Jeremy? I want to come to Seattle, get a good night's sleep, and fly to him the next morning. We need to be together."

I couldn't agree with him more, and my heart did a happy dance. "Well, I have a work meeting I can't miss, so it will have to be the following day." A flash of annoyance that work was in the way of us being together ran through me. We needed to figure the work situation out so we could be together more often. "And, uh... no, I fell asleep last night. I'm talking to him soon, so I'll tell him and let him know we're coming to see him."

"Okay, Love. I talked to him last night, so that's fine. I'm going to go get some dinner. Have fun playing with Jeremy."

We blew kisses to each other on the phone and said our goodbyes. After I disconnected, I selected a red lace negligee and laughed. I never said I was going to play with Jeremy, but Tristan knew me so well.

By the time I showered and put on the skimpy red wisp of lace, I was more than ready to play with some toys and see how long it took before Jeremy was a moaning puddle of mush. My pussy hummed at the thought of making Jeremy so fuzzy brained that he could barely speak. At some point, I planned on getting both my men so turned on that they couldn't think and were my mindless sex toys, willing to do my bidding. I knew which buttons to press to make Tristan a drooling mess, and it was going to be fun learning Jeremy's triggers. Whenever Tristan got that way, I felt like a sexual goddess. The thought of two drooling men... I shivered as I settled in on the couch.

At the appointed time, I started the video chat and called Jeremy. His haggard appearance alarmed me. He looked as if he hadn't slept.

I blurted out, "What's wrong? Are you sick?" as I was hit with a rush of concern for him.

Jeremy's brow furrowed. "Faith, I'm not ready to talk to you yet."

I blinked at him, bewildered, as my stomach clenched and my hands went clammy. "What's wrong, Beast?" I used my best soothing voice on him to keep him calm while I rubbed my hands on my nightie.

He didn't speak for a few seconds, and then mumbled, "I need time after a breakup. I'm sorry." He swiped across the screen and the video stream ended.

I stared at my tablet in shock, my legs weak. I was glad I was sitting down. What the fuck happened?

My hands shook as I pulled out my phone and dialed Tristan's number. He answered on the first ring and I could tell his mouth was full of food.

"Hey, Love... give me a moment. I grabbed Thai food for dinner. I thought you'd still be talking to Jeremy."

An icy fear clutched at my heart. "Tristan, what did you say to him?"

"What?" I heard him swallow and take a sip of something. "What are you talking about?"

My shoulders tightened and I started shaking. "Tristan, he thinks we broke up with him. You need to get to the resort, NOW."

"I don't think it was anything I said..." He sighed. "It's possible I may have said something not in the best way and he misunderstood it. I'll call him. Give me a moment."

He disconnected. I stared at the phone while my pulse sped up. He better fucking fix this. We didn't all go through all this upheaval to have a misunderstanding mess everything up.

Tristan called back in a few minutes. "He didn't answer his phone. I've got my laptop open and I'm arranging a flight out of here as soon as possible."

I fought the urge to snap at him he BETTER get there as soon as possible since he was the one who did this, but I reined in my temper. Tristan didn't mean for this to happen, and he didn't need me angry at him while anxious about Jeremy.

Tristan stayed silent. I heard his finger clicking away on his laptop keyboard.

"Okay, Love. I've booked the jet as early in the morning as I can. That's the best they could do. I'm going to get some sleep."

I was tense and my heart still pounded, but there wasn't anything more we could do if Jeremy wouldn't answer his phone. I purposely made my tone gentle, hoping to help him sleep. "Okay, Love. Text me when you land. I'm going to keep trying to call him and see if he'll eventually pick up." I tried to inject some humor into the shitty situation. "Maybe he'll answer to tell me to shove off and stop calling him, and then I can get him to listen."

Tristan chuckled unhappily at my poor attempt at a joke. "I love you. Text me if you reach him."

"I will, and I love you too. Never forget that." I made one last attempt to get him to smile for real. "I'll join you guys as soon as I can. When I get there, you better have kissed and made up with him. I want both of my men naked and waiting for me."

That earned me a soft laugh. "Okay, Love."

After we disconnected, I dropped my hand to the cushion, clutching my phone, and leaned back into the couch. Between the time zone difference and the long flight, this wouldn't be resolved fast unless Jeremy answered his phone.

The past few days had been a rollercoaster of emotions, and I felt overwhelmed. Whenever this happened in the past, I took a bath to clear my thoughts and help process what was going on. If that didn't work, Tristan would take me to bed and hold me until I could put words to my thoughts.

I was too anxious this time to want a bath, and Tristan wasn't here. I lifted my hand with the phone and pressed the speed dial for Jeremy. When I heard it ringing, I prayed he would answer.

CHAPTER 32

Jeremy

It was good that Lucy was busy at school that week, because I was an emotional wreck over the next day and a half. I hadn't meant to get so carried away with Faith that it ruined things for the two of them at work, and I felt awful about it.

Most of all, I missed them. The bond I shared with them had been stronger than any I'd experienced in my adult life, and it was like ripping out a piece of my soul to be torn away from them yet again. No matter how much I told myself I should have known it was coming, I couldn't imagine myself doing any of it any differently.

A knock on my front door startled me out of my musings. I wondered for a moment if it was worth answering, but then I heard the door creak open.

"Don't you lock your door?" Tristan's voice, his posh British accent. Everything made me smile. It was irrational, really, because he was probably here to discuss something to do with our business dealings.

I stood and walked into the hallway, leaning against the door frame to drink him in. He was wearing slim cut designer jeans and a black t-shirt that showed off his lean body nicely. He was so damn handsome, but his hair was a mess, like he had been tugging on it excessively. "What are you doing here?"

He was looking around, apparently distracted by my unlocked door. "Someone could barge into your house and rob you."

I chuckled. "It's a small town, and there's almost no crime. No one barges into people's houses unless they're there to deliver Girl Scout cookies because they're afraid to leave them out in the rain."

"People just walk into your house?"

"Yeah, like friends, or, you know, you. What are you doing here?" It was so good to see him. I wanted to touch him, but it wouldn't be appropriate. This was a business relationship now. Wasn't it? I found myself wishing it wasn't.

"You weren't answering your phone." Tristan's jaw was tight. "Why the fuck weren't you answering your phone?"

"I was kind of..." I scrubbed a hand over my forehead. "I needed a minute."

"Well, it made me feel like an arse for standing up for our relationship with my family." He crossed his arms over his chest and glared at me, his eyes challenging.

"Wait, what?" I asked, my heart stopping. "Our relationship? I thought we were done."

"You thought we'd give up that easily, after everything?" His words were tight, irritated, and I was pretty sure I needed to find out what was going on. More urgently, I needed his mouth on mine. I needed to touch him. I stepped in closer, backing him into the wall and capturing his jaw in my hand, forcing eye contact. Our lips were close enough that I could feel the heat of his breath, smell the expensive aftershave he used, and I paused.

"Why are you here, Tristan?" I asked.

He sighed. "I came to tell you I love you. We love you. And I'm sorry if what I said made you feel differently. That was not my intention. I was simply stressed—"

I cut him off with a kiss, and he groaned, lifting his hands to rest on either side of my face as he kissed me back, holding me there. I didn't realize how much I'd missed him until our bodies were pressed close, our lips locked together in desperate, hungry passion. After a moment, I pulled back, and his harsh breathing matched mine. "I missed you."

"I love you," he repeated, his eyes warm. "I told my board and my parents that they needed to respect our relationship with you and my sexuality, and if they can't handle that, they can fuck off."

Warmth spread through my body, making my cheeks feel flush. I felt giddy, a nervous rush of energy causing me to feel jittery. I kissed him again, roughly, then pulled back. "Where is Faith?"

"She'll be here tomorrow. She's very upset about your phone call the other day."

My heart dropped as I remembered how terse I had been with her, how I hadn't even given her a chance to talk. This was a bad habit of mine, and it was clear that I needed to stop assuming the worst.

"I'm sorry," I whispered. "I keep reacting instead of thinking things through. It's fucked up, and I don't know how to stop. I want to stop."

"There's nothing wrong with being angry or upset by things, but answer your damn phone, no matter how you're feeling." He dropped his forehead against mine, and I nodded. "We can always talk things through, Jeremy. If you need time, ask for time."

"You're right." I was failing at this, and it was too important to allow that to happen. I looked up at him and saw only concern and love in his eyes, no judgment. "Fuck, I'm so sorry."

"Promise me you won't cut us off again."

"I still sometimes feel like an interloper with you guys, like it can't possibly last. Not the way you've already lasted."

"We're going to make it last," he said fiercely, and I smiled. "It might not always be easy, and we need to know you won't disappear every time you get a little hurt."

"This is important to me. You guys are important to me." I looked away for a beat, trying to figure out how to explain it. "I just don't want to screw up what you already have."

"You won't. You make us better, teach us to chill out every once in a while. We're happier with you, no matter what that does to the company. But you have to recognize that you're happier with us as well."

"I am. So much happier. I've finally found a home and a family for Lucy and I."

"And you talk to your family when there's an issue."

"You have a point." I grinned up at him. "Do you want to punish me again?"

"So you're all better now, is that it?"

"No. But I started seeing a therapist. I have the type of trust issues that require professional help."

"Ah. Hadn't noticed that."

"She hasn't fixed me yet, but I've only been to two sessions. The therapist would probably suggest that you spank me better," I said. "Just saying."

He narrowed his eyes and I could tell he was trying to look stern, but his lips twitched with barely contained laughter. He leaned in and kissed me, cupping my chin as he spun me around and took control. Now I was slammed against the wall, forced to take his rough kiss, and I liked it. He backed off, breathing harshly.

"We need to talk to Faith. She's waiting for news." He raised an eyebrow at me, and I nodded, so he set up a video call to Faith. She was sitting in her office, light shining in on her from the window, and her eyes were a little red. Even so, she was so beautiful that my chest ached. Her face softened when she saw how we were standing.

"You fixed it." She smiled tentatively.

"I'm sorry, I'm an idiot. I should have talked it through with you, but the thought that being with me was hurting you..."

"Being with you would never hurt us," Faith said, leaning forward as if she wanted to be closer to us. "We want to be with you, and we'll fight for it."

My cheeks felt hot as I nodded. Talking to a therapist had helped me realize that I often backed out of things too soon. Better to run than be disappointed. I had been that way for as long as I could remember, maybe since Lucy's mom had left me alone and afraid and way too young to care for my child. Tristan and Faith were the only people who'd ever pushed me outside my comfort zone like this, forcing me to deal with my feelings. Everyone else in my life let me go the moment I backed off. I took a shaky breath and glanced at Tristan. "I'm ready to fight for it, too."

A slow smile spread across Faith's lips. "I wish I was there. I want to touch you, both of you."

"We can get naked for you and touch each other if you like."

"Oh." Her eyes widened, and I wouldn't mind being more naked, really. "You should have gotten naked before you called. That would have been a delightful surprise."

"We'll keep that in mind next time. Apologies can come with some eye candy."

Tristan rubbed a hand over his face. "Guys. This is our romantic moment here, and you've already gone straight to horny."

"Right." Faith nodded agreeably. Then she froze, staring out at us through the phone screen, slowly blinking as realization dawned. "Wait. It is?" She paused and combed her fingers through her hair, adjusting her pose to be sultrier. "Okay. I'm ready. Be romantic."

"Well, now it feels sort of awkward," I said, scratching the back of my head. "Couldn't you just come to Tahoe now so I can tell you I love you?"

"You love me?" she whispered. "You love me." She bounced a little in her chair, her smile contagious. I couldn't stop smiling either.

"Of course. I love you." The happier she looked the easier it was to say. I turned towards Tristan. "I love you." I gave him a quick kiss.

Faith ducked her head, fiddling with her little notebook. I recognized it as the same notebook which convinced me to see them as something different.

"I want to kiss you so badly right now. I love you both so much. Fuck. Why did I stay in Seattle to work?"

"I'm questioning your decision as well." Tristan softened his words with the twinkle in his eye. "But you'll be here tomorrow, and we'll have a lovely day. Once you're here, we can take care of your fantasy about having both of us at once."

That sounded like an excellent fantasy. I needed details about where specifically she wanted both of us to be at once, but someone knocked on her office door, interrupting us. She rolled her eyes, complained about being in the office a little more, and signed off.

She left us with instructions to take pictures of anything sexy she might want to see. The image of her in her bed, making herself come to a video of Tristan fucking me, was a good one, too. We needed to make it happen. My body responded to the thought of him inside me. I'd been playing more and more with my anal toys, unable to stop thinking about the time that he'd fucked me. No more vibrators and dildos. I had the real thing again.

Well, okay, occasional dildos and vibrators, because they were really fun, and I was in a long distance relationship, but not when he was here in my house.

Tristan cleared his throat, and I realized I had completely zoned out for who the fuck knows how long. "Sorry. I was having a vivid daydream about taking your cock in my ass again."

He laughed, and we were back to kissing, stumbling up the stairs to my bedroom, tearing at each other's clothes. He set his phone on the nightstand, keeping it ready to send Faith her kinky photos. We tumbled into the bed together, kissing and touching.

They loved me, and the relief of knowing that set me free. Free to explore him, to love him back with all my heart. They had no intention of ever leaving, and everything felt deeper and more meaningful.

This was the body of the man I loved, and I wanted to worship every inch of him.

I pushed him back onto the bed, kissing my way down his throat, across his chest. I wrapped my hand around his cock as I sucked his nipple into my mouth, biting a little, finding the pressure that made him moan. I kissed my way down his stomach, teasing at his thighs, knowing what he really wanted. He spread his legs, trying to guide my head to his cock, and I nipped at his inner thigh.

"I love you." I finally made my way to him, hard and leaking for me. I licked a bead of pre-cum off the top of his cock, lifting my eyes to meet his.

"Fuck," he groaned. "I love you so much." He reached for his phone, taking a picture of me as I pushed him between my lips, then setting it aside, grabbing my head and thrusting up into my mouth a few times. He seemed close to losing it already, so I backed off.

"I want this inside me, now." I sucked his balls. "You feel so good inside me." I kissed my way up his shaft and licked him again. He was so delicious, and I loved the way he moaned for me. He shoved me onto my back, pinning me with my legs spread wide, and kissed me roughly, pressing his cock against mine. I shuddered, enjoying the heady rush of giving myself over to him. He was bigger than any toy I'd ever put inside me, though I'd been stretching myself out for him over the past two weeks. I wanted to take him without pain. I whimpered as he slicked lube over both of us, then rocked his hips, letting his shaft glide along mine.

He shifted and pressed two slick fingers at my hole, pushing inside me. It was so much better than my own fingers, and I couldn't wait for the pleasure of him stretching me open. I needed it, and I wasn't above begging. He laughed, leaning forward to kiss me as he lined the head of his cock up with my ass.

"You've been preparing yourself for me," he murmured.

"Yes," I whispered. "If we're being honest, I can't stop masturbating with toys and thinking about you."

He held my eyes as he lined up his cock and thrust into me. I loved the intense stretch of him entering me, my eyes rolling back as he pushed further. He paused for a moment, letting me adjust to his girth, watching me closely. I didn't know how to explain how good it felt, how much I liked it. Hell, as he pulled out a little and drove in deeper, I wasn't even sure if I could speak. He leaned forward, seating himself fully inside me as he grabbed me around the back of my neck and kissed me wildly. I had the man I loved, the man who loved me, and that made it even better.

He stroked my cock as he fucked me. The pleasure was so intense I felt a deep pressure building inside me. I was writhing against him, begging for more, and he gave it to me, moving my legs onto his shoulders and fucking me in long, rough strokes. I needed to come so badly, needed a release from whatever was building, and reached for my cock. The pleasure intensified as I touched myself. He held eye contact as he thrust into me until I threw back my head with a shout of pleasure and came, shuddering against him. Closing his eyes, he followed me over the edge into oblivion, his movements becoming fast and jerky as he unloaded deep inside me.

Tristan let my legs drop and lay on top of me for a moment, breathing hard. "Holy shit," I said, laughing. "That was unbelievable."

"Crap, we forgot to text Faith more photos," he muttered. "I was so lost in you, I forgot everything."

I smiled, wrapping my legs around his waist as his cock slipped out of me. Using the bed, I pushed off and rolled us over, sitting on top of him and kissing him tenderly. "Lucy's bus doesn't drop her off until 4:45, so we have three hours to get Faith the footage she needs. I'm willing to try again. And again. As many times as necessary, really." I kissed him between each statement, and he laughed against my lips, kissing me back.

"Hell, Faith might even want a video of you inside me," he said, and I laughed. I was definitely on board for attempting that one.

"I'm willing to do whatever it takes to get our girl off."

CHAPTER 33

Tristan

We met Faith at the airport. She was almost bouncing with joy when she saw us, running up to me and throwing herself into my arms, then grabbing Jeremy and pulling him into the hug.

"OH, it's my boys. I am so happy to see you."

She kissed Jeremy long and deep, then broke away to do the same to me.

"Can one of you help with my bags?" she asked.

Jeremy took her hand and turned her round.

"That's been taken care of. Someone's going to put them in the car. What you need to do is come with us."

I hadn't heard him use his commanding voice much, but I loved the effect it had on Faith. I wouldn't have been surprised if even just that hint of command had her wet.

"Remember how we agreed that every time we came here, someone else would be in charge?" I asked. She nodded. "This time we're in charge, and you are going to be our obedient little pet."

I watched as her eyes went wide and her mouth dropped open. She recovered quickly and smiled.

"Yes, Sirs."

We led her off without another word, knowing not telling her what was happening would get her all worked up. When we stopped outside the family restroom, she gave us a confused look.

"In here?" she asked.

"Now," I barked, and she quickly went in, followed by Jeremy. As I stepped inside, I locked the door behind me.

Jeremy was wasting no time, having already pushed her up against the wall. He opened her jacket, his hand squeezing her breast as he kissed her.

"Well now, that looks like fun." I grinned as I stepped over and pulled her top up, exposing her breasts. No bra meant she had an idea something like this might happen.

We each grabbed an arm and pinned her to the wall. We took her nipples in our mouths and sucked, making her moan and gasp, unable to do anything except let us. I made sure that my teeth grazed over her nipple, getting the expected "Oh god," in response.

"On your knees," I commanded as we let her go.

She went straight down, looking between the two of us, desperate to find out what was next.

Jeremy leaned over and stroked her hair, his fingers trailing through it till they reached her neck and gave the softest of rubs. Then he pulled down the zip of my trousers, reaching inside and pulling my hardness free.

"Faith, I want you to give Tristan a nice sloppy blowjob. Since he'll be driving us back to the condo, he won't be able to join in any fun in the car. Give him something to keep him hard. I'm going to be staying overnight with you two to make sure that you get all the attention you deserve."

"What about Lucy?" she asked.

"She's staying with a friend tonight. Don't you worry, just do what you're told."

"Yes, Beast."

Her hand wrapped around my cock like it had a hundred times before, but this time felt different, as it was Jeremy commanding her to do it. Her lips slipped over the tip and sank down as Jeremy kissed me. His tongue darting and pressing against mine, mixed with the feel of her taking me deeply, made my body ache for more attention. As we broke our kiss, I could see he had rested his hand on the back of her head and was guiding it as she bobbed up and down.

"Seems a shame for you not to use her mouth while we're here." I grinned at Jeremy.

With a popping noise, my cock slipped from her mouth, and I could hear her gasping.

"Do you want to suck Jeremy's cock?" I asked her.

She nodded eagerly and watched as he got it out, the tip already wet. As she moved towards him, I took her hand and placed it on my shaft.

"You're always saying you're the best in the company at multitasking, so make sure you keep me nice and hard."

She did well, stroking me as Jeremy thrust into her mouth. By the time we started taking turns with her mouth, she was too far gone, happily taking whichever cock was offered her.

"You want to touch yourself right now, don't you?" I didn't expect a reply but got one as her head shot straight up to look at me.

"Please, please, Tristan. Let me rub myself, or one of you could fill me up?"

The desperation in her voice made my cock throb in her hand. Glancing at Jeremy to see him nod, I pulled her up to her feet.

"Time to go to the car."

I got in the front and adjusted the mirror so I would have a good view of what was happening behind me. Jeremy had slipped in the back and already pulled his cock out. For a moment I wished I could sink my mouth down over it and feel him pulse for me, but I remembered we were doing this for Faith.

She slipped in behind me, her hands eagerly reaching for Jeremy's shaft.

"Faith," I said sternly, seeing her glance up at the mirror in response.

"On all fours. You can suck on Jeremy's cock as much as you want, you can even see if you can get him to coat your throat in cum. You may touch yourself, but you may not come yet. Do you understand?"

She let out a sad little moan, but nodded her head.

"And Faith, if I look back and don't see your mouth on his cock and a smile on his face, you will be punished."

Already she had wrapped her fingers around his shaft and was working them up and down. Her other hand squeezed his balls, making his eyes roll back in his head.

"Yes, Tristan."

Her head sunk down, then immediately snapped back up again.

"I mean yes, Sir."

With that, she took Jeremy as deep as she could into her throat.

I pulled into traffic, trying to concentrate on the road ahead while listening to Jeremy call my wife a good little cock sucker.

Not for the first time, I wondered how my life had become so wonderful.

When we arrived at the condo, Faith was as desperate as I've ever seen her.

There was no messing about. We went straight to the bedroom. Jeremy told her to strip and sit at the end of the bed, which she did straight away, discarding the clothes on the floor.

I turned to Jeremy and started stripping him, taking my time getting him out of his jeans and t-shirt, enjoying his happy sighs as my fingers moved over his body and the matching moans from Faith as she watched and touched herself. When I freed his cock, it bounced up and some pre-cum dripped over my fingers, sticky and wet and perfect for stroking him with.

"My turn now," I said when he started drifting off, lost in my fingers stroking his shaft. It was still early in the day and I didn't want him getting all fuzzy-headed.

He nodded and gently pushed me up against the wall, slowly opening my shirt as we kissed. His hand sneaked down and pulled my trousers open, dropping them and wrapping his fingers round me. We stood there kissing and stroking each other for what seemed like hours until Faith's moans brought us back.

"Please, Sirs, I can't wait any longer," she begged.

"Poor little thing, are you feeling neglected?" asked Jeremy, walking over to her and taking her hand, leading her round to the side of the bed.

I walked around the other side and climbed onto it, lying down and stroking my cock. Faith wore a hungry look. I knew I wouldn't need to tell her what to do. She climbed onto the bed on all fours, seizing my cock in her hand, and lowered her lips over me, groaning so hard I could feel the vibrations against my shaft.

"Mmmm, good girl," I gasped.

Jeremy rooted around under the bed and pulled out a tube of lube that I had placed there earlier. We both knew exactly what we were going to do to her.

"Let's see how good a girl she is," he replied.

Faith drew my attention away again as she looked up at me, my cock still fully in her mouth. Her eyes were slightly glazed but I could see she was enjoying herself.

"You okay there?" I asked.

She gave a small nod, which turned into her head bobbing up and down on the tip of my cock, her tongue swirling and driving me crazy.

"Oh, fuck."

I glanced up but knew what had happened. Jeremy had sunk himself into Faith's ass and let out a cry. The thought of her tightness on his thick cock made me pulse, the tip of my head hitting the top of

Faith's mouth. Not that she noticed; she was lost in a series of moans and enthusiastically swallowing my cock.

I lifted her hair and looked her in the eyes.

"You know what is happening, don't you?" I asked her.

She smiled a lazy smile and nodded, releasing my cock for a breath.

"Jeremy is fucking my ass," she gasped as he slammed into her, picking up speed.

I slipped my hand over her breast, my thumb rubbing her hard nipple and sending shivers through her body.

"Faith, I want you to ask for it."

I didn't need to explain what "it" was. She knew. She had been wanting it badly, and I wanted her to say it, so she knew it was real and going to happen.

Jeremy slowed down, giving her a chance to breathe.

"I want you inside me. I want you both inside me, both my men, both my loves."

She gasped as Jeremy pulled out of her, climbing onto the bed. Gently, he helped her move on top of me, her leg swinging over mine and her head resting on my shoulder.

"You want this?" I asked her, as she guided me into her pussy.

We locked eyes, and I saw nothing but love.

"Yes, more than anything. I want you both."

It started slowly, with her straddling me and riding my cock. Her little movements drove me wild and made her gasp and groan. Jeremy was saying something in a soothing voice, but I couldn't hear for the noises she was making. I saw him move to the end of the bed behind her, pushing her forward, leaning against her till his chest was against her back, and then I felt him thrust inside her.

She came almost straight away. After all the teasing and playing with her, having both of us inside her tipped her over the edge. Her head dropped and her hands clutched at me, keeping her safe as she rode out her orgasm. She was breathless and her makeup was smeared across her face, but she had never looked more beautiful.

"Now it's our turn," said Jeremy, leaning down to kiss her back and filling her again. I barely had to move, able to feel his thrusts deep inside her, the friction pushing me closer and close to the edge. All this time Faith was kissing my neck and moaning "Oh god," and telling me how much she loved us.

I don't know if I came first or Jeremy, but it was a close thing. His groans echoed with mine as I came as hard as I ever had, pumping load after load of cum into her, my hand reaching out and taking Jeremy's as he gave his final push and collapsed onto her, spent and exhausted.

The air was filled with the sound of our breathing and the thumping of our hearts.

Jeremy rolled to the side, and Faith followed, lying between the two of us. She had a look on her face I had only seen a few times before. This smile couldn't merely light up a room, it could illuminate an entire world.,

She leaned over to Jeremy, kissing him deeply, her body pressed against him. Already my body was recovering, reacting to the sight of the two of them together. Then she turned round and kissed me with all the passion and love she had shown me over the years.

"That was... everything." She sighed, collapsing back against the bed, staring up at the ceiling.

"Hell yes it was." Jeremy pulled himself up, so he was leaning on his elbow. He looked so cute, I wanted to take his face in my hands and kiss him till he couldn't breathe.

"Tristan," Faith said, looking at me. "Are you okay? Was that good for you?"

With my new family lying beside me and my heart beating hard with love for them, I couldn't help but laugh, startling both of them.

"I think I may be happier than I have ever been in my entire life."

CHAPTER 34

Faith

Tristan's comment about being happier than he's been in his entire life echoed in my head as I floated in a contented daze between my two men. My heart sang with delight at his words. Joy infused my entire body. There were so many ways this could have gone badly. For me and Tristan to have found someone we both clicked with, and for all three of us to love each other, was nothing short of amazing. I knew Tristan didn't believe in fate, but there was zero doubt in my mind that meeting Jeremy, everything we went through to get to this moment, couldn't be random.

The guys each caressed one of my hands as we snuggled together, and I smiled softly when Jeremy kissed the one he was holding. My sexual high was gone, the intense orgasm after a long day catching up with me. Before my eyes drifted closed, I twined my fingers with theirs and fell asleep holding their hands.

I woke the next morning to the smell of bacon. I was alone in bed, and a quick glance at my phone told me I slept longer than I intended. Climbing from bed, I slipped on a robe and followed my nose to the kitchen. Tristan was at the stove flipping pancakes, but I didn't see Jeremy anywhere.

Tristan glanced over his shoulder as I walked in. "Morning, sleepy-head. I was going to wake you as soon as these pancakes were done."

Spying the plate of bacon warming on the stovetop, I carefully avoided the pancake skillet and snatched a couple of strips of bacon while Tristan laughed at me. I stifled a yawn and snuggled behind him, hugging him and kissing his shoulder. "Where's Jeremy? I gotta kiss both my men good morning."

"You slept so long he had to go pick up Lucy. We're supposed to pack whatever we want from the condo and meet them back at their house later. He and Lucy are going to spend some time clearing out space for our stuff."

I spied a shiny silver key on the counter. It looked brand new, and I realized it was a key to Jeremy's house. *Holy shit.* The implication of that tiny piece of silver metal and the thought of moving our stuff from the condo made my brain blip out. I slid into a kitchen chair, slightly breathless.

Tristan set a steaming plate of pancakes down in front of me, along with butter, syrup, and the bacon. As I prepared my pancakes, I thought about Jeremy's house. Maybe we should look into building our dream house for all of us. I was sure Lucy would get a kick out of being able to dictate exactly how she wanted her bedroom. If Jeremy was an unplanned life event, Lucy was an even bigger one, but I was excited for our future.

Lost in thought while I mechanically ate, it took me a while to realize that Tristan was sitting at the table. He fiddled with a piece of bacon and curiously watched me, I stopped with a forkful of pancakes halfway to my mouth.

A defensive, "What?" popped out as I self-consciously moved the fork to my mouth.

Tristan shrugged. "Nothing. I could tell you were thinking, so I was waiting for you to talk."

"Oh." I relaxed, swallowed, and gave him a playful smile. "I was wondering if we should build a house with enough room for everyone." Before he could say anything, I continued on. "What are we going to do with the condo? Though I suppose your mom might want to visit once she adjusts to the new reality, and she could stay here. It's not like this was a terrible investment. It'll get used."

Tristan came over to kiss me. "We'll find plenty of uses for the condo. You know some of our friends will want to come visit and get away from the city."

He was right, and I relaxed as a warmth spread through my belly. He tasted like bacon and I wanted to gobble him up, but we had a busy morning ahead. We had a new house to move into.

The thought of his mother amused him, and he brought it up while he cleaned the skillets. I finished eating, and we chatted about his family's reaction to our happy threesome. His mother may seem stodgy, but I would bet money that her icy heart would eventually melt. She wanted Tristan to be happy. We could always set Lucy loose on her, and she'd thaw out right quick. Lucy was so adorable and impossible to dislike.

After breakfast, Tristan went to get some moving boxes. It didn't take long to pack up what we wanted to take with us. As we loaded up the car, I glimpsed the mountain and paused with the final box in my hands.

Taking a deep breath, I inhaled the crisp mountain air and thought back to the first trip to Lake Tahoe less than a year ago. I hadn't even wanted to come here. Life was so amazingly different now.

Tristan wanted me to take a vacation and relax. That one decision set off a chain of events that changed our lives. If someone had told me I would meet Jeremy and we would all fall in love, I would have laughed my ass off. Yet, it felt right. This was exactly how it was supposed to happen.

Tristan took the box from me and grinned. "You ready for this?"

I smiled at him as happy butterflies swirled in my stomach.

I was ready.

EPILOGUE

Jeremy

"Ah, you guys can't watch that!" Lucy yelled, diving for the remote. "It's so embarrassing."

Evelyn Vaughn held the remote out of Lucy's reach, shaking her head. Tristan's mother was quick and she narrowed her eyes at Lucy.

"My granddaughter got a gold medal in the Olympics. I'm going to watch her interview on national television again if I so desire." Evelyn's voice was cool and collected, a voice that left no room for argument. Even after years of hearing her, I still found her a little terrifying. I still couldn't quite believe Tristan stood up to his mother when she tried to stop him from seeing me.

Evelyn adjusted her prim Chanel jacket and patted the seat next to her. "Lucy. Come sit with me. Let's celebrate your triumph!"

"Besides, it's exciting, not embarrassing," Faith said, also coming to sit with Evelyn. "I can't believe you were on the Late Show." She gave Lucy a little high five with a fist bump, their secret handshake.

"The twins finally went to sleep," Tristan said, appearing from a back bedroom. "They were wired." I wasn't surprised, but Tristan had volunteered to take them back himself, while we all celebrated with Lucy.

We'd splurged on a hotel suite in Manhattan for Lucy's big day, but the twins had been overstimulated and cranky by the end of our celebration. Lucy's full cheering squad had been there for her. I leaned against the back of the couch and ruffled my daughter's hair as the show came on the enormous television screen.

"I can't believe you thanked Tristan's mother before you thanked us," I teased, shaking my head. "Who taught you to snowboard?"

We'd all watched Lucy talk to the late night host from backstage, but the twins had gotten antsy halfway through it. Faith and I missed part of the show, so I was excited to see the rest. On the screen, a slightly bashful Lucy was being interviewed. The host had a talent for making people comfortable, though. Soon, Lucy was opening up about the excitement and struggles of earning a gold medal in the Winter Olympics at only fifteen.

"This is my favorite part," Tristan said, walking up behind me and resting his chin on my shoulder. "It's classic." His hands roamed around my waist, pulling me close.

On screen, Lucy was saying, "My twin baby brothers are here too. They're only eighteen months, though, so they're probably backstage making trouble. Even my Nana is here with us tonight! Do you want to meet her?"

For some reason, the host said yes.

Faith and I turned towards Evelyn, who huffed. "Well, he asked me to talk about my granddaughter. I couldn't very well say no." With plenty of laughter and jokes, we watched as Evelyn was hustled onto the couch with a late night television host, discussing snowboard slang.

"Never in a million years did I think I'd see my mother on national television explaining to a talk show host what a backside rodeo was," Tristan said. We all laughed as on stage, Evelyn and Lucy tried to demonstrate a backside rodeo with gymnastics, much to the crowd's delight.

I shook my head, then turned and gave my husband a quick kiss on the lips. Sometimes, even though I'd been with Tristan and Faith for over three years, it seemed impossible. I reached forward and rubbed Faith's shoulder, like I needed to touch her to make sure she was actually there. Tristan pulled me closer against his chest, and on screen, the show wrapped up to wild cheers from the audience. Evelyn and my daughter had been a hit. Evelyn stood and popped out the DVD recording of Lucy's interview, putting it into a plastic case, and Lucy stood and yawned.

"Time for bed?" I asked. "Big day of shopping tomorrow, and you're supposed to be on another talk show."

Lucy, who looked exhausted, didn't even put up her usual fight. Instead, she yawned and trudged toward her room, while Evelyn grabbed her purse and headed to hers, leaving us alone. Faith turned to us, grinning.

"The twins are asleep. Everyone's in their own room. You know what that means, right?"

"Sleep?" I asked, yawning.

"No. Some sexy fun." She winked and jumped up, turning and unbuttoning her shirt as she walked backwards towards our room. She bit her bottom lip, and that was about all the sexy I needed to get moving. As she tugged her shirt open and showed us her cute black bra, she tripped over a toy the twins had left behind.

"Crap," she yelped, flailing as she went down. I lunged forward and caught her, laughing a little, and hauled her up over my shoulder, swatting her ass. Tristan shook his head and followed, carefully closing the door behind him. We all glanced at the baby monitor, wondering if we'd made too much noise, but the twins seemed to be deeply asleep.

I tossed Faith on the bed and reached for the waistband of her jeans, tugging them off as Tristan stripped. Since having small children, we'd learned to be efficient, and we were naked within seconds, which was all the better, really. Faith pulled us both on top of her, and our hands skimmed over her body, worshipping her. She wasn't as slim as she was when we'd met, but I loved her all the more. She was the mother of our children now, and unlike Lucy's mom, she was all in. I kissed her stomach, working my way across her navel and down between her legs, circling her clit with my tongue as our husband sucked on her nipples. She whimpered, trying to stay quiet, and I had the sudden wicked urge to make her scream.

Surely this hotel room was sound-proofed, right? I reached for the lube, slicking it over a finger and pushing two fingers into her ass as I continued to suck her clit. It was my favorite, being inside her together. I could feel Tristan, and felt like I was fucking him, too. Faith completely lost her mind between us.

I glanced up at Tristan. He saw what I was doing and winked. Her body shuddered as if every part of her knew her favorite thing was coming. I kissed my way back up her stomach, stopping to lave attention on one of her breasts, all the while fucking her ass with my fingers, making sure she was slick and ready for me.

Finally, it was time, and I pulled back, stroking a stream of lube over myself. We lifted her on top of Tristan, and I leaned down, sucking his balls and cock as I guided her down. I had been so tentative when we'd met, but now I was in love, and I spent hours sucking him, enjoying the feel of him inside my mouth, the warm rush of his cum as I found the right rhythm.

Now was not the time. I gave the tip of his cock a loving kiss before pushing him inside Faith, listening to their groans as he disappeared inside her. I licked them where they were joined, exploring them. This was a taste and sight that would never get old: my husband stretching my wife open.

After a moment, I shifted, nudging my cock against Faith's ass as I pulled her face around to kiss her. She rocked on Tristan, and I smiled down at him. His hands were gripping her thighs. His face was a mask of pleasure.

"I love you," I whispered as I sunk into her, pushing into the tight channel of her ass.

She made the pleading little whimpering noise she always made when she had both of us. I gently gripped the base of her throat and held her as I fucked her in long strokes, relishing in the snug fit. I could feel the ridge of Tristan's cock, right through the thin wall between her ass and pussy. Our bodies pressed together intimately as we moved inside her. Faith whimpered again, crying out softly as her muscles tightened like a bow ready to fire, then exploded in a wild shudder. Tristan's hands roamed her breasts, mine over her stomach and hips, and we held her as we used her, as we made her come again and again with our bodies.

It had been too long between the twins and the chaos of getting Lucy to the Olympics. I couldn't hold on for long, but it didn't matter. Tristan shouted, slamming his hips up into her, and she was still coming in our arms, making soft, breathless little sounds with each thrust. I closed my eyes and let go, feeling the dam burst, my cock jolting deep inside her as I filled her up.

We stayed there, me kneeling behind Faith as she flopped over on Tristan's chest, breathing hard. After a moment, she laughed softly, reaching back to hold me in place longer. "Fuck, I love my husbands so much."

"We love you, too, wife," Tristan said, his voice gruff and sexy.

As we cleaned up and brushed our teeth, then fell in to bed together, I thought about our unconventional family and all the ways which it worked. Sometimes it was harder, maybe, but so much of the time, I couldn't imagine my life without them. I couldn't imagine life without Lucy, or our twin boys, one who looked like me, and one who looked like Tristan. Hell, I couldn't imagine life without Tristan's mom or Faith's sweet family, or the random assortment of found family Lucy and I had collected around us at Emerald Bay Resort.

After this, we'd go home to the new house we'd had built, high on the hill with views of Lake Tahoe. In the end, Tristan and Faith had sacrificed some of their jet-setter lifestyle for our family and for me. Together, they were working on the new Tahoe division of Vaughn group, while I still ran Emerald Bay Resort.

And life was pretty damn perfect.

The End

About the Authors

Kristin Lance

Kristin writes sexy stories with funny bits in them. Or maybe funny stories with sexy bits in them? Her stories take place in quirky mountain towns and are full of heart, awkward moments, and humor. Okay, and a whole lot of three-ways. She loves subverting alpha males and turning tropes a little upside-down. She also writes alien erotic romances under the pen name Kaylee Pike.

She currently lives in the mountains of Oregon with her husband and two daughters, three chickens, and two dogs. In her spare time, she play snowboards and rides bikes.

Books: https://author.to/kristinlance
Website: https://kristinklance.com/

April Cross

April is the erotic romance pen name for Lacey Cross. She writes ghost pepper spice romances that are really just an excuse to write a ton of sex — preferably with a hint of BDSM. On Lacey Cross she writes wife sharing and BDSM short stories. She's all about the woman experiencing as much pleasure as possible. She also writes short story alien erotica under the pen name Kyra Keys.

She currently lives in the Pacific Northwest and loves it.

Books: https://geni.us/aprilcrossbooks
Website: https://www.april-cross.com/

Alec Lake

Alec likes to say he's a writer of fact and fiction that he blends together into Erotica. He focuses on short stories that include freeuse, BDSM, and really anything that pops into his filthy mind.

He currently lives in the UK, with his new guinea pigs, Pumpkin and Pretzel.

Books: http://author.to/aleclakebooks
Website: https://signup.aleclake.co.uk/

Ingram Content Group UK Ltd.
Milton Keynes UK
UKHW022003130323
418485UK00015B/938